Sylvia

In the Cellar

-by-
Melissa Dawn Brown

ACKNOWLEDGMENT

Thank you to my mom, Carolyn, who was one of my biggest supporters, my mentor, and my friend. When I wrote this story about a girl battling life without her mother, I had no idea I would end up losing my mother before I finished writing the book. Completing the story was one of the most difficult things, but I know she would have wanted me to. She was a bright light in my life, and I miss her every day!

Thank you to my dad, Jerry, for your love and support. Thanks for being a great marketer too!

Thank you to my husband, Eric, for your love, support, and encouragement throughout this process.

Thank you to my son, Braden, for your love and support. You're a true joy in my life! You make me smile every day.

Thank you, Kristen Miller, for the fantastic cover!

Thank you, Katie Post, for the author's photo.

Thank you, Karen, for your friendship, inspiration, prayers, and faith. You're a true blessing in my life, and I couldn't have made it through this last year without your support! Also, thanks for reassuring me, making me believe in my writing.

Thank you, Jacqueline Franklin, for your editing, advice, and friendship. This wouldn't have been completed without your help!

DEDICATION

In loving memory of my mom, Carolyn—
My biggest supporter, mentor, and friend

Printed in the
United States of America
First Printing, 2018
~
©Copyright '2018' (LOC)
Melissa Dawn Brown

REVISED: 7.5.2020

~
ISBN-13: 978-0-692-95717-2
ISBN-10: 0-692-95717-0

TABLE of CONTENTS

CHAPTER ONE
Darkness

1880's
Clintok Missouri

Sylvia was startled awake and blinked several times. Had she really opened her eyes? She rubbed them, and then her face, but she couldn't see a thing. Bleak darkness prevailed everywhere. With her heart pounding and a racing pulse, panic took hold. *Where am I? Apples... I smell apples.*

After turning her head from side-to-side, there was still no light anywhere. She became aware of something underneath her head, but she felt a cold substance when reaching for it and then picked up a fistful. Still unknowing as to what it was, she sifted it between her fingers. Is this *dirt? Where am I? And why?*

Her attention went back to what had been beneath her head. She realized after moving her fingers over the soft texture, it was some kind of fabric. Then she discovered a short, narrow piece, along with a longer one. *Two? Ties of some kind, maybe? That's it—my bonnet. Yes ... I used it for a pillow before dozing off.*

While trying to sit up, a slow aching pain coursed through her whole body. Sylvia strained to remember through the throbbing pain in her head. *Why does it hurt?* She reached up to feel the source of discomfort. It was a lump. Also, there was something moist caked in her hair. Dropping her hand to her nose, she sniffed... *dried blood?*

Overwhelming nausea overtook her at the same time she felt the urge to relieve herself. *Now what?* As lost memories crept in again, she recalled anger in the man's voice—how he shouted and called her names. *Did he slap me? No. He had to have hit me with something since I have the bump on my head. But why?* Chills began to travel up and down her spine as she relived how he had moved closer toward her with rage-filled eyes. In fact, it seemed more like pure hatred, which seemed to flow from his body into hers.

She remembered being terrified. *Oh, it's coming back to me. When I turned to run, I was grabbed by the arm, then wheeled around to face the man. That's when he slapped me. Then, I remember being struck from behind with something before everything went black. But what... what did he hit me with? Oh... I need to pee.* She stifled her welling tears. *Where am I? Why do I keep recollecting sliding and bumping on something? B... but what? Then downward... more bumping... and footsteps... there were a lot of steps.*

The aching in her body worsened, along with the mounting pain in her head. Given her desolate circumstances, she still found it difficult to believe it was happening. Sylvia forced herself to recall how she ended up in this place. *That's it! He dragged me down some steps.*

With stretched out hands, she began searching the area all around her. Then, she scrunched her face when her fingers hit something. *What is this? A handle, maybe?* Whatever she found, she realized it was round, smooth, and fit in the palm of her hand. As she lifted it to her nose, the smell filled her senses. *Apples?*

Realizing her surroundings, she was caught off guard when something crawled across her hand. "Oh, no!" She jerked it back as if she had felt hot coals. "Wha... what was that?" She wiped at her tears. Then, with bent knees and arms wrapped around her legs, she let her forehead rest on her knees. "Oh, why am I here?" She looked up as if to will the darkness away. "Plea—"

The sudden opening of a door above startled her. Blinding pain hit Sylvia in the eyes as she squinted when drawing her hand up to block the sunlight from finding its way into the darkness. As her eyes adjusted, the silhouette of someone stood at the top of the door... a man, but who could it be?

"Sylvia, get up here. I want t' eat," he ordered, then moved out of sight.

A look of confusion crossed her face. *The voice... oh, no, it couldn't be... not—*

"SYLVIA! Don't dawdle, child. Chores need doin'."

"Pa... Papa?"

The shadow shifted back in front of the door. "Child, ain't gonna tell ya 'gain. Get the ladder, then get up here."

"Yes, Papa. Where is the ladder?"

"Look to yer right."

She looked around and noted several baskets of apples on the floor with the light fanning out over the dirt floor. And potatoes from the garden were in a bin across from the apples. To her right, the ladder leaned against the wall, just like Papa had said. It dawned on her that she had never been in the cellar before since he had always put the apples and potatoes in baskets and then brought them down to store.

She started to get up, but a piercing pain soared throughout her head and body. So much so, she catapulted backward on her heels. However, forcing herself to place one hand on the floor and the other on her head, she willed away the discomfort penetrating every muscle in her body. Yet, she wasn't fooling herself—the pain remained.

"SYLVIA!"

She flinched. "Y... yes... Papa. I'm getting the ladder now." After succeeding in pushing herself up into a semi-upright position, she then stood, zigzagged, and shuffled her feet over to the wall. She paused a moment and rested her head on the cool dirt wall. Above her, she heard the loud clattering of metal and the shifting of footsteps. It was so difficult for her to comprehend her father's anger with the person who could lock her up in the cellar—it just made no sense. He'd never done anything like this before. She knew him to be aloof and unsmiling, even... but not hardhearted.

Exhausted, she ceased her thoughts for the moment, forced her head away from the wall, and then grabbed the ladder. After a few attempts, it stayed in position at the top. Even though her eyes had somewhat adjusted, looking up into the light was painful. She placed her arm through the rungs of the ladder and then pulled herself up one step at a time.

After reaching the top, she started to place both hands on the floor, but something clasped around her wrists like a vice, jolting her body upward. When looking up, she saw her father's scowling face at the same time her feet hit the floor. She began to wobble and would have toppled over had it not been for his tight grip. He released his hold and walked over to the kitchen table to seat himself.

"Got water fer coffee and washin'. Coffee's started."

"Thank you, Papa. I'll go out and gather eggs."

"Gathered 'em. Pan's on the stove. Wash up, so you can fix breakfast. Then, get to yer Saturday chores."

"Thank you, Papa. I'll have breakfast ready soon." The cool water in the bowl felt refreshing on her dirty face. But trying to clean the dried blood out of her long dark hair proved to make the pain surge, and tears stung her eyes. Deciding it could wait until later—lest she aggravated and become a target for her father's irritation again, she muffled her anguish and qualms. She needed to finish quickly.

As Sylvia cracked the first egg into the pan, a loud bang startled her. She turned to see her father had gotten up, walked over, closed the cellar door, and then moved the kitchen table and chairs back over the door. As their eyes met, she turned back to the stove—and then continued cracking eggs. Although her distress mounted while feeling as if his cold eyes seared into her back. After serving eggs, biscuits with jam, and coffee, they ate in silence.

When her father finished, he got up, grabbed his hat, and placed it on his head. With his hand on the doorknob, he halted but didn't turn to face her. "Be tendin' to the fields. Bess not forget all yer chores."

"Yes, Papa. Right away."

Willing away her aches and pains while finishing her work, she moved slower than she could remember.

Later, when it was time to fix lunch, her father came in right after she had put a pan with leftovers on the stove to heat up. Dawning struck through her flustered brain, as having served it on Friday meant she'd only been locked in the dank cellar overnight. She sighed that at least it hadn't been longer.

"What's fer lunch?"

"The stew will be ready shortly, Papa. I think there might be some cornbread left. Would you like coffee? I just made it."

"Hmm."

After the stew was hot, Sylvia poured it into two bowls and sat down at the table, across from her father. As she waited for hers to cool, she noticed he'd already started spooning it into his mouth. As he ate, she noted wrinkles on his face and the silver hair on his head. *How old is he? Maybe in his 50's? I don't even know when his birthday is. We've never celebrated one... his... or mine.* She tried to recall the last time he had smiled but couldn't think of a single instance.

While eating, he didn't look up from his bowl. Although when finished, he got up and walked over to the door. "Headin' back. 'Spect the cleanin' done and supper."

For the rest of the day, Sylvia concentrated on cleaning the house and sweeping the front porch. Her bedroom came last, and after she finished polishing the dresser, her bed looked too inviting. Against her better judgment, she curled up in the middle. *I'll just lie down for a few minutes.*

After drifting off to sleep, a vague but constant thumping, along with the darkness, invaded her thoughts of shouting, then turning to escape as her breathing grew heavier. She tried opening her eyes but could not—they felt like two heavy weights. Trying to free herself failed as past events of being dragged... the bumping... and footsteps... kept spiraling out of control. She began to feel helpless, mixed with a sense of futility.

A loud bang was followed by "Sylvia!" She jerked awake. *Oh, no, Papa!* As her eyes popped open, she managed to roll off the bed but fell to her knees. Even though every muscle in her body had tightened up while she relaxed. Still, she willed herself to push through the pain by pulling herself up by hanging onto the bed. Once standing, she smoothed all the wrinkles out of the bedspread.

"Sylvia?"

"In here, Papa."

"What're ya doing?"

"Just making the bed."

"Brought chicken. Get to fixin'."

"Right away, Papa."

After another meal in deafening silence, her father went to his room. She soon sought out her own when the supper dishes were washed and put away. After reclining atop her bed, she removed a gold chain from around her neck, which had a small locket attached—she opened it with a smile. It warmed her heart when gazing at the picture inside. Her mother, Sophia, was a beautiful woman with long dark hair and brown eyes. Sylvia savored the fact she was the mirror image of her mother, down to the turned-up nose and long lashes.

She yearned to know any tidbit about her mother. However, talking about her was never permitted. Therefore, the locket contained the only picture she'd ever seen. It was her most prized possession. And her father didn't know she had it.

She grew up aware of her mother having difficulty in bringing her into the world. In turn, she, herself, had barely survived. Her sadness worsened as thoughts wandered to one actual reality. She was the reason her mother died, although her father had never said as much. Nonetheless, he didn't have to—she felt it anyway. The weariness of such veracity lay heavy on her heart. She often wondered why she had never learned anything about the rest of her family. Or if there were any other living relatives except for her mother's sister in California. Her father wouldn't say anything but scowl and say there was nothing to know. So, that was it. Not to be talked about again. Exhausting, she slowly drifted to sleep.

The next morning, Sylvia jolted awake when she looked up to see her father towering over her with his piercing glare.

"Bess get ready fer church. Waitin' in the wagon."

She jumped out of bed and traded her nightgown for her simple Sunday dress of burgundy. After brushing her hair, she took care when putting her bonnet on by avoiding the lump on her head that had reduced in size. She slipped into her boots and put her jacket on while rushing to the kitchen. With clumsy hands, she wrapped a piece of cornbread in some cheesecloth, slid it into her jacket pocket, then out the door, but careful not to slam it. The last thing she wanted to do was anger her father and risk facing more of his wrath. She raced to the wagon and then took her seat beside him.

Her hand unconsciously reached for the chain around her neck. *Oh, no, my locket! I must have left it on the bed. I'll have to get it as soon as we get back. Papa can never see it.*

En route to town, the sun was shining, but the air had a cool crispness to it. It enhanced the autumn leaves that were changing to vibrant colors of yellow, brown, and red, but she didn't care—her thoughts were centered on her locket.

While nibbling on the cornbread during the somber ride to town, the awkward silence between father and daughter hung heavy in the air until they arrived in town.

"Bess keep yer bonnet on, so folks won't talk."

"Okay, Papa."

CHAPTER TWO
Green Apples

Before church started, Patrick Ryan, a 15-year-old boy with brown wavy hair, dimples, and kind brown eyes, was shooting marbles with some other boys from school. It was the usual morning activity before the services started.

His friend, Timmy Logan, said, "Ain't that the White girl?"

"I hear ole man White's downright crazy," added one of the younger boys.

"How so?" asked Patrick.

Timmy said, "Ya ain't lived here all yer life, so don't know the story."

Patrick looked puzzled. "What story?"

"The ole man used to be nice, but after his wife died, he ain't been the same since. Folks said he snapped. You know, looney," Timmy answered, making circles near his temple with his index finger.

"Still got him a looker of a daughter, though," noted Robbie, an older boy.

Patrick glanced over at Sylvia just as she stepped down from the wagon. *I have to agree with Robbie. There is no doubt about it, she is pretty. But then, so are a lot of other girls in school.*

~

As Sylvia placed both feet on the ground, she looked up, and her eyes met Patrick's. At the same moment, the organ music started inside, which signaled them to take their seats, so the momentary connection was severed.

Her father growled. "Come on. Late enough 'cause of you."

"Morning, Bernhard... Sylvia." The reverend nodded when they approached.

She smiled. "Good morning, Reverend Brooks."

"Reveren'," Bernhard said gruffly, with his scowl remaining intact.

As they walked through the doors, Sylvia's father grabbed her arm and whispered in her ear, "Leave yer bonnet on."

"Yes, sir." She noted a strange, putrid odor on her father's breath. *What's that smell? It's familiar, but...?* After taking her seat, she had a strange feeling of being watched but wasn't sure why.

~

Not only did William Stoope operate the bank in Clintok, but he also owned the mercantile, which his wife, Eliza, ran. It gave her the chance to know everyone and everything around town. And if there was a bit of juicy gossip to pique her interest, she made it her business to find out all about it.

"I wonder why the White girl is wearing her bonnet inside the church," Eliza said to her husband with a curious eye. "Doesn't she know it's disrespectful? Just because she has no mother does not mean her father shouldn't teach her simple manners befitting a young woman."

William grimaced. "I don't know, dear. Furthermore, it isn't our concern."

"Well, I agree with Mother," Abigail said in a snide way.

After services were over, Eliza made her way to Sylvia. "Are you feeling ill, Miss White?"

"No, ma'am. Why?"

"Well, I think it odd you wouldn't remove your bonnet inside the church if you aren't sick?"

"None yer business," Bernhard scoffed. Then grabbed Sylvia's arm and proceeded to usher her toward the back door.

"Well, Mr. White, I don't think it's proper—"

"Don't care what ya think."

"Well... such terrible treatment of a lady!"

William urged his wife onward with a nudge to her arm. "I told you not to stick your nose where it doesn't belong, Eliza."

"Hmpf! I do no such thing, William. Goodness, but simple deportment of one's dress is not too much to ask. Come along, Abigail. I will not be treated this way, and in the Lord's house no less." Eliza turned and stormed off.

~

Bernhard and Sylvia marched out of the church, climbed into the wagon, and then headed toward home. The only sounds she heard were the clompity-clomp of the horses' hooves and the crickety-crack of the wagon as the team pulled it.

Bernhard continued to seethe from Eliza's pesky remark. *Stoope kept 'er in line, wouldn't be in folk's business.*

Upon arriving home, no sooner had her father stopped the wagon than Sylvia jumped out of it. Nonetheless, no matter that she could feel his eyes on her back with his usual skeptical expression burning into her receding backside, she hurried off.

"'Spect lunch."

"Yes, Papa," she said, unwisely ignoring him while running to the house and all but slamming the door behind her. Sylvia had one ultimate goal—it was to find her locket.

Meanwhile, Bernhard unhitched the horses and put them in the barn. When entering the house, he scowled to find the kitchen was empty.

"Tarnation... SYLVIA!"

"I'll be right there, Papa." With a quick search for the locket proving unsuccessful, she hurried and changed from her Sunday dress to an everyday one and then rushed into the kitchen. Her untied shoelaces caused her to trip and fall flat on her face, multiplying the pain of existing bumps and bruises. Nevertheless, she knew better than to acknowledge that fact.

"Tie 'em... get to fixin'."

Picking herself up off the floor, her father's meanspirited glare was evident from his chair at the table. After standing, she busied herself with preparing breakfast while sensing his unforgiving black eyes. They continued to reveal no emotion as they bore into her. She could even envision the right one with its familiar twitch.

"Yes, Papa."

After church and then lunch, Sylvia did her Sunday jobs to make bread and biscuits for the week. It was the only time because of chores and homework otherwise.

Later in the day, while preparing an early supper, Sylvia's relentless pursuit in every nook and cranny of her room continued in mind's eye. *I know I had my locket before I went to sleep. It has to be there somewhere.*

After eating in silence, Bernhard went back out to the barn to do some repairs.

Meanwhile, Sylvia quickly cleaned up the dishes, then went back to her room for another search before starting her chores. *Did he find it? He couldn't have since he hasn't been in here—or has he? Maybe before waking me? I must find it.*

"Sylvia?"

Oh, no. What does Papa want now? Since finishing her work early, she had gone to her room, as exhaustion claimed her. *Maybe, if I pretend to be asleep, he'll leave.*

"SYLVIA."

Upon hearing footsteps approach her room, she kept her eyes closed and remained still. As the door creaked open, her pulse raced, with her heart beating like a drum. *Oh, God, please make him go away. Please—please—please.*"Aaak!" Her eyes popped open when his hands gripped her neck so tightly that she nearly choked.

"Tryin' to fool me?"

The tighter he squeezed, the more her breathing labored. Unable to make a sound as her eyes begged him to release his hold, terror-filled her entire body. The more lightheaded she felt gave her cause to believe the end was near. But when she was about to give in, he released his chokehold. She bolted upward, swung her legs over the side of the bed, and gasped for air while coughing.

Her father waited for the fit to end—yet never taking his eyes off her. Although the lack of tolerance shown in the scowl on his face.

"Two apples... cellar."

"But you usually go to the cellar."

"Get 'em!"

"There are red apples in the kitchen."

"Want green."

"I think there are green apples, too."

"Get two."

Once on her feet but on unsteady legs, she made her way to the kitchen. Then, after locating the requested apples in the pantry, she grabbed two of the green ones. However, before she could turn around and hand them to her father, a loud WHACK stung her head from behind. Once again, she was in a never-ending tumble, mixed with the sounds of thumping. The feeling of plummeting down steps came over her. Suddenly, she descended into the familiar darkness.

With every breath taken, the next one came harder as her heartbeat increased. The faster it pumped, the more she relived the thumping... darkness... and her father's heavy breathing. With closed eyes darting back and forth like a sideways yo-yo, her mouth opened for a scream to escape. Instead, her eyes flew open as she sat up, blinking and gasping. *Oh! It must have been a nightmare.*

With sweaty palms, a gritty substance stuck to them—and sweat tickled the tiny hairs on her neck to stand on end. As well, her dress stuck to her skin like the tightly woven fabric on display at the mercantile. Adding to her discomfort was a slow, dull ache, growing into a searing pain on the already existing lump to her head.

Rolling her fingers over the handful of substance in her hand, she sniffed it... dirt. Déjà vu struck her when there was no light. Inhaling again... *apples.* Her spirit became deflated. *I'm really in the cellar—not a nightmare at all.*

Sylvia stifled sobs since it wouldn't help her predicament but add to it. While trying to collect herself as much as possible, she brushed the dirt off both hands. Then she reached behind her head to feel a new raised knot next to the already existing one. It was hard and painful, but no blood.

Her throat felt dry as cotton, and she felt queasy as anxiety grew. "Pa... Pa... Papa?"

She listened, but no sound as she looked up at the door. "Papa? Help!" No matter how much she called, an eerie silence prevailed.

After what seemed like hours, she ceased calling when her voice was reduced to a whisper. And with parched lips, she was desperate for a drink of water.

Memories surfaced from her last time in the cellar when creepy-crawlers flittered over her body. She scooted back toward the corner, then huddled by wrapping her arms around her bent legs. While she was used to the skittering and scratching of mice in the old farmhouse walls when doing chores, now she tried to block them from her mind. A shudder ran through her. *Oh, please, Lord, let there be no snakes down here.*

When something crawled up the calf of her leg, she shrieked unlike anything she could have imagined would spew from her mouth. Sylvia swatted at it with her hands before it could get past her knee. She knew whatever it was, had to be dead, as wet goo ran down her leg. Whimpers of distress flowed while wiping her leg with the hem of her dress. Unable to stop her snuffling and numb to the bone, she gathered another section of her dress and blotted at her runny nose.

Left with no recourse, she shook her head in weariness, willing her mind to shut down from sheer fatigue. She tilted her head back until it touched the damp, sod wall, where she soon drifted into a troubled sleep.

How much later, she couldn't be sure, but a door slammed shut, startling her awake. Heavy footsteps followed—then voices. *Do I hear a woman?* She shook her head. *Oh, dear, now I'm must be imagining things. Outside of traveling salesmen, nobody else comes calling.*

As time passed, moments began to feel like hours, lulling Sylvia into hopelessness. Soon, she heard more footsteps, followed by the moving of furniture, but the door opening got her full attention. Although this time, she knew better than looking into the direct light—subdued though it was.

"Sylvia," Bernhard called in a gruff voice.

She found herself speechless while twitching on the earth floor as a rope plummeted downward—just missing her. When splashing water hit her in the face, nothing short of pure joy made her cry out in surprise, "W... water!"

Even so, before she thought of moving, the door slammed shut, leaving her bewildered, which caused a sob of distress. *What did I do so wrong that Papa keeps me down here?*

A little ray of hope sprang up when her father didn't cover the door with the table, although his footsteps faded away. Sylvia managed to sit up, and since the bucket dropped not far from her, she crawled over to it and found a ladle inside. After savoring the flow of water over her cracked lips, she continued to gulp several ladles full. Since Sylvia did it on an empty stomach, it caused it to flip-flop from drinking too fast. She didn't care. After cleaning her hands, she poured another ladle of water over her face, but at the expense of disregarding the muddy effect from the water on the earthen floor where she sat.

After resting a few moments, hunger pains began to twist in her stomach. *Apples. I know they're here. I can smell them. I hope Papa didn't move the baskets.* She crawled to the left until running into one, reached inside, grabbed the fruit and took a bite, and then savored the tangy flavor. *Green ... the reason he sent me down here, even though I was in my room.*

She huddled in the corner like before, as if she could see in the dark while watching... waiting... fearing another creepy crawler or something worse would find her. The nightmare just wouldn't go away.

More memories about what happened plagued her as a shiver ran down her spine. She could still feel her father's hands around her neck as he began to snuff out her life. *Let me think. I went to the kitchen for his green apples, but I don't remember anything else. How did I get down here? Is it day or night? I don't even know what day it is. Oh, when will he let me out of here?*

"Huh! No! A mouse." Scratching and skittering came from the potato bin, so she scooted away on her backside. "Papa! Papa!"

Nothing.

Thump... bumping... the stairs... then darkness.

"Tryin' to fool me?"

Her father's beady black eyes were fixed on her, and his large hands closed around her neck.

"No, Papa."

His heavy breathing came with glaring eyes of anger while he shouted.

"Help... no..."

WHAACK!

"Get 'em... green ones."

WHAACK!

"Tryin' to fool me?"

"No, Papa... no."

After an abrupt noise, the door opened. However, this time, Sylvia knew not to look into the direct light. She used her hand as a visor and then saw the silhouette of her father.

"Grab the ladder," he said in a piercing demand.

The sudden sound of his harsh voice surprised her but also warned her not to linger—pain or not. Wincing, she reached for the wall, felt her way to the ladder, and then centered it at the opening of the cellar. He held it steady while she climbed upward but was hesitant when he offered his large and calloused hand before clasping her small, delicate one.

She stood in a death-like stillness while he closed the door to the cellar and then moved the table and chairs back over it. While glancing out the window, she took a deep breath. *I can't remember the daylight ever looking so beautiful.* She noted a book atop the table but stood unmoving until her father finished moving the table and chairs over the cellar.

Bernhard noticed she saw the book. "Teacher stopped."

"Miss Kimball was here?"

"Just now."

"What day is it?"

"Monday."

"What did she want?"

"Dropped off yer readin'."

"What did you tell her?"

"Don't matter. She'll 'spect ya in the mornin'."

"I better get my chores done."

"Tendin' to the fields. Back fer supper."

CHAPTER THREE
Miss Kimball

After opening the book, Sylvia saw a note but treated it as if it would fall to pieces in her hand while unfolding it.

You were missed at school today, Sylvia. Please read the first chapter since we read it in class.

Miss Kimball

Sylvia smiled. *It was nice of Miss Kimball to bring homework to me. Not only is she beautiful with her blonde hair, but her eyes are as blue as the sky. Even her skin is perfect, like the porcelain dolls sold at the mercantile.* She sighed. *If only I had beautiful dresses like hers. And her perfume—she always smells like fresh spring flowers.*

Sylvia frowned, thinking how different her life could be if she had a life like Miss Kimball. She wondered if her teacher had a beau. If not, she would soon enough—no doubt about it.

Unable to shake her melancholia, she went outside to do her chores. Starting with mucking out the horses' stalls, along with the cow's, too. Then, she scattered straw for bedding and cleaned out the chicken coop. She finished by watering the livestock.

Before going back inside, Sylvia leaned back against the barn wall, unable to quit fantasizing about being just like Emma Kimball. *I'd wear a beautiful new dress every day, with a matching bonnet. I'd also walk over to the dressing table, dab perfume on my neck and behind my ears. While at the schoolhouse, of course, my day would be perfect. I would teach children who would be on their best behavior.*

A dreamy warmth covered her face. *After school, a tall, well-dressed man with black hair, kind eyes, and a warm smile would be waiting in the doorway, just to escort me home.*

She turned toward the door of the barn while having a vision of the schoolhouse. The handsome man was ready to speak to her.

"Sylvia!"

She jumped. "Oh! You startled me, Papa."

All of a sudden, the handsome man's image faded away because reality hit her smack in the face. The gray-haired man standing in the doorway had familiar beady, black eyes, with an ever-constant scowl on his face. He glared at her for what seemed like an eternity before his dictatorial voice boomed, "Bess fix supper."

"Yes, sir."

Later, with the meal over, dishes washed, and the floor swept, Sylvia retired to her room. With some fresh water, she was eager to sponge away the grime from the cellar and the gooey mess from the creepy-crawler on her leg. She just wished washing away the memory of her horrid ordeal could be as easy. Since it was not the day for her weekly bath, this was not the time to test her father by fixing one. A sponge bath would have to do.

Once finished, she felt somewhat revived, so Sylvia put on a freshly laundered nightgown. After snuggling into bed, she settled in and read the assigned chapter of her homework. Once she finished, her bed became too inviting, so her eyes grew heavy after such a grueling ordeal. In no time, her dreams drifted back to Miss Kimball and the handsome stranger as he walked into Stoope's Mercantile.

"Good morning, Mrs. Stoope."

"Good morning, Miss Kimball. How can I help you?"

"I'd like to see your dress fabric, please."

"Of course." Mrs. Stoope grabbed a tan calico print off the shelf and placed it on the counter. "This is a very good fabric for every day."

Miss Kimball gave the shelves of other material a good look. "I'd like to see the burgundy one, please."

"As I said, this cotton calico print is much more practical."

"I'm not looking for practical, Mrs. Stoope. I want the burgundy one."

Mrs. Stoope spun on her heels and returned with the lovely burgundy taffeta. "I must remind you how the calico is more suited for—"

"I like the burgundy fabric, Mrs. Stoope."

The tall, tan man with dark hair and brown eyes, who had been watching, moved to the counter. "Excuse me, ladies, but if you don't mind me saying so, the burgundy is most appealing." He smiled at Emma. "In fact, it may be the prettiest thing I've ever seen."

Miss Kimball blushed.

With a grimace, Eliza Stoope stood more daunting. "How can I help you, Mr.?"

"James... I'm James Thurston. I'll take a pouch of your tobacco when you have a moment." He turned back to Miss Kimball.

"And you are?"

"Miss Kimball... Emma Kimball."

"Did you say... Miss?"

"Yes." She blushed.

Eliza slammed the tobacco on the counter. "Shall I add it to your account?"

"That'd be fine," he answered, although his attention was elsewhere. "Miss Emma Kimball, it has been a pleasure to meet you. Maybe we'll meet again sometime."

"It was a pleasure to meet you, too."

He tipped his hat to Eliza. "Ma'am."

She smirked. "Good day, Mr. Thurston."

James stood at the front of the church while waiting for his beautiful bride-to-be walk down the aisle. When she stepped inside the church, however, it wasn't Miss Kimball.

"Sylvia."

"Yes, my love."

"Sylvia! Yer late."

Jerked awake, Sylvia blinked and looked around the room, quickly realizing night had turned into day, and she was still in bed. It was so unlike her since she was used to getting up at dawn. At least, it was a relief to realize she was in her room and not the cold, dank cellar. Nonetheless, the sudden awareness of her father's endless, sour disposition that was never far from mind's eye urged her to spring up and out of bed. She speedily changed into her everyday dress, brushed her hair, and scooted off to the kitchen.

"Would you like some eggs, Papa?"

"Fixed 'em. Some left."

"Thank you, Papa."

She got a plate, dished out a helping, then grabbed a biscuit and some jam. Aware her father watched with a scrupulous eye while she scarfed down her food, she was relieved he didn't say anything while she cleared the dishes off the table.

"Teacher asks—you were sick. Hear?"

"Yes, Papa."

An hour later, Sylvia arrived at school and was greeted by one of Miss Kimball's pleasant smiles.

"Glad you're feeling better, Sylvia."

"Thank you, ma'am."

When school was over for the day, Miss Kimball detained her by pointing to a chair. "Sylvia, would you stay after class? I have something I want to ask you."

"Yes, ma'am." Nervousness made her stomach flip-flop while taking her seat. *Oh, no, what does she want? Could she have guessed what happened?* As the rest of the kids scurried outside, Sylvia remained frozen in her seat until she and her teacher were alone.

Miss Kimball finished erasing the board, then turned around. "Thanks for staying, Sylvia. I have a favor to ask you?"

"A favor, ma'am?"

"Yes. Susie Evans is ill, and I'm not sure how long she'll be gone. Until she can return, would you like to take her place by erasing the boards and help grade papers?"

"You want me?"

"Yes, if you'd like to do it."

"Um, yes, ma'am. But I will have to ask Papa."

"But of course. I'd be happy to ask your father if you'd like."

"No, ma'am. I better do it."

"Okay, then. Can you let me know by tomorrow?"

"Yes, ma'am."

"Okay, I will see you then."

Sylvia smiled. "See you tomorrow. Uhhh, Miss Kimball."

"Yes, Sylvia."

"Thank you."

"You're welcome."

Sylvia's enthusiasm grew as she left the room. *Miss Kimball could have asked anyone to help her, but she picked me instead. No one's ever asked me to do anything.* Aggravation set in when seeing Abigail Stoope walking toward her.

"Did you get in trouble?"

"No."

"What did Miss Kimball want with you?"

"She just wanted to ask me something."

"What?"

"She wanted to know if I would help her after school."

Abigail made a smart-aleck face. "Why would she ask you?"

"I don't know. I have to get home. Move, Abigail."

~

Abigail smirked in irritation while watching her classmate rush down the road. *Well, it's obvious as the nose on your face, Sylvia White. Why wouldn't Miss Kimball ask me to grade papers? After all, I am the smartest girl in school.*

~

Sylvia hurried home to do her outside chores, then went inside to tidy up the house. Glancing at the clock, warned her she had no time for any dawdling, so she prepared their supper. When her father walked in the door, she took a deep breath to calm her nerves. "Hi, Papa, we can eat soon."

"Chores done?"

"Yes, sir."

Bernhard hung up his hat on the hook by the door.

"I have the water ready for you, Paps. It's in the bowl on the table by the stove."

"Hmmm." Bernhard turned and squinted at his daughter.

"I made your favorite stew and cornbread."

"Sounds fine." Bernhard washed and dried his hands with the towel Sylvia left next to the bowl. Then he pulled out his chair to sit.

Sylvia served the food and then took her seat across from him. She had rehearsed in her mind all afternoon the best way to ask him about helping Miss Kimball.

"How's the stew, Papa?"

"Fine."

"Miss Kimball asked me to stay after school today."

"Hmm." Bernhard continued to shovel in his food.

"She had a favor to ask of me."

"Favor?"

"Susie Evans stays after school to help, but she's sick, and Miss Kimball isn't sure how long she'll be absent, so she needs some help."

Bernhard looked at his daughter with beady, quizzical eyes.

"So, Miss Kimball wants to know if I can stay after school and help her until Susie comes back. It wouldn't take long, and I would still have plenty of time to do my chores."

"Doin' what?"

"Erasing the blackboards and helping her grade papers."

"Plenty t' do here." His attention turned back to his meal.

"But Miss Kimball said it would only take a half-hour each day."

"Answer's no."

"But, Papa, Miss Kimball needs—"

"Ain't gonna say it again."

With a sigh, Sylvia slumped in her chair, and any appetite she may have had vanished in the blink of an eye. "May I be excused?"

"Umm-hmm."

She got up and put her plate on the stove for later—maybe. After hurrying to her room, she threw herself face down on the bed as tears rolled down her cheeks like rain beading down a windowpane. *Why is Papa so mean to me? Why won't he let me help Miss Kimball? Why does he hate me so much? What did I ever do to him? I try to be good and do everything he wants. I don't understand him at all.*

Sylvia sat up on the bed and wiped tear-stained eyes when she heard his footsteps coming closer to her room. *Maybe he has changed his mind.* She wrung her hands in hopeful anticipation as the door opened.

"Bess get to them dishes."

She frowned. "Yes, sir."

Filled with dread and feeling worse but unsure why it was so, Sylvia dragged herself into the kitchen to do her work.

Sylvia had a restless night, but walking to school the next day, she dreaded telling Miss Kimball her father's decision. She thought about faking illness but knew it wouldn't work. Although skipping school crossed her mind, but only for a fleeting moment, because, should her father find out, his wrath would be a high price to pay.

~

The next day at school, Emma Kimball could tell Sylvia's downcast expression that something was wrong at home. Or her father refused to let her help after school. Deciding if her intuition about Bernhard White was right, she had ideas to change his mind racing around in her head.

At recess, she saw Sylvia sitting underneath the big oak tree by herself, looking sad and a million miles away.

Later, when school let out, all the kids scurried from the building, except Sylvia.

"Hello, dear, you've been so quiet today. I'm guessing your father didn't agree to you staying after school to help me?"

"No, ma'am. He says I have too much work to do, so I have to go home right away."

"I understand."

"I'm so sorry, Miss Kimball."

"There's nothing to be sorry about, Sylvia. It's okay."

Sylvia left the schoolhouse without looking back, although just outside the door, tears ran down her cheeks.

"That poor girl. I've got to do something."

CHAPTER FOUR
Apple Pie

Over the weekend, Emma Kimball continued to run scenarios over in her mind about how to convince Bernhard White to change his mind and allow Sylvia to help after school.

She'd heard the story about Sophia Bowden. How she had come from a well-to-do family who was connected to the railroad. The forbidden romance with Bernhard White, a lowly farmer's son, rose many an eyebrow. Within six months, the couple married, despite Thomas and Ann Bowden's adamant disapproval.

Unable to prevent the inevitable, they were resolute about their daughter not living in less than the best conditions. So, as a wedding present, they purchased twenty acres of land, where they had a two-story house built.

A year later, due to complications, Sophia died giving birth to Sylvia. Thomas and Ann took the news hard, and in a short time, moved away, using the expansion of the railroad as their excuse. Further gossip told of how the Bowden's never returned to see their granddaughter. Some even said it was because Bernhard White's blood running through her veins considered her inferior.

If I could get him to agree to let Sylvia help me, I could have time alone with her. She's a beautiful girl, but there's something so sad and haunting about her behavior. I must find out why—come up with a plan. I could invite them over for supper. No, I don't want to make Sylvia feel uneasy. I could invite Mr. White for supper. But if the rumors about him are true. No... maybe just flowers. Wait... there's something about an old saying—like, the way to a man's heart. I've got it!

While Emma had been tempted to hitch up the horse and buggy, and then venture to the White place after church on Sunday, or later in the evening, she decided to wait until after school on Monday.

When the time came to carry out her plan, she erased the boards, then stopped home to pick up the surprise for Mr. White, and then went on her way.

Dear Lord, please help me say something to change Mr. White's mind. Somehow, I have to reach Sylvia. I sense something isn't right, but what? Please, Lord, help me.

She noticed Bernhard White walking from the house and was convinced he had glanced her way—most likely when hearing her horse and buggy. Nonetheless, she felt as if he tried to ignore her when he continued toward the field. She rode a little faster.

"Hello, Mr. White."

"Sylvia's inside."

"Thank you, but I'm here to see you."

"Can I do fer ya?"

"Well, I... um... I made these yesterday." Smiling, she picked up the box beside her, then handed it to Bernhard. "I made a couple of pies since I had extra apples. However, I didn't stop to think that I'm alone. I can hardly eat them both, so I wanted to share."

A smile threatened to form. "Apple's my favorite."

"Thank goodness," Emma said under her breath while she looked toward the sky.

"What?"

"Huh... my goodness, I was lucky to have extra apples."

Bernhard's half-smile faded, and then he abruptly handed the box back to Emma, almost shoving her. "Headin' t' the fields. Give it t' Sylvia."

"Mr. White, I need to ask you something."

"'Bout her helpin'? Answer's no."

"But, Mr. White, I could use her help."

"Plenty t' do here."

"Mr. White, our new school program requires each child to help after school for a specified time..."

"'Fraid I can't spare 'er."

"It would only take a half-hour after school at most. It's a part of Sylvia's grade. Each parent has agreed to allow their child to be a part of the program. I just haven't had a chance to ask you yet. Mr. White, Sylvia would be the only child—"

"Bess get t' the fields."

"Mr. White, I'm not leaving until you agree to allow Sylvia to be a part of—"

"I say yes, ya stop chatterin'?"

"Yes, of course!"

"Bess not take more 'en a half-hour."

She smiled. "You have my word. May I go tell Sylvia?"

He nodded.

"Oh, thank you."

"Umm-hmm."

"Oh, Mr. White?"

He frowned. "Yeah."

"Can Sylvia start tomorrow?"

Bernhard nodded.

"Thank you!"

Bernhard headed back to the fields without hesitation.

An excited Emma climbed out of the buggy. She wanted to run like a schoolgirl, although most improper for a teacher.

~

Hearing the horse and buggy, a curious Sylvia had watched and heard the conversation taking place between her father and teacher through the window. She wasn't sure how to feel about it as she answered the door before hearing the knock. "Hello, ma'am. It's nice to see you."

The teacher smiled. "Hello, Sylvia. I came to bring you and your father this apple pie I made yesterday."

"Thank you, ma'am. Apple pie is his favorite."

"He said as much, too."

"You came all the way out here to bring us a pie?"

"Not exactly. I came to ask your father to allow you to help me after school."

"Oh." Sylvia's smile vanished.

"I'm so happy to tell you, he's changed his mind."

Sylvia looked surprised. "He has?"

"Yes."

"Oh, Miss Kimball, are you sure? I mean, how did you ever convince Papa to let me help you?"

She smiled. "Well, I simply wasn't going to take no for an answer. I can be quite persuasive if need be, you know."

Sylvia hugged her teacher. "Oh, thank you, ma'am, thank you very much."

"Well, I look forward to seeing you tomorrow, dear."

"Oh, I'll be there."

Later, while preparing supper, Sylvia could hardly contain her enthusiasm. She wondered if thanking her father for allowing her to help Miss Kimball would be a good idea. *Maybe, I better not. I don't want to anger him.*

Bernhard came in and washed for supper, sat down at the table, and as usual, said not one word while shoveling food into his mouth. After a while, he glanced up at Sylvia with an unscrupulous eye. "Teacher's meddlin'."

"Well... um... all the kids are volunteering, Papa."

"Said no before."

"It won't take long, and I will be right home."

He shook his head, scowling. "Womenfolk and meddlin'."

Sylvia pushed her chair back and then stood. "Would you like a slice of Miss Kimball's apple pie, Papa? It sure does smell good."

"Umm-hmm. When yer done, come straight home."

"Yes, Papa." Sylvia smiled while placing the slice of pie in front of him. While cleaning up the kitchen, she had the urge to whistle, so she finally got the hang of it with some practice. Sylvia couldn't think of any other time when her father had allowed her to do anything of her own choosing. Oh, how she loved Miss Kimball for helping her.

Sylvia tossed and turned and hardly slept a wink all night. But the next morning, when Bernhard came to wake her, she was already up and dressed for school.

He opened her door and looked startled. "Oh... yer awake."

"Yes. I will get breakfast started."

"Eggs gathered."

"Thank you, Papa."

After a breakfast of eggs, biscuits, and peach preserves, she washed dishes, then was off to school. Sylvia hurried so fast, it felt as if her legs might fall off, but she didn't want to miss the big day. She even ended up being the first one to arrive at school. She saw Patrick Ryan and Timmy Logan walking up the road with their books and fishing poles in hand.

~

Timmy nodded in Sylvia's direction. "Hey, ain't that the White girl? What's she doin' at school already?"

Patrick looked at her with a shrug. "I don't know."

"Maybe, she killed her crazy 'ole man and ain't got nowhere else t' go."

Patrick shook his head. "Timmy, only you would come up with such a story."

"What? It could happen."

Patrick walked faster, with Timmy trying to catch him. He was just about to say hello to Sylvia when Abigail Stoope approached them.

Patrick smiled at Sylvia but kept walking.

"How do you like my new dress, Sylvia?"

"Oh, it's pretty, Abigail."

"My mother ordered it just for me. There are none others like it in the mercantile. Mother says I shouldn't wear what the common folk around here wear. It would be beneath me, she added."

"Yer ma's a snob," Timmy said as he walked past.

Sylvia couldn't help but smile.

"Timmy Logan, you're just a country hick," Abigail shouted after him.

"Rather be a hick than a stuck-up snob," Timmy teased while walking backward.

Abigail sneered while turning away from the boy. "My mother says you're going to help after school for a while?"

"Yes. How does she know?"

"Miss Kimball came into the restaurant last night. My mother overheard her talking to one of the other parents."

Abigail had a smirk on her face. "Well, you must know, she only asked because she feels sorry for you."

Sylvia's heart sank. "What do you mean?"

"My mother says it's the only reason there could be for her to do so. Otherwise, Miss Kimball would have asked me. It's clear to see I am the best choice. In fact, Mother even says I am the smartest one in the whole school."

The sound of the bell interrupted the snobbish girl.

A disheartened Sylvia frowned as she stood. "We better get to class." With each step taken toward the schoolhouse, her earlier excitement was replaced with disappointment. She sat at her desk without saying anything unless called upon.

~

Emma noticed Sylvia's melancholy tone and wondered what had happened since last night to cause such a change in her demeanor. Things just didn't add up at all.

At lunchtime, she dismissed the other children but asked Sylvia to remain at her desk. "Are you still going to help after school today, dear? I do hope so because I'm looking forward to it."

"Yes, ma'am." She didn't look up from her desk.

"Are you okay?"

"Yes, Miss Kimball."

"It's just... well, you seemed so happy about it last night. But now, I'm not so sure."

"Yes, ma'am, I'm fine."

"Well, something must have changed?"

"No, ma'am."

"Well, all right then. Go on out and eat your lunch with everyone else. We can talk more later."

"Yes, Miss Kimball."

Emma couldn't help but notice a dejected Sylvia who got up from her desk and walked to the door. She was so excited last night. I wonder what has changed since then?

CHAPTER FIVE
Sylvia -vs- Abigail

Sylvia walked over to the big oak tree and seated herself in the grass. However, after looking at her lunch pail, she was no longer hungry, since every time she tried to get Abigail's words out of her head, they came back to her. *She only asked you because she feels sorry for you.* Her frown grew. *I thought Miss Kimball wanted my help. Maybe, Abigail was right.*

Her nemesis appeared. "Did you get into trouble?"

"No, why?"

"Well, Miss Kimball dismissed everyone but you. So, it stands to reason something is wrong."

"She just needed to ask me if I was still planning on helping her today."

"I told you she felt sorry for you."

Sylvia thought to change the subject. "Don't you want to go eat your lunch?"

Abigail took her sandwich out and then sat down next to Sylvia. "If you want to get out of helping after school, I could always stay in your place."

"I don't know. I promised Miss Kimball that I would."

"Oh, she won't mind. It's not like it's hard to erase the blackboards. I could tell her if you want me to."

Jessica Potter, a younger girl, ran up to them. "Abigail, I've been waiting for you by the teeter-totter."

"Oh, I'm not going to teeter-totter today, Jessica. I have to help Sylvia with a problem. Run along now, and maybe I will play with you tomorrow at recess."

Jessica frowned. "But you promised to teeter-totter today. I can't do it by myself."

"Oh, scat, little girl. You're bothering us!"

"Miiiiiss Kiiiiimmmbaaaaal!" Jessica sobbed all the way to the schoolhouse.

Sylvia gasped. "You weren't very nice, Abigail."

"Oh, she'll get over it. Now back to this problem of yours."

Miss Kimball stepped outside. "Abigail, may I see you inside, please."

She hurried to the schoolhouse. "Yes, Miss Kimball."

"Did you tell Jessica you'd teeter-totter with her today?"

"No, ma'am."

Jessica snuffled. "She's lying."

"Well, she says differently."

"I play with her sometimes, but I couldn't today. I was helping a friend with a problem."

"She told me she would today, Miss Kimball," Jessica said.

"Did you get your friend's problem resolved, Abigail?"

"Yes, ma'am."

"Very well. But I will ask you to never again yell at Jessica or any of the other children."

"Oh, I didn't yell at her, Miss Kimball."

"So, you didn't tell her to scat?"

"No, ma'am."

"Abigail, I stood by the window and saw the entire thing, and I distinctly heard you tell her to scat because she bothered you." She fisted her hands on her hips. "I also believe you told Jessica you would teeter-totter with her today. When you say you're going to do something, you need to stand by your word."

"But—"

"Since you've been dishonest, you'll stay after school today."

She smirked. "Oh, I'd be glad to help you, Miss Kimball. Then, you won't need Sylvia since she is needed at home."

"On the contrary, Sylvia will be helping me grade papers. I have something different in mind for you."

Miss Kimball reached over for the bell and then rang it. "Okay, children, recess is over."

Later, when school was finished, only Sylvia and Abigail remained in their seats.

"Sylvia, would you start erasing the blackboards? Then, I would like to have your help with grading papers."

"Yes, ma'am."

Abigail looked expectantly. "What about me, Miss Kimball?"

"You can stand in the corner until all of the blackboards are erased, Abigail. And then, you'll write on all of the clean blackboards... *I will not yell at others. And I will keep my word.*"

As Sylvia turned her back toward Abigail and picked up the eraser, she couldn't help but smile.

Abigail's expression was one of stubbornness. "My mother won't like this."

"Well, your mother is welcome to come and talk with me. I will be happy to explain the situation."

"She'll worry if I don't come straight home. I have to tell her I'll be here for a while."

"Yes, Abigail. You may hurry across the street and tell your mother, but I want you to come right back. If you don't, I'm afraid you'll have to stay late again tomorrow."

Abigail scowled. "Yes, Miss Kimball." And then she was off.

Abigail returned in no time, and while she wrote on the blackboards, Sylvia helped grade papers. After Miss Kimball checked her pocket watch, she looked up. "Okay, Sylvia, it's been thirty minutes, so you must be on your way home. We don't want you to be late."

"Okay, Miss Kimball."

"I should go home, too," Abigail said in a matter-of-fact tone. "I don't want Mother to worry."

"I don't think you're quite done yet, Abigail."

"But, Miss Kimball, I have filled the whole board."

"I'm afraid you are only half-way done. You will continue to write; *I will not yell at others. And I will keep my word*, on the other blackboard."

"But, Miss Kimball, my arm is tired."

"I'm afraid it's going to get more tired, dear."

Sylvia had grabbed her books, lunch pail and then started to walk toward the door.

"You have done a great job today, Sylvia. Thank you for your help."

"Yes, ma'am. See you tomorrow."

"Okay, dear."

Abigail looked dejected while walking to the other board.

"Goodbye, Abigail," Sylvia said.

The pouting girl with her turned up lip gave Sylvia a disgusted look.

Sylvia was just about to walk through the doorway but bumped into Eliza Stoope instead.

She gasped while splaying her hand over her chest. "Oh, Mrs. Stoope, you startled me."

"Well, I should have known this would involve the likes of you, Sylvia White."

"Hello, Mrs. Stoope," greeted Miss Kimball, irritated at the woman's rudeness. "You may leave, Sylvia."

"Yes, ma'am." She hurried out the door.

Eliza stood in a confident stance. "Miss Kimball, I wanted to see my darling daughter grading papers. Why is she at the chalkboard?"

"Because I asked Sylvia to help me grade papers."

Eliza looked at her daughter. "Whatever are you doing, child?"

"Helping... Mother," Abigail answered unconvincingly.

"Helping? But you are not erasing—you're writing." She turned away from her daughter. "Miss Kimball, what is going on here? My daughter should be helping you grade papers, so why would you have Sylvia instead?"

"Mrs. Stoope, I—"

Eliza's impatience began to show. "What is going on here? Why do you have Abigail writing all over this board? I insist you tell me this instant."

"Because we had an incident at recess today, and I asked her to stay after school."

"An incident? Well, surely, you don't mean to say my daughter was involved in any way?"

"Yes, she was. The incident occurred between Abigail and another student."

"And you're punishing my baby girl?"

"If I may explain—"

"Well, where is the other student?"

"Mrs. Stoope, your daughter promised one of the younger girls she would teeter-totter with her today at recess. When the little girl asked Abigail about it, your daughter denied making the promise to play. She also yelled at the other girl to go away since she was bothering her."

"Well, it's clear to see the girl must have misunderstood."

"No, she didn't, Mrs. Stoope."

"Well, how do you know, Miss Kimball?"

"Because I stood by the window and heard Abigail."

"Well, maybe you didn't hear it as well as you thought."

"Mrs. Stoope, I assure you, I saw and heard your daughter yell at the little girl, who came running and crying straight to me for help."

Eliza turned to her daughter. "Abigail, is this true?"

"Uh..."

Her mother grimaced. "Uh... uh... what?"

"Y... Yesss."

"Oh, for cryin' out loud! Well, I will deal with you at home." She turned to the teacher. "Good day, Miss Kimball." A very angry Eliza Stoope stomped to the door.

"Good day, Mrs. Stoope," Emma sighed, aggravated at the woman, then went back to grading papers. But due to Abigail's frequent stops, she didn't finish for forty-minutes.

"Miss Kimball, I'm done."

"Well, it took longer than I had hoped it would, Abigail. Now you may erase the boards."

"Erase? I just got done with all this writing!"

"Yes, I know, but I still need clean boards for tomorrow."

"Ugh... I don't know if I can lift my arms, ma'am."

"I'm sure you can manage for just a few more minutes, then you may go home. But only after the boards are clean."

Abigail sighed while picking up the eraser. "Yes, ma'am." When finished, she grabbed her books and lunch pail. "May I go home now?"

"Yes, Abigail. I hope you learned an important lesson here today."

"Yes, Miss Kimball."

After Abigail left, Emma gathered her things in readiness to leave. *I hope I can spend time alone with Sylvia tomorrow. I've got to figure out what's going on.*

CHAPTER SIX
Meddlers

Sylvia left school and hurried home to avoid upset with her father. Arriving home on time every day meant a better chance of being able to continue helping Miss Kimball.

As she came down the path to her house, she saw her father working in the fields. He looked up for a brief moment but went back to work.

She continued with daily chores, made supper, and set the table since her father would be returning soon.

Later, he walked through the door, washed up, and sat at the table without saying a word. Halfway through the meal, he stopped eating. "Teacher ask 'bout anythin'?"

"No, sir."

"Good. She does you keep quiet."

"Yes, Papa. One girl had to stay after school today for getting into trouble at recess."

"Fer what?"

"She made a promise to play with Jessica at recess, but broke it, and then yelled at the little girl. Miss Kimball made her stay after school and write on the board."

"Who?"

"Who do you mean, Papa?"

"Which girl?"

"Oh... it was Abigail."

"Stoope?"

"Yes."

"Stay 'way from 'em Stoope's. Nothin' but trouble."

"Oh, I try Papa. But Abigail just isn't a nice person. Not many kids like her."

"Meddlers."

"Would you like some coffee and dessert, Papa? I made a pie."

"Umm-hmm."

The rest of the evening went as usual. Once dishes were washed and the kitchen in order, they retired to their own rooms, where Sylvia did her homework. Afterward, she changed into her nightgown and then decided to read for a while in bed. Before long, her eyes felt heavy, and she drifted off to sleep.

Soon, dreams of writing on the blackboard intervened, where Mrs. Stoope stood in the doorway of the schoolhouse. "Huh. I should have known this would involve the likes of you, Sylvia."

Next, Abigail appeared, standing at Miss Kimball's desk, looking just like her—and wearing their teacher's clothes, too. "rite on the boards, Sylvia. *Miss Kimball feels sorry for you*. Do it. Write it."

Mrs. Stoope joined her daughter. "Yes, Sylvia. Since your teacher feels so sorry for you, write on the boards. *Miss Kimball feels sorry for you*. Go ahead and write it." They both kept at Sylvia. "Write it... write it. *Miss Kimball feels sorry for you.*"

They both started cackling with sinister laughs.

Then, her father appeared—angry and pointing his finger at Mrs. Stoope first... then Abigail. "**MEDDLERS!**"

In an instant, the cackling stopped.

An angry, glaring Bernhard turned his attention to Sylvia, who had stopped writing. "Keep writin', *She feels sorry fer you.*"

Then she saw Miss Kimball's face appear. "Keep writing, Sylvia. *I feel sorry for you.*"

All their faces started to flash before her eyes in rapid succession. "Write it. *Miss Kimball feels sorry for you*. Write it. Sylvia, *I feel sorry for you*. Go ahead, write it, child; *Miss Kimball feels sorry fer you.*"

Sylvia's head thrashed about, "No! No! No!" Her eyes popped open, and she sat up in bed. Minuscule droplets of perspiration formed on her forehead. And her breathing was labored. Reaching for the nightstand, she lit the oil lamp. Sylvia looked around her room and started to calm herself. *Oh, just a dream. But it seemed so real.* After taking a few deep breaths, she grabbed the book again and opened it to take her mind off the nightmare.

After reading a chapter, her eyes became heavy. She put the book back on the nightstand, extinguished the oil lamp, and snuggled into bed. *I sure do hope I sleep in peace tonight.*

The next thing she remembered was opening her eyes to the morning sun and how it shone brightly through her window. It put a smile on her face. Sylvia hurried with her usual morning routine and was dressed soon enough, then off to school. *I wonder if today will be as hectic as yesterday? Oh, well, it doesn't' matter.*

As she walked up the school path, she saw a large cloud of dust in the sky. *What's that?* Once closer, she realized it came from the schoolyard. Children were chanting, "Get 'em! Get 'em!" She saw two boys who were intertwined while rolling around in the dirt.

When Sylvia was close enough to see better, she recognized rowdy Johnny Prescott, a 15-year-old boy who managed to instigate getting into a fight with someone at least once a week. The other boy was Patrick Ryan, who she had never seen get into a wrangle.

Miss Kimball came running out of the schoolhouse and stopped in front of the dust cloud of boys. "BOYS... STOP IT! THAT'S ENOUGH! BOYS... ENOUGH!"

When the boys stopped their scuffling and stood up, she grabbed them both by their shirt collars. "What is going on here?"

Johnny scowled. "He attacked me, Miss Kimball."

Patrick stood with fisted hands at his sides. "I did not. You attacked me first."

"Boys, why did you attack each other?"

"He was cheating," Patrick answered first.

Johnny shook his head. "Was not."

"Since we're not getting to the truth here, both of you will have to stay after school. By then, maybe you'll remember what happened. Right now, it's time for class, everyone, so let's go inside and tend to our lessons."

With the excitement over, all the children filed into the schoolhouse. Miss Kimball looked down at her pale, yellow dress and dusted it off, which caused a large puff of dust to fly into the air. While choking and coughing, she looked down to find patches of yellow next to tannish-brown dirt ground all over it.

Emma looked up at the sky and sighed. "So much for my new dress." *Why did I insist on having them stay after school? I should have just made them stand in the corner. No doubt, I am having the most difficult time finding any alone time with Sylvia. It's already been a hectic start to the day.*

After the morning chaos, the rest of the day went without incidents in class or fights at recess—the children seemed to play well together. Even so, she kept a close watch on Johnny and Patrick. They must have known they were in trouble, as they avoided each other like the other had scarlet fever.

Miss Kimball checked her pocket watch. "All right, children, you may be dismissed."

Everyone stood and started for the door, including the boys who were required to stay.

"Excuse me, Johnny... Patrick... you will remain here, as I still would like to speak with you."

They both stopped, and as if they had been caught stealing, replied in a misery-laden tone, "Yes, Miss Kimball."

Emma turned around to face the desks. "Sylvia?"

"Yes, ma'am."

"Would you please erase the boards, dear, while I'm outside having a chat with Johnny and Patrick?"

"Oh, yes, ma'am." She walked to the board and started cleaning.

Miss Kimball moved toward the door where the boys were standing frozen like two mannequins. Then she walked past them and turned around. "Follow me, boys."

They glanced at each other and then followed their teacher down the steps.

After stopping, she turned to them and paused, but neither boy offered an explanation. "Well... tell me what happened between the two of you this morning. Johnny, you go first."

"He attacked me, Miss Kimball."

"No, I didn't, Johnny, you attacked me first."

"Boys, I feel like we're starting the day all over here."

"What were you doing this morning before you got into a fight?"

"We were shooting marbles," Patrick answered.

"So, I can assume no one else is involved then, and it was just you two shooting marbles together?"

Johnny nodded. "Yes, Miss Kimball."

"Good. At least you both agree on something. Now, who would like to tell me what happened next?"

When both started talking at the same time, she raised her hand. "Boys! I only want one of you speaking at a time. So, Johnny, you may begin."

"Well, we was—"

"Were."

Johnny scrunched up his face. "What?"

"Were... we were," Miss Kimball corrected.

Johnny nodded. "Well, we was... were... shootin' marbles. I beat him fair and square, but he got mad and attacked me."

"I did not. You attacked me first."

"Patrick, you will have a chance to explain in a moment. Do you want to add anything else, Johnny?"

"Nope."

The teacher puckered her lips. "It's no, ma'am."

"Oh... nope, ma'am."

She rolled her eyes at his almost correct response. "Okay, Patrick, you may explain."

"Well, ma'am, we were shooting marbles, and he did win, but only because he cheated."

"DID NOT!"

"While I was shooting, you stole my cloudies."

"DID NOT."

"Johnny, please do not interrupt one more time. You've had your chance to speak. Patrick, how do you know he stole your cloudies?"

"When I got done shooting, they were gone."

"Was anyone else around you, Patrick?"

"No, Miss Kimball."

"I didn't steal 'em."

"Johnny, I will not warn you again about interrupting!"

"Patrick's got them. All you have to do is check his pockets."

"All right, Patrick, we'll start with you. Please empty your pockets first."

"Yes, ma'am." After reaching into his pockets, all Patrick came up with was some fuzz from his trousers, along with a few clear marbles, but no cloudies.

She turned to Johnny with a stern expression. "Now, I want you to do the same."

The boy stood with his mouth agape.

"Johnny, please empty your pockets... now!"

He did so, but something catapulted out of his pocket as if shot from a slingshot.

Miss Kimball screamed and covered her mouth.

Sylvia hurried out of the schoolhouse. "Are you okay, Miss Kimball?"

The teacher closed her eyes while exhaling. "Yes, dear, I'm fine. You can start grading the papers on my desk, though, if you're finished with the boards."

"Yes, ma'am." Sylvia then went back inside.

Miss Kimball looked in the direction the object flew and saw a fat, green frog sitting in the dirt. Her hand flew up to her chest and to cover her racing heart. "Oh, my goodness."

Johnny grinned. "It's just a frog."

Miss Kimball forced a smile. "Yes, so I see. Do you have any other creatures in your pockets?"

"Nope."

Her irritation with Johnny was clear to see as her smile faded while correcting him. "No, ma'am."

"Uh... right... No, ma'am."

"Thank you. Now, will you remove any items you have in the other pocket?"

Johnny did as asked, then opened his hand to reveal a few clear marbles, but nothing else.

Patrick gasped. "What? He has them, Miss Kimball. I know he does."

"All right, are you sure you've removed everything from your pockets, Johnny?"

"Yep."

Miss Kimball glared at Johnny for his incorrect response.

Patrick puckered his lips. "I remember. He wore his jacket this morning. I bet the cloudies are in those pockets."

"Let's go." Miss Kimball pointed to the schoolhouse.

Johnny stopped in front of his jacket but looked at the floor.

Miss Kimball held her hand out. "Please give the jacket to me." She paused for a moment before handing it to Patrick. "Would you mind checking?"

Patrick searched the outside pockets first but didn't find anything. This time he tried the two pockets inside the coat, with the first hand coming up empty. Patrick's expression was intense as he pulled his hand out of the second pocket to reveal marbles... five cloudies.

"Thank you, Patrick. Now, I would like you to stand in the front corner today. I won't tolerate fighting at this school."

"Yes, ma'am," Patrick said, downcast, as he moved to the front of the room.

"As for you, Johnny, you will write on the boards; *I will not lie and steal*."

"How long will it take me?"

"It depends how long you dawdle," Miss Kimball snapped.

CHAPTER SEVEN
Patrick

Patrick strutted to the front of the room with a smile on his face. While approaching Miss Kimball's desk, he gazed at Sylvia.

Their eyes met, giving her a twisting feeling in the pit of her stomach. Nonetheless, she tried to refocus on grading the papers as Patrick moved to the right of the desk, then stood in the corner.

While checking papers, Sylvia had a premonition someone was watching her but looked up to find Johnny writing on the board in the back of the room. She realized then, their teacher was nowhere around. *I wonder where Miss Kimball is. Maybe she went to the outhouse.*

Sylvia went back to her papers, but with an uncomfortable sensation remaining. She looked around the room again, but nothing. This time, she turned her attention to Patrick, who wore a broad smile. As soon as their eyes met, he was startled and turned his gaze back to the wall.

~

When Miss Kimball walked back into the schoolhouse, she found Johnny had filled one chalkboard and started on the second one. Nonetheless, she was hard-pressed to read it, which was usually the case when it came to his work. But she decided it wasn't a battle she wanted to face today.

Emma redirected her attention and studied the girl for a moment. *Maybe I should attempt talking to Sylvia now, but*

Patrick is in the corner next to my desk. He is so close to her. For heaven's sake! Why do these kids keep acting up this week? Honestly, but I feel like I have not accomplished one thing. She shook her head and forced herself to pay attention to the situation at hand. "How are things going, Sylvia? Do you have any questions?"

"No, ma'am."

Emma checked her pocket watch. "You have around fifteen minutes left."

"Thank you, Miss Kimball."

"You are welcome. Now, I have a quick errand to run at the mercantile, so I'll be right back."

"Okay."

"Would you mind watching to make sure Johnny completes his writing on the board?"

"Sure, Miss Kimball."

"Thank you, dear."

"As for you, Johnny, since Sylvia will be monitoring that all goes well, I want you to complete this board before you leave. Is that understood?"

"All right, Miss Kimball," Johnny answered with a frown while turning back to his task.

"What about me, Miss Kimball?"

"Oh, goodness, Patrick. I almost forgot that you were still there. If I'm not back in time, then you may leave along with Sylvia."

He smiled. "Okay. Thank you, ma'am."

Emma rushed off to the mercantile.

Sylvia glanced in Patrick's direction, who still had a grin on his face. It stirred something inside her, and it wasn't panic. This time, a new and undefined feeling sent a sense of warmth flowing throughout her body. Her smile grew with tenderness. *Could he be feeling the same things as me?*

She and Patrick hadn't noticed Johnny finished erasing the board and left the schoolhouse. Their game of visual cat and mouse continued until their teacher returned. "Oh... Sylvia, you should've left ten minutes ago!"

Sylvia's smile disappeared and turned to panic. "Oh, no! Yes, I have to get going, ma'am." She jumped up so fast, it sent the chair flying into the wall. Nonetheless, she rushed to the door without stopping to say goodbye and then started running for home.

"See you tomorrow, dear," Miss Kimball called out to her, but Sylvia had sped off.

Patrick had moved from the corner and already picked up the chair. "Boy, she sure is in a hurry."

"Yes, she—"

"Hey, she forgot her books."

"Oh, dear, I'll walk home and hitch up the horse and buggy so I can take them to her."

Patrick grinned. "I can catch her."

"Ok—"

He didn't hear his teacher since he had already grabbed the books and was out the door.

She grinned. "Okay."

~

Patrick raced out of the schoolyard, but Sylvia was farther away than he had thought. However, he continued on until spotting her running ahead.

"Sylvia... wait! SYLVIA!"

She stopped and turned toward him. "Yes?"

He smiled. "Boy, I never knew a girl could run so fast."

"What is it?"

"You forgot your books," he said with a lopsided grin.

"Thanks, Patrick."

"Sure, no problem. Can I walk you home?"

"I have to go. I can't be late," Sylvia said while backing away.

"Okay, maybe another time then."

"Maybe," she answered, hurrying on her way.

"See ya tomorrow!"

Sylvia gave a backward wave while running as fast as her legs would carry her all the way home. She only hoped her father would be far out in the field or working in the barn. Then she'd slip past him and into the house.

~

Patrick turned, and with a whistle, headed for home, but in the opposite direction. *For the first time ever, I am looking forward to school tomorrow.*

~

Mary Ryan, a kind woman and well-respected member of the community, hung clothes on the wash-line when Patrick walked around the corner of the house. "Hi, Ma."

"Hi, son. You're late, aren't you?"

"Yes, ma'am."

"Mind explaining?"

"Miss Kimball asked me and Johnny to stay after school."

"Johnny Prescott?"

"Yes, ma'am."

"What happened?"

"We were shooting marbles, but Johnny stole my cloudies. I knew he did cuz he was the only one there. Miss Kimball and I found the cloudies in Johnny's jacket."

"So, why did both of you have to stay after school?"

"Well, we kinda got into a fight."

"A fight? You know your pa, and I don't encourage fighting."

"Well, he took a swing at me, so I tackled him. I never even got a chance to hit him because Miss Kimball came outside right away."

"Oh, yes, I imagine she did." Mary chuckled. "So, what was the punishment?"

"I had to stand in the corner, and Johnny had to write on the boards that he wouldn't lie or cheat anymore."

"Sounds like he got the worst of it."

"Yes, ma'am. Well, I guess I better get to my chores."

"All right, son. And no more fighting."

"Yes, Ma."

~.~.~

Sylvia ran up the path and halted, attempting to catch her breath. With no sign of her father anywhere, she sprinted down the hill towards the barn. Her eyes darted back and forth from the field to the house and all around. Still, he was not to be found. *Where could he be? House or barn? Maybe the outhouse? If he's in the house, I'm dead.*

After reaching the barn, she slipped through the doorway, then stopped to catch her breath. From the window, she scanned the area again. She felt a sense of relief, believing if her father was in the house, then maybe he hadn't seen her arrive late. She started her chores but nearly jumped out of her flesh when looking up to meet her father's terrifying expression. Her face went flush, and her mouth gaped. "Papa... I... the time... it won't happen—"

"Hidin' from me?" he asked in a harsh voice while walking over to her. Then encircling her throat, he tightened his squeeze while leaning to within inches of her face.

Sylvia tried to respond but couldn't make a sound.

"Yer late."

Since she couldn't speak, she tried shaking her head, but to no avail. His hand tightened, constricting her throat until she choked. Terror reflected in her eyes as she began to see spots. Then, with a sudden release, he shoved her hard enough to send her careening across the barn's earthen floor. She landed face down in the straw bedding, nearly hitting her head on the side of the horse's stall.

"Told ya not to be late."

Willing herself not to cry from the onslaught of her father's anger and the pain that the fall caused, she pushed herself up but remained seated in the straw.

"Warned ya."

Sylvia was about to speak when the sound of quickened hoofbeats drew close.

Bernhard peaked out the window. "Ugh... 'at woman." He turned to Sylvia and shook his finger. "Keep quiet."

When her father went out to meet the horse and buggy, Sylvia stood and tried to gather herself. Then, trying her best not to think about what was taking place, she grabbed a pitchfork to start cleaning out the horses' stalls.

~

Meanwhile, Miss Kimball's horse came to an abrupt stop, and when she stepped down out of the buggy, she turned and almost ran into Bernhard.

"Ma'am."

Emma jumped and placed her right hand over her heart. "Oh, my goodness, Mr. White, you startled me."

"Can I do fer ya?"

"Well, I wanted to stop by and make sure Sylvia made it home on time."

"She's here... late."

"Oh, well, then I owe you an apology. You see, I had to run an errand at the mercantile, and I... well, you know how Mrs. Stoope is."

Bernhard didn't respond—just continued to glare.

"Well, I'm sorry to say that Mrs. Stoope and I had a disagreement, so it kept me from getting back to school. You see, I forgot that I should have left my pocket watch with Sylvia. So, she didn't know the time since I told her I'd be back before she had to leave."

"Hmm."

"So, you see, it was my fault she was late. Anyway, I hope you can forgive me and continue to let Sylvia lend me a hand after school. She is such a wonderful help. At least until Susie returns."

Bernhard turned away. "Got chores need tendin'."

"Mr. White?"

Bernhard stopped with a scowl.

"May she continue?"

"Bess not happen again."

"Oh, thank you, Mr. White." She climbed back into the buggy and seated herself. "Good day to you." By the time she looked up, he had vanished.

~

Bernhard walked back to the barn, stopped at the door to look back at his daughter, where he lingered for a moment while watching as she raked the straw. He recalled the day his beautiful Sophia brought Sylvia into the world—it was one of the happiest times of his life. One corner of his mouth turned upward. No sooner did the memory flash in his mind, it was replaced with the doctor's haunting words. "I'm sorry. I did everything I could do to stop the bleeding, but she's gone. It was a long labor and birth. I'm afraid Sophia hemorrhaged."

A mere few hours after his daughter's birth, his wife was dead, and he was left with a tiny life, dependent on him to survive. Bernhard's eyes bore right through Sylvia while thinking over the difficult years of raising a young girl who was the exact replica of his lovely bride.

~

While working, Sylvia got the distinct impression she was being watched, but no one was there when turning toward the door. She walked over to it, peered out, but still saw nothing in either direction. Petrified and feeling as if he might come back and do something else, or worse, throw her back in the dreaded cellar after talking to Miss Kimball. *I wonder what she wanted. Whatever she said sure seemed to work.*

After the father and daughter finished their chores, they had a quiet supper. Sylvia was tempted to ask about Miss Kimball's visit, but she knew better, even though she was desperate to know if he would still permit her to help at school. Nonetheless, the risk was far too great. *Maybe I should just plan on coming straight home unless Miss Kimball says otherwise.* After supper and clean-up, they both retired to their respective rooms.

CHAPTER EIGHT
Getting to Know You

The next day, Sylvia awoke, dressed, made breakfast, and then served hotcakes and sausage to her father.

He looked in her direction with his eyes nearly bulging. Then Bernhard made an about-face and went back into his room.

She heard him rustling through something in his room while mumbling to himself. *What was the look he gave her? What's he doing?*

"It's ready, Papa." Then she sat down and poured syrup on her hotcakes.

When Bernhard returned to the kitchen, he carried some light blue fabric, which he tossed onto the table. "Put it on."

"It's a dress... it's beautiful. Was it Mama's?"

He nodded, and without a word, sat down and ate.

Sylvia picked up the garment, ran to her room, slipped out of her drab brown dress, and hurried into the beautiful baby-blue one. It was sure to make her look older with the ruffled sleeves and white lace scarf on the bodice.

Grabbing the hand-held mirror on the vanity and raising it to see herself, she gasped as tears welled. Protruding from under the neckline were dark, purplish-black bruises, and they wrapped around the sides of her neck. *Maybe, I should stay home. No... Papa won't allow it. It would only anger him again. I could pretend to go to school and hide somewhere. But where? Oh, no, I better go.* She pulled the neckline up as high as it would go, but it didn't work because as soon as she'd move, it would slide down again, exposing the black marks.

Even the scarf sewn on it didn't allow her to maneuver it around her neck. At last, she resigned herself to reality, cut the scarf off, and then tied it around her neck. "I'm sorry, Mama."

Later, as Sylvia approached the schoolyard, she saw Abigail Stoope talking to a group of girls. *Oh, please, not today.* She shifted to the left, which was behind the other girls, and happier Abigail was too busy bragging about something new her mother had bought her.

However, her good fortune ran out at lunchtime when the snooty classmate approached her. "Where'd you get that scarf?"

"It was my mother's."

"We have them at the mercantile. I've got to go."

"Go where?"

"I have to tell my mother because I want her to order me some," Abigail answered while running across the street to the mercantile.

A few minutes later, Miss Kimball called the children back into the schoolhouse. Sylvia was the last one to enter, but with a smile on her face. "Oh, what a lovely scarf, dear."

"Thank you, ma'am."

"I'll have to admire it more closely after school."

"But... I... I didn't think—"

"That your father would let you?"

Sylvia nodded.

Miss Kimball chuckled. "Well, I clarified it was my fault, or rather Mrs. Stoope's for detaining me at the mercantile. I also explained the mishap and got him to agree that you could continue helping me, which I am looking forward to."

Sylvia smiled. "Yes, ma'am. Me, too."

After school, while Sylvia erased the boards, Emma admired the scarf while seated at her desk. "It's beautiful."

"Thank you. It was my mother's."

"Oh, I'm sorry, Sylvia."

"It's okay."

"You were quite young when she died?"

"I'm the reason she died."

"Oh, no. Why do you think such a thing?"

"She died while having me."

"Sylvia, it's not your fault. Sometimes these things just happen, but I certainly can imagine it is difficult without a mother."

"Yes, ma'am. But I don't remember her."

"Do you have any pictures?"

"No. I had a picture in my locket, but I haven't been able to find it for a while."

"Oh, that's too bad. Does your father have any pictures of her for you?"

"I don't know. I've never seen any. Just the one in the locket. It was a gift from my aunt—her sister."

"Where does she live?"

"She's in California."

"So, you have no other family nearby?"

"No, ma'am."

Emma glanced at the open pocket watch she had placed atop her desk. "Oh, no, the time has flown by. I'm afraid you must leave already."

"Okay, Miss Kimball. See you tomorrow."

"Bye, dear, and thank you."

"Yes, ma'am." Sylvia placed her bonnet on, and no sooner got outside the door when she heard someone calling out her name. She turned to find a smiling Patrick leaning up against the tree.

"How 'bout I walk you home?"

"Oh, I don't know. I can't be late."

He kept smiling. "But you promised."

She grinned. "Oh, no, I didn't."

"You mean I waited all this time, and now you're not going to keep your promise?"

She giggled. "I think my exact word was... maybe. That does not mean yes."

"Well, I would be honored if you would allow me to walk you home." Patrick approached and held out his arm.

"You make it hard for a girl to say no."

He grinned. "That's the plan."

She hadn't noticed before, but he had dimples on both cheeks when he smiled. He was quite handsome.

"Well, maybe just part of the way. I can't be late."

"So, you said. Is your pa real strict or something?"

"Yeah, sort of."

"Oh, well, I wouldn't want to make you late then." He held out his arm like he was an escort at a dance.

She giggled and wrapped her arm around his. After a few steps, they unlocked their arms and continued walking.

"Would you like me to carry your books?"

"Okay," she said while handing them to him.

"So, you've lived in this town your whole life?"

"Yes. And you moved here a year ago?"

He nodded. "We did."

"Where did you live before you moved here?"

"California."

"I have an aunt and uncle who live in California."

"Whereabouts?"

"Bakersfield."

"We moved here from Riverside."

"Did you like it there?"

Patrick turned and smiled at Sylvia. "It was okay, but I'm beginning to think I like it here a lot more."

At the sound of those words, she felt a pleasant wave of warmth flow through her—she smiled back. Engrossed with getting to know more about Patrick, she came close to missing the ridge at the top of the hill, which would put them in very dangerous territory. If her father were to see them, she couldn't bear the result of his anger. With a racing heart, her breathing became agitated, so she halted. "Stop! Please stop, Patrick."

His smile faded. "What's wrong?"

"Sorry, I mean, this is far enough. If we get to the top of the ridge, Papa might see us and get mad."

"Oh, okay. Well, I don't want to get you into trouble."

"Thanks, I appreciate you walking me home, though, but I better go."

"Okay, see you tomorrow?"

"See you then."

Patrick placed the books back in her hands, started to walk away, and then turned back. "Hey, Sylvia?"

"Yes?"

"Would it be okay if we talk at recess tomorrow?"

She grinned. "Sure."

He smiled back. "Great. See you then."

"Bye." She disappeared over the ridge.

~

Never seen a girl run so fast. Patrick's smile faded to a sigh with confusion about Sylvia's evident dilemma with her father. His racing emotions spiraled as well while he headed for home.

~

When Sylvia reached the barn, she continued in an all-out sprint toward the house, where her father watched as she walked through the door. She jumped in surprise, causing her books to scatter as they hit the ground.

"Minute shy a late," he said while surveying the mess in front of him, then continued walking back out to the field.

She sighed, bent down to pick up her books, and then placed them on an end table inside the house. She walked over to the fireplace mantle, picked up her father's pocket watch, and opened it—3:01 p.m. She was to be home at 3:00 p.m. *Too close. I have to be careful. If I'm late again, I won't be able to help Miss Kimball.*

As she continued her nightly chores, her thoughts were of Patrick Ryan and how he made her feel safe. As if she didn't have a care in the world. And his smile sparkled and reached her soul, which made her feel as if she were a real person.

Her father was so unlike him, with his heartless stare, which made her feel as if she were a piece of excrement and disposable. He had no love in his soul—just hatred for any and all, or so it seemed to her.

She couldn't help herself as new-found feelings niggled at her as they were unfamiliar to Sylvia. It warmed her to think of Patrick's dimples—irresistible. *When he smiles at me, I think my heart might melt. Oh, no... I think I'm in trouble, but I just don't know what kind.*

It was pleasant to sit through supper since it was rare when her father had nothing to say. She barely nibbled on her food because her mind wandered to more thoughts of Patrick and their conversation earlier. However, when she looked up at her father, she was met with a quizzical stare.

"Somethin' wrong?"

"Huh?"

"With yer food?"

"Uh, no, sir."

He stared between bites. "How long 'at teacher need ya?"

"Huh?"

"At school?"

"Oh, I'm not sure."

Sylvia didn't notice her father's watchful eye during supper, as her mind was on Patrick and school the next day. After eating, she washed the dishes, then retired to her room to do her homework. At last, she finished and turned off the lamp. *The sooner I get to sleep, the quicker tomorrow will get here.* As darkness filled the room, she closed her eyes and saw his face—his warm smile while drifting off to sleep.

The next day she woke up more rested than ever before. After opening the drapes and then cracking the window open a smidge, she stretched while breathing in the cool, crisp air. While dressing for school, she heard the fire's crackling, which suggested her father had already started it. After breakfast, she cleaned up the kitchen, grabbed her books, and then raced out of the house, but forgetting to shut the door.

Bernhard growled. "Door!"

She ran back and grabbed the handle. "Sorry, Papa."

~

Bernhard sipped his coffee, paused, and then got up from the table. He grabbed his cup, walked over to the window, and noticed Sylvia racing over the ridge for school. *Why's she runnin'?*

~

Sylvia slowed to a walk the last third of the way to school because she didn't want to arrive out of breath and looking unkempt. As she approached the schoolhouse, it looked like Patrick, and Timmy Logan walked up the path in the opposite direction. At the same moment, Patrick looked up from the ground and smiled—his eyes stayed locked on her until they met in front of the schoolyard.

"Good morning, Patrick... Timmy."

"Hi, Sylvia." Timmy looked away from her. "Patrick, wanna shoot marbles?"

Patrick smiled while his eyes fixed on Sylvia. "No, you go ahead. I think I'll sit out today."

"Huh? Uh, well, okay. A dejected Timmy walked in the direction of the other boys. However, not before giving them both a quizzical look, as if questioning what happened to his friend before he joined Johnny Prescott and another boy for a game of marbles.

~

Patrick smiled. "Good morning. I hope I didn't get you in any trouble yesterday."

"No, but I was almost late."

"So, what happens if you're late?"

"I won't be allowed to give Miss Kimball any help at school anymore."

"Well, it's not as bad as being locked up or something."

Sylvia's smile faded.

Patrick noted her face turn from a pleasant smile to a look of terror. He put his hand on her shoulder. "Not to worry. I'm sure nothing like that happens in this town."

She softened and managed a slight smile.

The bell rang for school to begin.

"Can we talk more at recess, Sylvia?"

"Sure."

They walked into the schoolhouse and took their seats on opposite sides of the room.

At lunchtime, Sylvia went to her usual spot under the big oak tree and took her lunch out of her pail. She wondered where

Patrick had gone but then spotted him talking to Timmy near the playground. She was just about to take her first bite of lunch, but Patrick appeared instead.

"May I sit with you?"

"Of course."

"So, how's your day going?"

"Good. And yours?"

"Okay, but Timmy's sore since I haven't shot marbles lately."

"I hope I'm not keeping you."

"Nah, I can play after school."

"Okay."

"Can I ask you something, Sylvia?"

"Sure."

"Is it hard without your ma?"

"I guess so. I mean, I've never had one, so I don't know."

"Folks say your pa kinda changed after your ma died."

"Changed?"

"Yeah."

Sylvia scrunched her nose. "How?"

"Well, they say he was nice, and then when she died, he kinda... uh... well... never mind."

Patrick grimaced. "He kinda, what? Wait, if it makes you uncomfortable, then we don't have to talk about it. Only if you want to."

She frowned. "I want to know what folks say."

"Well, they say—"

Just then, the bell rang, signaling lunchtime was finished.

"You'll tell me later?" Sylvia asked with a sad, faraway tone.

"Uh... sure," Patrick answered.

~

They stood at the same time, but he noticed the change in her demeanor—how she seemed low-spirited all of a sudden. With a perplexed expression, he watched as she walked ahead of him toward the schoolhouse.

CHAPTER NINE
Stay 'Way From 'Im!

When class was dismissed, Sylvia erased the boards and then helped Miss Kimball grade papers.

"You're doing a fine job, Sylvia."

"Thank you, ma'am."

"Are things okay at home?"

"Uh... yes. Why?"

"Oh, well... I just wondered since explaining to your father how it was my fault the other day for you getting home late."

"He just asked me how much longer you needed me."

"He wasn't too excited about you helping at first until I explained the other children would be taking a turn, as well."

"Well, there is a lot to do on the farm, so he needs my help."

"Yes, I can see he does. Your father doesn't have much to say, does he?"

Sylvia paused. "No, ma'am, I guess he doesn't. He's always been that way."

"Well, folks in town think he was different before your mother died. Have you ever heard anything about it?"

"As a matter of fact, someone else mentioned it today." Sylvia paused. "Miss Kimball, what do people say about my pa?"

"They just say he was different, but then he, well... he changed."

"What do you mean—changed?"

Miss Kimball fidgeted and checked her pocket watch. "Oh, goodness, it's time for you to head home, Sylvia. Please, I don't want you to be late again and get into trouble. I'll see you tomorrow—okay?"

"Yes, ma'am," Sylvia said while grabbing her jacket and bonnet to put on, then exited the schoolhouse.

When she got outside, she noticed a peripheral shadow near the big tree by the schoolhouse window. There was Patrick, leaning his back against it with arms crossed and a smile on his face.

"Hello, Sylvia."

She beamed. "Hi, Patrick."

"May I walk you home?"

"Of course."

They talked about their likes, dislikes, and their families. She thought about how Patrick's family sounded terrific. In turn, it made her think about the different life she might have had if her mother was still alive.

"Patrick?"

"Yeah."

"Earlier, you mentioned my pa being different or changed. Miss Kimball said so too. What did you mean?"

"Well, what did Miss Kimball say?"

"She was about to tell me something, but time ran out."

Patrick's confusion showed. "Oh, so she didn't say anything about your pa?"

"Tell me what? You said, folks say he's different or changed since my mother died?"

"So, I've heard."

"Well, how was he before she died?"

Patrick hesitated. "Uh... well... decent... good."

"Good... how?"

"Folks just say he was... different."

"You mean good... like nice?"

"Yeah, I guess so."

The next few minutes were filled with the wind blowing and the rustling of leaves.

"Sylvia?"

"Hmm."

"What are you thinking?"

"I'm just trying to imagine it."

"What do you mean?"

"Him... being... nice."

He stopped, turned to hold her hand, and then moved closer. "Well, I think you're nice."

She smiled while gazing at him. "You do?"

He nodded.

"I think you're nice too, Patrick."

~

Lost in the moment, he wanted to pull her into his arms for a kiss, but he wasn't sure if he should. *She thinks I'm nice, but maybe she doesn't feel the same way about me. Then, again, maybe I should. No... it might be too soon.*

~

He's handsome, with eyes that are so kind. I love his smile and those dimples. And he thinks I'm nice too. Oh, but maybe he just wants to be my friend—nothing more.

"Well, we better get you home, Sylvia, so you're not late getting home."

They walked on for a few more minutes until they reached the ridge, where she turned to face him.

"Well, off you go, Miss." He lifted her left hand to his lips for a kiss.

She giggled and blushed. "Why, thank you, kind sir."

"Until tomorrow, Sylvia."

"Until tomorrow, Patrick." After running home, she shut the door behind her and then leaned against it as her heart raced.

With eyes closed, she relived his warm lips on her hand. However, for her own good, she knew not to dawdle. Sylvia hurried into her room, changed out of her school dress, and then put on her threadbare one, so she could do evening chores. Although hard as she tried to concentrate on them, daydreaming about Patrick as she worked seemed to be uppermost in her mind. At least, it made the time fly by. Before realizing it, the sound of her father's approaching footsteps forced her back to reality. She raced off to the kitchen to start supper.

Bernhard closed the door, hung up his hat before washing his hands, then sat at the table without saying a word.

"The soup is almost ready, Papa."

Sylvia served her father before sitting, then they both ate a piece of cornbread while waiting for the soup to heat.

"How long teacher need ya?"

"I don't know."

"Do anything at lunch?"

"No, sir. Just ate under the tree."

"Alone?"

"Yes, sir."

"Sure 'bout that?"

She stopped chewing while looking up at him, along with her heart racing and quickening pulse.

"At the mercantile t'day, 'round lunch. Saw you and 'at boy. Flirtin'?"

"No, sir."

"FLIRTIN'?"

"No, Papa."

Bernhard swiped the table, sending his bowl of soup flying onto the kitchen floor. He jumped to his feet, knocked over the chair, then backhanded her across the cheek.

Her mouth gaped while cradling her face.

"Stay 'way from 'im!"

"We were only talking."

He bolted toward her and grabbed her by the throat. "STAY 'WAY FROM 'IM."

Tears welled as Sylvia nodded at the rage in his eyes, while the right twitched so much, a vein bulged at his temple—it was terrifying.

Bernhard loosened his grip and then backed away.

Even though tears streamed down her face, she was relieved when sensing there was no immediate danger, so she relaxed.

Bernhard grunted and then pointed at his daughter. "No teasin' 'em boys."

Sylvia wanted to scream because she didn't do to any boy, as he claimed. She liked talking to Patrick but didn't say so—she thought better of it.

Bernhard nodded toward the mess he'd made on the floor. "Clean it." Then he retired to his room.

When her father closed his bedroom door, Sylvia plopped on a chair, closed her eyes, and then took a couple of deep breaths. She remained unmoving for a few minutes while attempting to calm her nerves. *I can't imagine how folks ever thought he was nice. I wish I could run away, but where would I go? Oh, how I wish my Mama were here. Maybe he would be kind to me then—with no more hate.*

After pulling a handkerchief out of her dress pocket, she dried her eyes, then blew her nose. While she stuffed the handkerchief back in her pocket, she bent over and picked up the soup bowl and spoon from off the floor. Then, Sylvia collected the bucket of water she hauled in before supper, where she had hung it on a hook above the fireplace to heat up. Since it was now warm enough to wash the dishes, she took a small amount of it to clean up the splattered mess her father had made when he flung his supper off the table.

After finishing in the kitchen, she escaped to her bedroom. She tried to complete her homework, but focusing did not cooperate. Instead, dreamy thoughts drifted to Patrick and how much she cared for him.

Nonetheless, her father's warning to stay away from him echoed in her ear. *Yet, how can I do as he says at school?* Her heart ached at the thought of not being near Patrick. She felt helpless and didn't know what to do. If she obeyed her father, it would take every ounce of willpower she had to stay away from Patrick. And if she followed her heart, she would have to be ever so careful since there was no telling what her father would do if he knew. He could lock her in the cellar forever, and then she'd never again see Patrick.

Sighing, she reached over and snuffed the oil lamp on the nightstand. After climbing into bed, her heart remained torn, so slumber didn't come easy. However, she soon slipped into a dream—it was a beautiful summer day, where the sun was bright, and a gentle breeze caressed her face. Sylvia and Patrick held hands as they walked down the road. She carried a picnic basket on her free arm.

After finding the perfect spot under a gigantic oak tree, Patrick spread out a blanket, and then they seated themselves on it. After enjoying smoked ham and cheese sandwiches, blackberries, and some milk, they talked and teased one another as laughter filled the air.

She could feel the warmth on her face. "It's such a beautiful day."

Patrick's smile matched hers. "Yes, it is."

She looked out over the rolling green hills. "Have you ever seen anything so breathtaking?"

His gaze never left Sylvia's. "No, I don't think I have."

She smacked him on the arm. "You're not even looking and paying attention."

"I can't. There's a breathtaking beauty sitting in front of me."

She smiled with a blush when with tenderness, leaned in, placed his right hand on her cheek, and then gave her a kiss on the lips.

A shock of electricity shot through her from their kiss, but Sylvia pulled away first. "Shall we have dessert?"

He sighed while reaching for her. "I thought we already were."

She giggled while leaning into him. "You are so bad."

"Not bad… just crazy."

"Crazy?"

"Yep. Crazy in love."

He leaned in for another kiss. Although Sylvia didn't want it to end, she pulled away again, but with regret. "How about some apple pie?"

"Sounds great."

Once they had finished dessert, she cleaned up and packed the dishes into the basket.

"Sylvia?"

She turned back toward him. "Yes?"

"I have something to ask you."

"What?"

"You're so beautiful. And I am undoubtedly the happiest guy in the world."

"You make me happy, too, Patrick."

"I can't imagine my life without you, Sylvia."

"Me either... without you, I mean."

"From the moment we met, I have been in love with you."

"I feel the same way. You mentioned you have a question?"

"I'm getting to it."

"Okay."

"Well, beautiful, captivating lady, would you do me the honor of becoming my bride?"

"Ooohh, Patrick!" She jumped into his lap to plant kisses over his face.

He pushed her back for a moment. "Does this mean... yes?"

"Yes... yes... yes, I will marry you!"

A dark, eerie cloud overshadowed Sylvia's day when in an instant, it turned dark as night. She tried savoring her bliss-filled fantasy, but when she tried to look into Patrick's eyes, he had vanished.

"Patrick?" It's no use because the blanket and picnic basket was nowhere in sight. "What's happening?" Even the grass and big oak tree were gone.

"Where are you, Patrick?"

The darkness permeated everywhere—then a voice. "Saw you and 'at boy t'day."

"Patrick?"

"Flirtin'."

"Papa? No... no, I wasn't."

"Stay 'way from 'im."

"He likes me."

"STAY 'WAY FROM 'IM."

"We're getting married."

Sylvia saw Bernhard's angry face with his eye twitching. She could feel the hatred spewing from them as words rapid-fired through her mind. "Tease... stay 'way... flirtin'... don't tease 'em... stay 'way from 'im... flirtin'."

"NO!" Her eyes flew open as she catapulted upright in a cold sweat.

Sylvia crawled out of bed, dressed, then sat in front of the mirror to fix her hair. She saw it—a red mark on the cheek where her father had struck her yesterday, still feeling the sting, how his hands locked around her neck. She pulled down the collar of her dress and noted some new bruises as well. However, not as bad as the ones left on her the last time. At least, they were also lower and hidden underneath the collar. She winced while rubbing her fingertips over her inflamed cheek. *How will I ever explain this?* Full of anxiety, she finished brushing her hair and then hurried into the kitchen to make breakfast.

Sylvia set the table while the bacon fried. After she placed biscuits and blackberry jam on the table, she made fresh coffee before preparing the omelets.

While pouring coffee, her father came into the kitchen and seated himself at the table. He was silent through most of their breakfast until he glanced at his daughter. "Might stay home t'day."

"Why?"

"Don't need folks talkin'."

"But, Papa, I have to help Miss Kimball. She doesn't have anyone else."

"Friday. Teacher'll make it."

"She needs me. And you promised I could help, Papa! I can make up something. I'll say I fell on the steps and scraped my face on them. Or, I had trouble with one of the animals in the barn, so I fell against the wall and hit my cheek. I can make her believe me."

He smirked. "Horse charged ya and ran into a post?"

"Yes, it's perfect. It will look more suspicious if I don't go to school. What if Miss Kimball came to the house and started asking questions?"

Bernhard pondered for a minute and then nodded his head. "Keep quiet."

"Yes, I will, Papa. Thank you." Sylvia cleaned up, grabbed her books, and hurried out the door before he changed his mind. She recited her story all the way to school—it had to be convincing.

CHAPTER TEN
Secrets

Upon arriving at school, she saw Patrick approaching with a big smile on his face. But when he reached her, his smile disappeared into something else. Instead, he grabbed her by the arms to look at the right side of her face. "Sylvia, what happened?"

"Oh, just my clumsiness. A mishap in the barn is all."

"What kind of mishap?"

"While leading the horses into the barn, one of them got spooked. When I jumped out of the way, I forgot about the post and ran right into it."

"With your face?"

She demonstrated this by turning her head. "Yes, I watched the horses, and I was afraid they were going to run me over, so I ran right into the post."

"Why doesn't your pa bring in the horses?"

"He usually does, but he asked me to bring them in last night since he was busy."

"I bet it hurt."

"It did." Sylvia sighed with relief after Patrick seemed to believe her story.

The bell rang, and it was time for school.

"Can we talk more at recess?"

She smiled. "Okay."

They walked in together but went to their separate sides of the classroom. Sylvia noticed kids staring at her face. She hoped she could convince others, and Miss Kimball, too, as she knew the consequences if they didn't buy her story.

Throughout the morning, she could tell each time Miss Kimball looked at her, she was running the possibilities through her mind. After they were dismissed for lunch, Sylvia stood and walked to the door with the others.

"Sylvia, may I see you for a moment?"

She stopped dead in her tracks, closed her eyes while taking a deep breath, and then turned to approach her teacher's desk. "Yes, Miss Kimball."

"Sweetheart, are you okay?"

"Yes, ma'am. Why do you ask?"

"What happened to your face, dear?"

"Oh, I just had an accident in the barn last night."

"What kind of accident?"

"Just my silly clumsiness with one of our horses."

"Are you sure you're okay?"

"Yes, ma'am."

"Okay, then, you may go enjoy your lunch."

"Yes, ma'am."

When Sylvia reached the doorway, she found Patrick had waited for her outside.

"What did Miss Kimball want?"

"Same as you, to know what happened."

"I thought so. Want to eat lunch under the tree again?"

Everything in her screamed she should decline, but Patrick tugged at her heart. When looking toward the mercantile, she didn't see her father there. "Um... okay."

They ate lunch and talked as usual, but she sensed Patrick knew something was different about her demeanor.

"Why do you keep looking over there?"

"Over where?"

"At the mercantile?"

"Oh, do I? No reason."

"Sylvia, are you okay?"

"Yes, I'm fine. But it does sting."

"I'm sure it does. Are you okay at home?"

"What a silly question. Of course."

"You just seem... different. Distracted or something."

Sylvia was glad for the bell to ring—breaking the moment. "We better get back inside."

Hesitantly, he asked, "May I still walk you home today, Sylvia?"

"Uh... sure."

They walked back inside and finished the day.

Later, after school, Sylvia stayed to help Miss Kimball, as she had been doing.

"Does your cheek hurt, dear?"

"It stings some."

"How did you say it happened?"

An anxious Sylvia retold the same story she told Patrick.

"Sweetheart, is there anything you want to tell me?"

"No, ma'am."

"It's okay if there is—I will keep it confidential."

"No, ma'am."

"I'm sure things must be strained sometimes without a mother present—even difficult for you and your father."

"We manage."

"Sylvia, is your father... mean?"

"Mean?"

"Yes, sweetheart. Well ... there's no other way for me to ask you this. Does he hurt you?"

Her pulse raced. "No."

"Did he strike you?"

"No, ma'am." Sylvia's heart pounded without looking up from the paper she had graded. "May I be excused for a moment?"

"Sure."

Sylvia pushed the chair back, got up, and then exited out the back door. She bent over at the spigot, pumped water, and let it run over her cupped hands, but recoiled from the splashing water over her face and neck. It awakened the pain on her cheek. After taking a refreshing water drink, she let the water stream over her hands once again. It helped to calm her nerves. After a few deep breaths, she turned to go back inside, but Miss Kimball stood in the doorway with a look of concern. She was at a loss as to what more she could say to avoid suspicion.

"Sweetheart, are you sure you're okay?"

Her heart began to race. "Yes, ma'am. I'm fine."

"I promise, you can trust that whatever you say will remain between us."

Sylvia paused for a moment. "No... no, ma'am."

"Well, I intended to wait until it was time to go to tell you this, but I might as well now. Susie's father stopped by at lunch to say she's better and will be returning on Monday."

"Oh... so you won't need my help anymore?"

"Well, Susie did help before she got sick. I'll have to ask if she wants to continue. I can let you know on Monday."

"Okay."

"Shall we go back inside and finish up for today?"

"Yes, ma'am."

Sylvia walked toward the school, but as Miss Kimball grabbed the door handle, she had a strange feeling and perused the area for a sign of something or someone. She shook her head and closed the door. *It must be my overactive imagination.*

They both went back to grading papers, with neither one saying a word until it was time for Sylvia to head home. Nonetheless, Emma had glanced her way several times. *Why won't she tell me what's going on inside her house? I'm sure her father is up to no good, but how can I prove it's true? I thought I had more time, but now, with Susie returning. What shall I do?* Emma realized she should check her pocket watch. "Oh, dear, it's time already."

"Okay, ma'am. I just finished the last paper anyway."

"Thank you so much for your help, my dear. I appreciate your hard work. You have done a wonderful job."

Sylvia grabbed her books and stood. "Thank you, Miss Kimball."

"You're welcome. My offer will always stand. You know, about talking to me, because I'll always be here for you."

"Yes, ma'am."

"Have a wonderful weekend, Sylvia."

"You, too, Miss Kimball."

Sylvia walked to the door, grabbed her coat, and put it on to leave. It was a chilly, dreary fall day. And the wind had picked up since lunch. While pulling her bonnet on, she didn't see Patrick by the tree. After looking in all directions, there was still no sign of him, so she headed toward home. At the edge of town, she heard a familiar voice calling her name. She turned around to see Patrick running toward her.

"Hey, wait!"

She turned around. "Hi, Patrick."

"Hello, Sylvia."

"I didn't see you when I came out of school, so I thought maybe you had forgotten, or perhaps changed your mind to do something else."

"I would never do such a thing. You're leaving earlier today, which is why I wasn't there yet."

"Oh, I see," she said as they began walking.

"So, how did it go today with Miss Kimball?"

"Okay, I guess."

"Just okay?"

She sighed. "Yes."

"Did something happen?"

"I found out Susie is returning on Monday, so Miss Kimball won't need my help anymore."

"Oh, is that all?"

"I guess."

"You like helping her, don't you?"

"Yes, I do. And it was fun grading papers. I like Miss Kimball."

He smiled. "Yes, she's a nice teacher. I can tell she likes you, too."

"It was great to be needed for something other than chores, cooking, and cleaning."

"Hey, I have an idea."

"What do you mean?"

"Have you ever been fishing?"

"No."

"Why don't we go fishing after school on Monday?"

"I don't know. My pa will be expecting me."

"Does he know Susie will be back then?"

"I don't know. I don't think so."

"Well, if he doesn't know, you don't have to tell him. He'll think you are helping Miss Kimball, and we can go fishing."

"I have no way to keep track of the time."

"I have a pocket watch. I can check it and then walk you back at the same time."

"I don't know. If Papa finds out—"

"He won't."

"You don't know my pa."

He grinned. "It's only one day. It'll be our secret. Please?"

She giggled. "You make it hard for a girl to say no."

"So, you'll go?"

"Yes."

Patrick grabbed hold of her hand, and then they walked together the rest of the way while making small talk. When they neared the ridge, he spun her toward him and grabbed her other hand.

She hoped he would kiss her.

"I'm glad you're going fishing. I look forward to spending more time with you."

"I look forward to spending time with you, too, and um... learning to fish."

He released her hands. "Well, then, I'll see you first thing on Monday."

"I'd like that. See you then."

~

He turned and walked toward home after she disappeared over the ridge but glanced back and saw her running down the hill for a split-second, and then she was gone.

"Never seen a girl run so fast."

~

Sylvia expected to see her father in the field, but he came out of the barn as she sprinted past. It caused her to jump, which made her books go flying out of her hands—just like the last time he spooked her.

"Oh... you startled me, Papa!"

Bernhard's eyes traced from Sylvia, down to the mess of books, and then back up at her again.

"Pick 'em up."

"Yes, sir." She bent over and began to gather them one by one, then looked up at her father.

In turn, he glared at her as she stood upright. "Keepin' quiet at school?"

"Yes, Papa."

"Stayin' away from 'at boy?"

"Yes, Papa."

"Bess be, or ya know what'll happen."

"Yes, sir."

"Get to yer chores."

"Yes, sir." She turned and ran into the house, set her books down, and took off her coat and bonnet. After changing into her working dress, she finished her chores.

Later, while preparing supper, her thoughts were of Patrick and seeing him on Monday. She hoped the remainder of the week was calm.

When Bernhard retired to his room after supper, Sylvia hurried through cleaning up the kitchen, then retired to her room. Behind closed doors, she poured water from the pitcher into the bowl on the washstand. It felt relaxing to freshen up before slipping into her nightgown.

After brushing her hair and climbing into bed, Sylvia picked up a school book and read. However, before long, she began to yawn. Within minutes words blurred on the page, so she cast the book aside and soon drifted into a deep sleep.

She dreamt of another beautiful, sunny day with Patrick, where they enjoyed a delicious picnic and their growing love. He chased her through the forest, over the meadow of green grass, where the wildflowers were in bloom. They were so carefree and happy.

She giggled and kept checking to see if he would catch her, which she hoped he would. It didn't take long for him to grab her around the waist, thinking he had planned to swing her around but ended up knocking her down, then falling on top of her, instead. In a fast move, Patrick knelt and flipped her onto her back.

"Sylvia, are you okay?"

She laughed. "Yes, my love."

"I'm sorry. I didn't mean to hurt you. I was—"

She reached up and put her index finger over his mouth. "Shhh, it's okay. You'll just have to make it up to me."

He smiled. "Name it... anything."

"Kiss me."

His smile broadened. "I like the way you think." Then he leaned over and gave her a slow, passionate kiss, which she never wanted to end. Her breathing became heavier while her heart began to beat so fast, she thought it would burst. Then, out of nowhere, a dark shadow appeared, and in the blink of an eye... Patrick disappeared.

"Come back. Where are you? Don't leave me."

Sylvia heard noises, like the rustling of leaves—then her father's voice. "Stay 'way from 'im."

Then, there was a musty smell, with a familiar, pungent odor as things started to spin out of control. It caused Sylvia to be confused. Sylvia saw Patrick's face appear—and then he would vanish, as her father's face came into focus. They came and went, and with a brighter light for Patrick, but would fade to dark and grim when her father appeared.

"Come back. No. Don't go. No. Where are you?"

In an instant, the confusion, noises, and spinning stopped.

CHAPTER ELEVEN
The Best Catch

Morning came, and the sun streamed brightly through Sylvia's window. She opened her eyes, blinked several times as her eyes darted around the room. Yet, she felt so strange, like she'd been in a struggle, but couldn't remember anything.

She got up and looked into the mirror while brushing her hair and noted no new, strange, or unusual marks on her neck or face. Her body wasn't sore or bruised, either, as she checked while she changed out of her nightgown. *I must have had a nightmare last night. Why can't I remember anything?*

When Sylvia entered the kitchen to prepare breakfast, she noticed her father had already gathered eggs. They were in a basket on the kitchen table. With pan in one hand, a couple of eggs in the other, she turned and almost ran into him. Startled, she dropped the eggs and pan on the floor.

"Oh, Papa. You scared me!"

"Tarnation, girl. Wastin' eggs!"

"Sorry, Papa. I didn't hear you."

"Sittin' fer 'while."

While bending down to clean up the mess of eggs on the floor, she felt her father's eyes boring through her as she worked. She was thankful the pan hadn't broken. Her father would have been livid if he had to buy a new one at the mercantile.

He disliked dealing with the likes of Eliza Stoope more than necessary. Sylvia attempted to wash out the pan but burned her hand in the process. "Ouch!"

"What er ya doing?"

"Nothing, Papa. Just washing the pan."

She knew he watched her with intense eyes as she cleaned the pan and cooked more eggs. Even though her hand stung like the dickens, she didn't dare tend to it with him there.

Once he finished his breakfast and went outside, she let her guard down enough to finish cleaning up the kitchen and even indulged in a cup of tea. Although she knew it was a risky thing to do because should her father come into the house, he would think she was wasting time.

Afterward, she grabbed a towel and dampened it under the water faucet. Once she wrapped her hand in the towel, she stood in silence for a few minutes before tending to the rest of her chores.

She tried to recall her dream last night, but only minute details surfaced—faces. At first, her father's face haunted her, followed with the delight of seeing Patrick's, which is where her thoughts remained—she smiled.

There was no doubting it. Worry began to niggle at Sylvia. *Maybe I shouldn't go fishing on Monday. Yet, I want to spend time with Patrick. But what if Papa catches us? I would be doomed, and it would be back to the cellar. I know... maybe I should suggest going to the mercantile tomorrow after church since it is his day of rest from working in the fields. Then, come Monday, he would have no reason to go into town for supplies.*

The rest of the day went without incident, so Sylvia spent her day doing chores and then canned preserves.

Meanwhile, as was usual, Bernhard worked in the fields all day on Saturday.

With supper over and the dishes washed and put away by nightfall, an exhausted Sylvia passed out in no time. However, a repeat of her dream from the night before swirled around in her mind. The same feeling of being disoriented plagued her. She'd had these types of dreams before, but not two nights in a row.

They went through their Sunday morning ritual, then rode to church on the wagon, pulled by their team of horses. Sylvia tried to keep her attention on the reverend, but her thoughts kept wandering. She couldn't help but feel those dreams were a warning of something happening or the probability it would. The question was... what? She wasn't sure.

After searching for Patrick, she found him on the other side of the church, sitting with his family. Looking in her direction, he smiled and winked, and she couldn't help but be envious of how perfect the Ryan's appeared. *I wish I had a family like they do—with siblings and a mother. Oh, how I wish I would have known my mother.*

When church finished, she got back into the wagon, then Bernhard climbed in beside her.

"Papa, could we stop at the mercantile? We need to get some more flour?"

"Flour? Just bought some last week."

"Yes, but I want to make sure I have enough for pies."

"Ain't made none."

"But I plan to this week."

"What fer?"

"To eat."

"Make do." Without another word, he tapped the reins, then they were off.

Sylvia was disappointed she couldn't get him to stop at the mercantile. She feared he would need something on Monday, then find out she wasn't helping at school. Could she take that kind of risk? If he found out, he may lock her in the cellar for the rest of her life. She may never again see Patrick.

Upon returning home, Sylvia spent her day baking. She decided to make a mixed berry pie from the preserves she had stored and an apple pie.

Bernhard went down in the cellar to retrieve some apples for her. She watched as he moved the table and chairs off the trapdoor, then disappeared down the ladder. Chills went up and down her spine as she remembered her last stay in the dank, horrible place. *Maybe, I should shut the door and leave him down there. I wonder how he would like to be locked in a dark dungeon? Of course, there was no doubt he would have to remain down there forever because if I ever let him out, he would kill me.* She hardly had time to finish her thoughts before he was back with the apples.

While she baked, her father said he'd be in the barn fixing things and making repairs since he didn't work in the fields on Sundays. He felt it was a day of rest and not meant to do major work.

After coming inside for supper, he washed up and then ate. Only then did he break his silence. "Back soon."

"Where are you going, Papa?"

"None of yer affair." He grabbed his hat, went outside, hitched up the team, and then disappeared over the ridge. *Where's he going? Well, very strange. He doesn't go anywhere on Sunday... or does he?*

After cleaning up the kitchen, Sylvia covered the pies, put them away, and then finished her homework. Still, he wasn't home. So, she got ready for bed and began to read. Not long afterward, she heard the horses and wagon coming up the path.

She jumped out of bed and hurried to the window to make sure it was him. It was dark out, but from the shadows and movements, it appeared he was in, fact, home. She climbed back into bed and heard the door open and close.

Sylvia knew her father's footsteps, but she also heard strange noises, like something dragging, a loud crash, then something breaking. She wasn't sure if she should lie still and pretend to be asleep or get up and investigate.

Remembering her last attempt at pretending to sleep, she decided to investigate further—lest she suffered more of his rage. So, she scooted out of bed and tiptoed to the door. She cracked it open just enough to view the dining area with one eye.

Sylvia couldn't believe her eyes. A large male figure was sprawled out face down on the floor. He looked the same size as her father, but Sylvia couldn't be sure. Then the man muttered something to himself while scrambling to get on his feet.

She held her breath while the figure managed to get on his knees. She exhaled when realizing it was her father. *But I wonder where he goes to make him act this way?*

~

Lucky for Bernhard, when he reached for the lantern, it was in the correct position for him to easily pick it up off the floor. After placing it on the dining room table, he shoved the chair out of the way, then grabbed the edge of the table to pull himself up.

After picking up the lantern, he belched and then staggered down the hallway. Leaning against his bedroom door, he felt for the doorknob, turned it, then shuffled into his room. When he gave the door a shove, he didn't realize it remained open a slight bit.

~

Sylvia wanted to climb back into bed, but curiosity won out when hearing the strange noises, followed by her father's obscure mumbling. She cracked her door open just enough to peek out but noticed he had not shut his all the way. Even though having never considered doing it before, temptation niggled at her. Unable to resist, she tiptoed toward his room with her heart as it pounded harder with each step until reaching the threshold. Then, she took a deep breath and pushed the door open.

She stood in shock with a gaping mouth while taking in the room. She had never seen a mess like it in all her life. His clothes were scattered all over the floor. *Now, I can understand why his room is off-limits.* Even though he demanded the rest of the house be in perfect order—his room was anything but—more like a tornado had roared through it.

In one corner of the room, she saw what looked like a chair, but it was covered with dresses. However, she didn't recognize any of them. *They must belong to Mama.*

Against the wall to the right of the bed stood a bureau. Above it hung a mirror. Sylvia stepped closer for a better look. She saw the top was covered with pictures of him and her mother. It made her heart sink as she looked at them in longing. *Oh,*

Mama, I miss you even though I never knew you. For the first time in her life, she saw a trace of a smile on her father's face.

Although misty-eyed over what she never had, Sylvia noticed glass bottles strewn throughout the room. Some were long, round, and brown, then smaller square clear bottles as well.

She was distracted by the loud snoring in the middle of the room. Her father was flat on his back, sprawled across the bed. He was fully clothed and still wearing his boots. She stared at this man with intense eyes and couldn't help but think how frail he looked while sleeping. He appeared quite different than the brutal man who haunted her dreams. She took a few steps forward to get a closer look and kicked one of the bottles on the floor, sending it crashing into another bottle—she froze.

Bernhard stirred. "Wha... whaatya waaann?"

Sylvia ducked down beside the bed and didn't move. *Is he awake? Should I answer him? No. It will get me in trouble for being in his room. I don't want to think about how angry he would be.* She looked around for somewhere to hide. After waiting for what seemed like forever, she knelt to peer up at the lifeless body lying on the bed. Feeling it was safe enough, she stood and found he was still passed out—hadn't changed positions. His mouth was wide open, and drool ran down the left side of his cheek. Sylvia winced at the sight of her father in such an unkempt state. But at least he had resumed his snoring.

Sylvia decided it was safe to turn and leave the room, but she reached down and picked up one of the long dark bottles on her way out. The label was scrunched, but she smoothed it out with her fingertips—*Whiskey.* She sniffed the uncorked bottle, then stuck out her tongue. *Oh, he's drunk!* She placed the bottle back on the floor, then step by step, approached the nightstand, and extinguished the lamp.

Her body remained tense, filled with anxiety, and terrified that she might kick another bottle and wake the beast. She dropped to her knees, and moved bottles out of the way as needed, until reaching for the doorknob. She pulled herself up to her feet and then closed the door.

While walking back to her room, Sylvia remained stunned at what she had witnessed. There were so many bottles that were strewn about the room. It never occurred to her before, that this must have been going on for quite a while. It was a mystery why she had never suspected there was another side to her father.

With her thoughts racing hither-and yon, she crawled back into bed. *Maybe, this is why Papa is so mean. I wonder if it's the whiskey? But how do I stop him from drinking it? I can't. If he knew I was in his room—let alone saw what I did, I know all too well what he'd do to me.* It gave her chills to think of the consequences.

In no time, Sylvia couldn't fight the heaviness of her eyes and drifted off to sleep.

The next morning, she was in the kitchen by the time her father came inside. He set the basket on the table. "Eggs."

"Thank you, Papa. Breakfast will be ready soon."

"Good." Bernhard removed his hat and backtracked to hang it on the hook.

After pouring coffee, she set it down on the table.

Bernhard grabbed the cup without saying a word.

Sylvia served the meal before joining him at the table. While they ate, she stole quick glances at her father. The last one, she hesitated too long, and what looked back at her was nothing short of a scowl with beady slits glaring through her being.

She bounced out of her seat and started clearing the plates. When finished, she grabbed her school books, bonnet, along with her jacket, and rushed out the door. She didn't give her father a backward glance. Once outside, she set her books down on the steps to put on her bonnet and jacket, then grabbed her things and headed off to school.

It was a chilly, brisk morning, but she warmed up after the long walk to school and then saw him, which radiated a glow that filled her being.

"Good morning, Sylvia."

"Hi, Patrick."

"Are you okay?"

"Yes, why?"

"You don't seem happy to see me."

"Of course, I'm happy to see you."

"You haven't changed your mind about fishing after school, have you?"

"Well..."

"But you promised me."

"I shouldn't, but I will go."

"I've got my pocket watch, so you'll still get home at the same time. I promise."

"Okay. I'll see you at lunch."

"Would you be upset if I shoot marbles at lunch? Timmy is pretty sore at me because I've been spending my lunchtime with you."

"I don't mind at all."

"I'll see you after school."

"Okay."

Later in the day, Miss Kimball said, "Sylvia, it appears as if Susie wants to continue helping me after school. Although I want to keep my promise and start switching with other children. I do want to keep my word."

"Okay, Miss Kimball."

"Are you sure?"

"Yes, ma'am, I am."

"All right. Thank you for the wonderful job you did."

"You're welcome."

"See you tomorrow."

"All right."

When outside, she saw Patrick waiting with two fishing poles.

"Are you ready?"

Her eyes averted to the mercantile and back again, then she smiled. "Let's go."

Patrick grabbed her hand, then they rushed off to the lake.

They sat on two gigantic rocks while he dug up some worms in the dirt to use as bait. He baited both lines and showed her how to cast, then handed her the fishing pole.

"Sylvia, you've got one!"

"I do?"

Patrick set his pole down and then grabbed Sylvia's to reel in the fish. Then he strung it on a line and put it in the water to keep it fresh. After he baited the line again, the same thing happened.

"You got another one!"

She giggled.

"Hey, you're good at this!"

She beamed. "I think it must be beginner's luck."

Patrick frowned. "It must be because I haven't caught one yet."

"This is fun!"

"It's even better when you catch fish." Patrick checked his watch. "We better go."

"That was fast."

"Yes, it was, but I don't want you getting into trouble, or we'll never be able to do it again."

Patrick grabbed Sylvia's books so they could leave.

Halfway back, Sylvia noticed something missing. "Hey, you forgot the fish."

"I'll come back for them. I didn't figure you could take the fish home with you."

"No, I couldn't. My pa would know I wasn't helping Miss Kimball after school."

"That's okay. I'll just leave the fish here in the water where they will stay fresh for when I come back after I walk you home. Well, as close to home as I can."

"Patrick?"

"Yeah."

"I'd like to go fishing again, but I'm really afraid we may get caught."

"I just have to keep checking my watch to make sure you get back the same time as usual."

"Okay. But we have to be careful, because sometimes, Papa goes to the mercantile for supplies."

"Well, we can check by looking for his wagon from school. We'll just have to make sure it's clear before we leave, and then it'll be okay."

"Can we go again tomorrow?"

"Sure."

"All right, see you then."

"Bye, Sylvia."

Each day during the week, Sylvia surveyed the mercantile. When all checked out, she sat with Patrick while eating their lunch. After school, hand in hand, they would talk and make silly on their way to going fishing—just enjoy their precious time getting to know each other.

Sylvia chuckled. "I've never had so much fun."

He laughed along with her. "I can't remember when anyone else has caught so many fish."

"How many does Timmy catch?"

"He usually doesn't catch any."

"Oh! Oh, Patrick! I think I caught another one." Once again, she reeled in her biggest catch.

"I think you have passed beginner's luck."

"I don't know how." Off in the distance, it sounded as if a twig snapped. Sylvia panicked. "What was that?"

They looked in the direction of the noise but didn't notice anything out of place.

"Don't worry, Sylvia. It's probably an animal."

"Maybe, but we should go."

Patrick checked his watch. "We have fifteen minutes."

Sylvia looked worried. "I just have a feeling we should go."

"All right. Let's clean up, and we'll be on the way."

"Could we check the mercantile?"

"Sure."

"Thanks."

"You don't think it's your pa, do you?"

"I don't know."

"He can't know, Sylvia. Not even Miss Kimball is aware that we're together like this after school."

"Papa just knows things." She rushed ahead.

"Hey, slow down."

"I have to get home."

"Okay. Just let me walk with you."

They walked around the side of the school and peered from the corner to the mercantile. They saw a wagon parked outside. "Oh, we're lucky, Patrick. It isn't Papa's."

"See, everything's fine."

Sylvia sighed. "Okay. What time is it?"

Patrick rechecked his watch. "We have plenty of time, so we're still early."

Sylvia rushed off again.

"Hey, wait!"

"Sorry, I better get home."

"Do you want to go fishing again on Monday?"

"I don't know. I mean, I want to, but I know that Papa will be going to the mercantile soon."

"How mad would he get at you for fishing?"

"He needs my help at home."

"Would it help if I asked him?"

"Oh, no! It isn't necessary. He just needs my help."

When they reached the ridge, they stopped and faced each other. Patrick grabbed his watch, checked the time, and slipped it back into his pocket. "It looks like we still have a few minutes. I've wanted to do something for a while now."

"What?"

Smiling, he reached out and tucked a stray lock of hair behind her ears, then cradled her face to lean in for a kiss.

With eyes closed, Sylvia felt lightning bolts of electricity throughout her body. As the kiss deepened, she was sure he felt the same way.

He pulled away first as they opened their eyes.

She grinned. "You're my best catch of the day."

He smiled. "Definitely, the biggest one."

"See you on Monday."

"Bye, Sylvia."

After she disappeared over the ridge, Patrick turned—even hopped with a spring in his step as he started to whistle.

CHAPTER TWELVE
Liar

Sylvia thought she would enter the house and then hurry to her bedroom to change clothes. Nonetheless, she got no farther than the doorway before she was startled. Her father sat at the kitchen table while facing her.

"Early, aren't ya?"

"Yes."

"How long teacher need ya?"

"Not too long, Papa. We're getting caught up." Sylvia walked past him into the kitchen.

"Stopped at school t'day. Yer teacher said the same."

Sylvia's eyes widened as she held her breath and froze.

"Where were ya?"

"Um... nowhere, Papa. Just walking home."

"Didn't pass ya."

"I... I didn't walk on the main road today."

"Were you with 'im?"

"No... no, sir."

"Yesss."

"No."

Bernhard catapulted out of his seat, knocking the chair backward. In one step, he yanked on Sylvia's left arm, spun her around, then grabbed her by the throat. "Don't lie t' me!"

She attempted to shake her head but froze with fear while leaning back when looking at his hateful expression.

"You were with 'im!"

She shook her head.

Bernhard released his hold on her throat.

"Liar!" He backhanded her across the cheek.

With a light touch, she raised her hand to the sting and gave it a slight rub.

"Were you with 'im?"

Sylvia shook her head again while trying to stop the sobs threatening to escape her.

Bernhard backhanded her again. His piercing eyes twitched as large veins popped out on his forehead. "Were you with 'im? Tell, or so help me, I'll... I'll kill you!"

Sylvia bolted to the front door, turned the handle, and was thankful it opened. The front porch came into view, as did the road to freedom—it was within her grasp. She was suddenly jerked back by her hair as the door slammed shut. She cried out while feeling as if the roots of her hair had been pulled out of her head.

Bernhard latched onto Sylvia's arm and spun her around to face him. With a sucker punch, he sent her sailing across the floor, where she landed face down in front of her bedroom, smacking her head into the closed door—then everything went black.

"Sylvia?"

She remained motionless.

"Sylvia?"

Bernhard leered over his daughter's body and stared at the middle of her back.

"Told ya t' stay 'way from 'im."

He sprang into action before his daughter could begin to stir.

~.~.~

Sylvia attempted to open her eyes, but it felt like something had forced them shut. She tried several times, and when she did manage to open them, they were mere slits. Everything was somewhat blurry. After several minutes, she could open her eyes, with her vision clearing.

She became aware of pain throughout her body, like being trampled over by a runaway horse and wagon, although somehow, surviving. Her left cheek throbbed as penetrating pain attacked her head—then unconsciousness.

After several hours, she stirred again, but this time felt a wet, cooling sensation over her mouth. It took quite some time to open her eyes, but the view was still out of focus. Once the room came into view, at first, she didn't recognize her surroundings. She looked around the darkroom for several minutes before the nightmare came to life. *No... oh, no... not again. I'm in the cellar!*

Not only did Sylvia become aware of the dull ache in her head, but the left side of her face was also numb, too. She touched her cheek and traced the lines of her face to find the left side swollen. *That's right... he hit me.* With another swipe of her hand, she felt a tender spot on the top of her head. *Ouch! How'd this happen?*

While turning her head to the right, she discovered the all-too-familiar bucket of water hanging on the rope directly above her. With a throbbing pain in every part of her being, she still tried to sit up. Resigning herself to reaching inside the bucket, she fumbled to find the ladle. After grasping it, it was her hope it held fresh water. Sylvia was relieved when it did, so she lifted the filled ladle to her lips in the dark and tipped it so some would trickle into her mouth. However, without warning, the ladle fell out of her hand as things began to spin before losing consciousness.

Sylvia dreamt of beef stew cooking. The aroma awakened her palate, and she could hardly wait to eat. Her stomach churned and rumbled while both eyes fluttered before she awoke. *What is it I smell... beef stew?* Then she saw a bowl with a spoon in it. She had to roll over and stretch to reach it, then pulled it toward her body. After pulling the spoon out, she brought it close and inhaled. *Yes... beef stew.* She also found a piece of cornbread on the ground next to the bowl.

Sylvia had no idea of the time she had been in the cellar or how long she would be there. At least he brought her food and water. Still, after being held in captivity many times before, she became immune to the unsanitary conditions. She ate whatever was nearby, even though she heard the familiar scratching of mice. Soon, Sylvia felt herself drifting off again, but not so much she didn't feel something crawl over her bare leg. However, she felt useless in her lethargy. Just lifting a hand to swat at it was futile since her strength had waned as darkness led to her fading into a deep sleep.

~.~.~

Emma Kimball pinned her mother's cameo on her pale green dress, placed the matching bonnet on her head, and left her house. She climbed into the buggy and tapped the reins on her horse's backside. "Heupp, Chester."

Emma's mood was somber when she arrived at church and checked for the White wagon. *Maybe, they are on their way, or at least, I hope so.* As she reached the door, Patrick was approaching from the side of the building.

"Good morning, Patrick."

"Hi, Miss Kimball. By chance, did you happen to see Sylvia this morning?"

"No... haven't you?"

"No, ma'am."

"Patrick? Were you together on Friday?"

"Yes, ma'am. We went fishin'."

"Oh, dear."

"What is it?"

"Well, her father came looking for her."

"He did?"

"Yes. Sylvia's father thought she was still working after school."

Patrick swallowed hard. "Miss Kimball?"

"Yes, Patrick?"

"I think Sylvia may be in trouble."

"Did she tell her father she was staying after school? Or is there something I should know about, Patrick?"

"Well—"

"Patrick?"

"Yeah."

"Oh, no!" Miss Kimball became more distraught. "I've been worried about her since Friday."

"Why? Do you think he'll hurt her?"

"I certainly hope not, but I'm not sure. I've heard things about Bernhard."

"Me, too. Do you think there is any truth to the rumors?"

"I don't know, but something doesn't feel right."

"When we were fishin', we heard something, Miss Kimball."

"What did you hear?"

"There was some movement in the woods. I thought it was just an animal, but Sylvia got real spooked."

"Oh, dear."

"Do you think it was him?"

"I think it may have been."

"What do you think he will do to Sylvia?"

"I don't know, Patrick."

He looked dejected. "This is all my fault, ma'am."

"Don't blame yourself. Remember what folks say about Mr. White—how he hasn't been right for some time now."

"I have to know she's okay."

"Oh, Patrick. I don't think it's a good idea for you to go over there."

"I'll go later tonight. It'll be okay."

"What if he sees you coming?"

"I'll go through the field and then come up the back of the house."

"What if he catches you?"

He smirked. "I'm a fast runner."

"Well, I can see I'm not going to be able to talk you out of this."

"No, ma'am."

"Please be careful, Patrick."

"I will."

"Will you do me a favor?"

"What is it, ma'am?"

"Would you stop by after, then I'll know you're both okay?"

"Yes, ma'am."

"Thank you. And please be careful."

"I will."

After the church service, Emma made her way home. She tried to think of a reason to go to the White homestead but couldn't come up with anything on Sunday. *If Sylvia isn't in school on Monday, I can use homework as a reason to pay a visit. I do hope she comes to school.* "Dear Lord, please protect Patrick and Sylvia."

~.~.~

The Ryan family traveled out of town Sunday afternoon when they decided to stop at Hutchins Lake. The property had been deserted for years since Thomas Hutchins passed away. No kin surfaced to claim the property, which left an old, dilapidated house sitting adjacent to the lake. Since then, the house was branded haunted, and there had been no trace of anyone around the place.

Patrick's father spread out a blanket as his mother began unpacking the sandwiches. After an enjoyable lunch with a lot of conversing, mixed with laughter, Patrick, along with his 10-year-old twin sisters, Sadie and Sarah, played tag. After tidying up, Mary relieved Patrick from watching his sisters, so he and John could go fishing.

~

"Pa, can I ask you something?"

"Sure, son."

"What do you know about Mr. White?"

"You mean Bernhard White?"

"Yes."

"Not too much, other than things have been tough with raising his daughter by himself."

"What do you think he was like before his wife died?"

"Well, I can only go by what folks in town have said since I don't know firsthand. You know, son, hard times have a way of changing folks. I gather once he lost his wife—things just got harder. It's bound to have an effect on a person—some worse than others."

Patrick frowned. "I suppose."

"Why do you ask?"

"I was just wonderin'."

A concerned expression crossed John's face. "Well, we best get goin', son, so we can get back home and clean these fish for supper."

"Yes, sir."

When they returned, John walked over to his wife. "Mary, let's pack up and be on our way."

"All right, dear. Come on, girls, it's time to go."

They loaded up the wagon and then headed back home.

Later, after supper, John went out on the porch to smoke his pipe, with Patrick following to join him.

"Pa, I've got to check on Sylvia. I think I may have gotten her in trouble with her pa."

"What do you mean, son?"

"We were fishin', and Sylvia's pa didn't know about it. Friday, he came lookin' for her after school. She got real spooked when she heard some noises around where we were fishin'."

"Why didn't she tell him?"

"I don't think he lets her do too much."

"So, if she would have asked him, he would have said no?"

"I think so."

"Pa, something doesn't feel right about him."

"I'm not so sure you should go over there, son."

"I have to know she's okay."

"You'll see her at school on Monday."

"I just can't wait until then."

"If you talk to her father, things may get worse for Sylvia."

"I don't plan to talk with him, just Sylvia."

"What if your presence there makes him mad?"

"He's not going to see me."

"So, you're going to sneak over there?"

"Yes."

"I'm not so sure it's a good idea."

"Pa, I have to know she's okay."

"Yes, you've made yourself clear. But Bernhard White isn't what you'd call a stable man. There's no telling what he'll do if he finds you there."

"I'll be careful."

"Patrick... I—"

"Pa, I made a promise to Miss Kimball. Since I planned to check on Sylvia, she asked me if I would stop by afterward and give her an update."

"Maybe I should go with you."

"No, sir. I can handle it myself."

"Oh... all right. I hope I don't live to regret this."

"Thank you, sir."

"Please be careful."

"I will."

John continued to smoke his pipe while Patrick walked off through the field.

~

After Mary finished the dishes, she stepped onto the porch and sat down next to John.

"Where's Patrick off to?"

"He's off to the White place."

Mary did not look pleased. "Bernhard White's place?"

"Yes."

"Do you think it's a good idea?"

"No."

"Dear, I'm worried. I don't like the idea of him going there by himself."

John took the pipe out of his mouth. "I don't either, but he's near a man, Mary."

"He's still my boy!"

"And mine, too."

"Well, I don't like 'our' boy going over to a crazy man's house."

"He wanted to handle it on his own."

"John, either you head over there, or I'm going myself."

"All right, dear. I was contemplating it before you came out here."

"I'll get a lantern for you."

"Thank you."

While Mary went after the lantern, John walked to the barn and hitched the wagon's team. Then when his wife returned, she brought not only the lantern but a small basket.

"I put some fresh molasses cookies in there."

"Ah, my favorite. Thank you, dear."

"You're welcome."

He put the basket and lantern in the wagon and then climbed onto the seat.

"Please be careful, John."

"Yes, ma'am."

"And bring him back safe and sound."

He nodded. "Back soon."

Mary's expression was one of apprehension as she watched her husband leave. "Dear Lord, please keep my Patrick and John safe from that mad man. I couldn't take it if anything happened to either one of them."

~.~.~

Patrick made his way through the fields and came up to the back of the White homestead. He hid behind the giant oak tree, squatted down, and scanned the premises for any sign of Bernhard. When there was no indication, he snuck up to the window in the back of the house. Standing against the siding, he peeked inside for a perfect view into the kitchen and dining room area, but it was empty.

He straightened up and walked around the left side of the house, where there were no windows. However, when he walked to the front of the house, he found one, but it was covered by a curtain, which obstructed his view. Then, he noticed a small gap in the curtain at the top portion of the window, but he wasn't tall enough to see through it. Patrick thought it could be Bernhard's.

He saw a small woodpile to the right of the window, then debated about standing on it to get a closer look inside but decided against it. Then he noticed the covered porch with an entrance to the front of the house located in the middle. It had a window on the right side of it.

Upon looking around the barn and stable area to the right, adjacent to the house, he noted one horse in the stable and the wagon parked out front.

A quick scan of the field revealed no evidence of Bernhard either. Feeling safer... bolder, he tiptoed back to the corner of the house, looked here and there, but still no sign of anyone.

He snuck over to the other window and noticed a bed centered against the wall in the room, which appeared not to have been used. A small oak stood to the right of the bed, and a matching dresser in the corner of the room, which he assumed was Sylvia's—but it looked eerily undisturbed.

After he crept out to the barn, he peered into the window, but nothing. Patrick made his way to the door and entered. *Where are they?* The only thing out of place was the elusive nature of father and daughter. *Wait a minute. I remember seeing only one horse outside. Doesn't he have two? I was sure of it.*

When Patrick thought he heard a horse neigh, he stopped to listen, and then his suspicions were confirmed when heavy footsteps followed. He became panic-stricken, so he dove into some loose straw, then crawled to an open stall, where he entered just in time to see the door open.

He watched as Bernhard staggered toward the stall he was in—scaring Patrick, but at the last second, he turned right and approached the wall. He attempted to hang up a bridle but missed the hook, so it landed on the ground. Bernhard paused a moment, belched, and then made his way back out of the barn with sluggish steps—almost falling a couple of times.

After waiting a few minutes, Patrick looked out of the barn door, which Bernhard forgot to close. *Where can she be?* He knew he should go since Sylvia's father was home, but he couldn't will himself to do so without knowing if she was safe.

He retraced his steps to the window, which he believed was Sylvia's room, but still noticed no sign of activity. His worry began to multiply.

When he crossed the porch area, he sneaked back toward the room with the closed curtain—it remained in the same position. It would be dark soon, so he needed to find Sylvia fast. He could either circle around to the back of the house again or attempt standing on the woodpile. If luck served him right, he could reach the window upstairs and feel more at ease to know what was behind them.

With his decision made, each step taken, he placed a hand on the woodpile while bracing himself against the side of the house. After climbing as high as he could go, he stretched to his full length, trying to reach the windowsill. However, he fell short of success. Trying one more time, he wobbled a slight bit when hearing a clanking sound. It caused Patrick to lose his footing, causing the woodpile to collapse beneath him as he fell to the ground, which knocked the wind out of him. He remained flat on his back for a moment to collect himself.

"Whaa... whoooseit?"

Upon hearing Bernhard, his discomfort was forgotten. Patrick sprang to his feet and hurried around to the right side of the house. He came to an abrupt stop when the door flew open to see Sylvia's father squinting while eyeballing the area. Patrick realized that the man had noticed the fallen wood. But he was thankful when Bernhard staggered back, then inside the house. Nonetheless, he quickly returned. This time, her father held the shotgun Patrick had seen hanging over the mantle.

"Whereyaat?" Bernhard walked around the side of the house.

Patrick sprinted through the yard toward the opposite side but heard Bernhard call out, "Gotcha!" He turned back to see the man raise his rifle and take aim. The gunshot blasted through the air. He hopped over the fence and continued to run as fast as his legs could carry him until he began falling to the ground. Patrick looked back to see Bernhard staggering backward, so he felt his chest and arms but saw no blood. He popped up and began to run again, and as fast as possible.

Another shot pierced the air, causing Patrick to fall to the ground in terrible pain. He couldn't tell if he was hit or hurt from the fall. Although while trying to stand, Patrick collapsed. He was still unaware if he'd been shot, only that the discomfort in his left ankle worsened. Nonetheless, there was no alternative but to stand if he were to escape. "Ahhh!" His attempt went for naught as he fell to his knee. Luckily, he heard the sound of a wagon.

"PATRICK!"

As he stood on one foot, his father pulled the wagon up to him. "Whoa... whoa... there. Get in, son."

Patrick grabbed for the side of the wagon and then hobbled to the back, where he pulled himself up and catapulted into the back of the buckboard.

"Heeyaaa... let's go, boys!"

As the wagon moved forward, Patrick gave a sigh of relief— his heart pounding while rolling over on his back to check his body for any sign of blood.

"Have you been shot, son?"

"No, sir."

"Thank God. Are you okay otherwise?"

"Pa, my ankle hurts somethin' fierce."

"All right, I'll get you to the doc."

"Pa?"

"Yeah?"

"You were right."

"About what?"

"I shouldn't have gone by myself."

"Let's not worry about that right now."

"Thanks for coming, Pa."

"Just hang on, son."

CHAPTER THIRTEEN
He's Crazy

John raced the wagon through town and then stopped in front of Doctor Jedidiah Parker's office. "Whoa... there."

He turned to his son, "I'll get the doc." Then he stepped down from the wagon and hurried to the back of the office, where he banged on the door. "DOC! DOC! It's an emergency!"

There was no answer, so John ran down the street to the restaurant that closed for the evening. However, he raced up the steps to see two men walking through the doorway and recognized it was Doc, along with William Stoope. "Well, hello, John."

John nodded. "William."

"What's the hurry, John?" asked Doctor Parker.

"I've got an emergency."

"Since you're here, I'm guessing it's not you."

"It's Patrick. His leg hurts somethin' fierce, Doc."

"Then, let's not waste time, gentlemen, "Doc Parker said while John and William helped him as they rushed down the steps and over to the buckboard parked in front of his office.

A short time later, Doc walked to the back of the buckboard to find his patient lying down. Patrick had propped himself up on his elbows and forearms, painful though it was, as his expression reflect. "Well, young man, what's the problem?"

"My ankle, Doc."

"Let's get you inside my office, so I can have a closer look. William, can you lend a hand?"

"Sure, Doc, I'll be glad to help."

The two men lifted Patrick by placing each of his arms over one of their shoulders, then hoisted him off the back.

Meanwhile, Doctor Parker hurried to his office, unlocked the door, then began lighting lanterns. "Okay, men, put Patrick on the examination table." Then Doc washed his hands.

Once Patrick was on the table, John offered a handshake. "Thank you, William, for helping me with my son."

"You're welcome, John," said William while shaking hands. "Is there anything else I can do to lend a hand, Jedidiah?"

"No, thank you—we're good."

"Well, I hope it's not too serious," William said as he walked toward the door. After taking hold of the doorknob, he turned back with a nod. "You take care, Patrick."

"Thank you, Mr. Stoope."

"Yes, William, same goes for me. Thank you for supper and your help," Doc said while not looking up from his patient.

"You're more than welcome," William said and then left.

Doc continued to examine his patient's ankle. "Does anything else hurt, Patrick?"

"No, sir."

He began the exam by palpating the leg to determine if it was broken or just a sprain. "Are you having discomfort in your upper leg, son?"

"No, sir."

After the doctor finished examining both ankles, he took his vitals. "Well, Patrick, you are a fortunate young man. I don't believe you have a break—just a bad sprain. I'd like to see you again in a few days if the swelling doesn't go down or the pain increases."

John breathed a sigh of relief. "Well, I like the good news, Jedidiah."

Doctor Parker walked over to the medicine cabinet, raised his right index finger, and used it to sort through all of his medications. "John, how about pouring a glass of water from the pitcher on the desk behind you?"

John nodded. "Sure, Doc."

The doctor picked up a small white packet and then handed it to Patrick. "Take one of these now, and as needed for the pain. I think you'll feel much better in a few days."

Patrick took one of the pills out, popped it into his mouth, and downed the water. "Thank you, Doc."

John and the doctor helped Patrick back to the buckboard. "Thank you, Jedidiah."

"You're welcome, John. Remember, Patrick, rest for a few days, and then I'll recheck your ankle if needed."

"Yes, sir."

As they pulled away, Patrick said, "Pa?"

"Yes, son?"

"I promised Miss Kimball I would stop by and let her know what I found out about Sylvia."

"All right, son. We'll swing by, but then we better get you home. Your ma will be worried."

~.~.~

After Emma finished supper at the restaurant in town, she strolled home to grade papers. No matter that she tried to concentrate, her thoughts strayed to Sylvia and Patrick. *Oh, dear, something is wrong. I should have heard something from Patrick by now.*

A knock at the door interrupted her thoughts, so she hurried to answer it. "Oh... John? Where's Patrick? Is he okay?"

"Here I am, Miss Kimball." Patrick attempted to raise his head up from the floor of the buckboard. Although he was unsuccessful since the pain medication had taken hold and making him drowsy.

"What happened?"

John's expression showed his angst. "Bernhard White shot at him. That's what happened!"

Emma gasped as her hand flew up to cover her mouth. "Oh, goodness! Has he been shot?"

"No, just twisted his ankle when he stepped in a hole while dodging bullets."

"I'm glad it wasn't worse. I tried talking Patrick out of going."

"I agree with you. But your son was worried sick about the girl."

"Yes... well, I'm worried about Sylvia too. Is she doing okay?"

"I don't know. Patrick was in a lot of pain, so I had to rush him over to the doc's office."

"Thank you for letting me know. I do hope he feels well enough for school tomorrow."

"I hope so. Right now, I need to get Patrick home to rest."

"Give my best to Mary and the family."

"I will."

~.~.~

Bernhard stood over Sylvia's body.

"He was here. Told ya t' stay 'way. Wouldn't listen, would ya?"

He turned away, climbed up the ladder, and closed the cellar trap door. He didn't bother to move the table and chairs back, as there was no need to now. He carried on down the hall to his room and passed out on the bed.

~.~.~

After Mary tucked the twins in for the night, she walked into the kitchen and heard the wagon pulling up. She grabbed her shawl, wrapped it around her shoulders while hurrying to the door. After lighting the lantern, she stepped outside, then closed the door behind her. "John?"

"Mary, I need your help!" He stepped down from the wagon and rushed back to help his son out of the buckboard.

She hoisted her beige ankle-length skirt up then hurried over to the wagon. "John, what's wrong? Where's Patrick?"

"I'm right here, Ma."

"Doc just said it's a tender ankle, but he's okay. Help me get him into the house." Together, they lifted their son off the buckboard and then helped him to his room.

Once settled in bed, Patrick fell asleep since his medication was working.

Mary went about gathering firewood from the porch, stoked the fire, and warmed a kettle of water.

Meanwhile, John unhitched the team from the wagon and returned with the basket of leftover molasses cookies.

After Mary poured two cups of coffee, they sat and enjoyed the cookies while warming up by the fire. It wasn't long until she realized the evening had taken its toll on her husband from his weary expression. "What happened?"

"I'm guessing Bernhard White wasn't happy to see Patrick. When I got there, I heard gunshots and—"

"Huh! Gunshots?"

"Yes. By the time I caught up to the boy, he had bolted like a hunted deer through the field."

"What is so wrong with a man he would do such a thing? He must be as crazy as the rumors suggest." Mary shook her head. "Why would he choose to shoot at Patrick?"

"I don't know, Mary, but I aim to find out."

"You're not going there after this, are you?"

"Anyone who shoots at my boy is gonna answer to me!"

~.~.~

Sylvia stirred while opening her eyes. After a few minutes, she realized her dire circumstances hadn't changed, and she was still locked in the cellar with no idea if it was day or night. The familiar darkness surrounded her. Trembling and cold, she closed her eyes while a single tear rolled down her cheek. Not only was her hair matted, but her face felt gritty, along with a dry mouth. Worse, she was in desperate need of a hot bath.

"Papa... let me out... Papa." She kept calling for help until her throat was sore, and she had a raspy voice. Still, there was no answer or movement above in the kitchen.

She felt for the bucket of water to quench her thirst. Since her father hadn't brought her food, she crawled over to the baskets of apples and ate one. Still hungry but unable to eat one more apple, she reached into the potato bin and then ate a raw potato, hoping to squelch the hunger pains. Fear about her circumstances took its toll, so she did the only thing to comfort her... she closed her eyes and thought of Patrick.

~.~.~

Patrick awoke in the middle of the night with throbbing pain in his ankle. After he called out for help, his mother brought him a glass of water and then another dose of his prescribed laudanum. Once it took hold, he was able to rest all night.

Upon waking the next morning, he smelled the bacon his ma was cooking, even before opening his eyes.

Before long, his bedroom door opened to bring his mother in with a plateful of food. "Good morning, sleepyhead." She handed him a plate filled with scrambled eggs, biscuits, and honey. I imagine you have quite an appetite since you didn't have anything to eat since supper last night.

"I'll say. Mmmm, smells good, Ma."

"Well, I'm glad to hear you have an appetite, son." She smiled while setting a glass of milk on the nightstand. "How's your ankle feeling this morning?"

"Still hurts."

"Would you like more pain medication?" she asked while picking up the white packet.

"Yes, ma'am."

"Well, you should have plenty of time to rest today."

"No, I need to get to school."

"You're not going to be able to walk on your foot."

"I hoped Pa could give me a ride in the wagon."

"I think you should stay home today and rest."

"Ma, I need to go."

"Why?"

"I have to go—see if Sylvia is there, and okay."

"Your pa is already gone, but I'm sure he will take care of checking on Sylvia."

Patrick looked confused. "Gone where?"

"To see Mr. White."

"That man, he's crazy!"

"Yes, indeed. Your father told me what the man did to you."

"I hope Pa took his gun."

"I wouldn't worry. Your pa can handle himself."

~.~.~

John stopped the wagon in the driveway, marched up the front steps, then pounded on the door. "Bernhard! Open this door up, now! This is John Ryan—I'm not leaving until we talk!"

Moments passed before the door opened, bringing forth a scowling Bernhard. "Whataya want?"

"You shot at my boy last night!"

"What boy?"

"My boy, Patrick."

"Tresspassin'."

"He came over to see Sylvia."

"Don't want 'im near her?"

"He was worried about her not being in school."

"Don't care. Should stay 'way."

"Excuse me?"

"Don't want 'im near her." Bernhard tried to close the door.

John overpowered and knocked him onto the floor, then pointed at Bernhard. "Anything happens to my boy, I'll kill you with my bare hands! Understand me?"

Bernhard struggled to stand while staring—dumbfounded.

"Well? We got an understanding, White?"

Bernhard nodded.

John stomped back to his wagon, then left for home.

~.~.~

Emma rang the bell while searching through the children walking toward the schoolhouse, but there was no sign of Patrick or Sylvia. Of course, she understood why he was absent, but she could only hope her fears about Sylvia and her father were wrong. Now, she would have two stops to make after school instead of one.

After an uneventful day, she dismissed the children. Susie started erasing the chalkboards, but Miss Kimball sent her home, so she could make the necessary rounds.

After arriving at the Ryan home, she picked up Patrick's reader from the seat of her wagon, then stepped down.

Mary walked onto the porch while drying her hands on a cloth. "Well, hello, Emma. It's nice to see you."

"Thank you, Mary. I'm pleased to see you, too. How is Patrick? If he's up to it, might I speak with him?"

"Well, he's in some pain, but it could've been far worse."

"Yes, I'm glad to know it wasn't."

"Come on. I'll take you to my son."

"Oh, thank you." Then, Emma removed her bonnet while following down the hall.

When Mary reached her son's bedroom door, she knocked. "Patrick?"

"Yes, Ma."

She opened the door. Son, you have a visitor. "Miss Kimball is here to see you."

He grinned. "Hi, ma'am."

"It's nice to see you, Patrick."

"Emma, would you like some tea?"

"Yes, how nice of you, Mary." She walked further into the room and glanced at her student's puffy ankle. "Ohhh... it looks painful. I can see why you stayed home today."

He shrugged. "I wanted Pa to bring me to school in the wagon, but he had already left this morning."

"Oh, where did he go?"

"Sylvia's house."

"Oh, dear. Did Mr. White know he was shooting at you, Patrick?"

His growing agitation was clear to see. "Yeah, he's crazy!"

"How was Sylvia?"

"I don't know. It was strange because I couldn't find the girl anywhere."

"Oh, Patrick. I'm worried."

"What do you think he's done to her, Miss Kimb—?"

"Here's your tea... oh, I'm sorry for interrupting."

Emma took the tea. "Thank you, Mary. And not to worry—you didn't interrupt anything."

"I'm so glad," Mary said, pulling a chair up beside her son's bed. "Please, have a seat, Emma."

"Thank you again." While seating herself, she held the book in her lap, and with her free hand, sipped the tea.

"I couldn't help but overhear you talking, son. Do you really think Mr. White has done something to his own daughter?"

"Ma, I looked all over the place. She wasn't in her room, the house, or even the barn. Where would she go? It's like she's vanished into thin air."

Mary grimaced. "I don't know. Maybe your pa will have some answers when he returns."

Miss Kimball took a sip of her tea. "Well, I'm headed there when I leave here. Maybe, I will get some answers."

Patrick's brow furrowed. "Where is Pa? Shouldn't he be home by now?"

"He had errands to run and some work to finish up at the widow Barlow's. Well, I'm sure you need to discuss my son's lessons, so I'll leave you two," Mary said while leaving.

"Oh, my goodness, I almost forgot. Your mother's right." Emma set her teacup on the bedside table, stood, and then handed Patrick his book. "I wanted to drop off your reader. You'll need to read chapter 12."

"Okay. Thank you, Miss Kimball."

"You're welcome, Patrick. Will you be in class tomorrow?"

"Yes, as long as Pa can bring me."

"Then, I will let you know what I find out about Sylvia in the morning. Well, I should go. I'd like to be home before it gets dark." She turned toward the door.

"Oh... Miss Kimball?"

She turned back toward Patrick. "Yes?"

"Be careful."

She smiled with a nod. "I will."

Miss Kimball made her way through the kitchen to find Mary kneading bread dough. "Leaving so soon, Emma?"

"Yes, Mary. As I told Patrick, I'd like to check on Sylvia and then be home before nightfall. Thank you again for the wonderful tea."

"You're welcome. I appreciate your stopping by to see my son."

"I was happy to. I'm just glad Patrick is all right."

"Please be careful, Emma. Something's not right about Bernhard White."

"I agree with you, Mary."

CHAPTER FOURTEEN
'Tagious

Miss Kimball walked outside, climbed into her buggy, then circled Chester around the yard and down the two-way track path. Once on the main road, she saw John Ryan.

"Hello, Emma. A beautiful day isn't it?"

"Hello, John. Yes, indeed, it is."

"What brings you out?"

"I dropped off Patrick's reader."

"Well, thank you. I'm sure he'll appreciate it."

"I didn't want him to fall behind in his reading."

"Not much else he can do right now, I'm afraid."

"Mary tells me you went to the White place today."

"Yes, I did."

"Did you see any sign of Sylvia?"

John scratched his head. "You know, I had every intention of asking about the girl, but when I saw him, I couldn't get past the fact he shot at my boy. I sort of lost my temper."

"Oh, my. Did you harm the man? Or did he, you?"

"No. Although there is no doubt in my mind that I caught the man dumbstruck. It was my intention to just threaten him more than anything. Maybe my visit rattled him enough, though, to send a message that many people are concerned for Sylvia. At least, I'd like to think so."

"Well, I can't fault you for being angry, John. We just have to hope and pray you're right, and she's okay."

"You bet." He nodded while tipping his hat. "I best be on my way, or Mary will worry. Good day, Emma."

Miss Kimball smiled. "Goodbye, John." Then they both rode off in opposite directions.

~.~.~

John arrived home and unhitched the team. As he approached the front porch, he noticed the basin full of water, soap, and towels that Mary had left for him, which made him smile. His wife always thought of the right things to do to make her man feel appreciated. He washed his face, arms, and hands in the warm water, then dried them with a towel. After emptying the dirty water basin, he placed the soap and soiled towel inside, then carried it into the house. "Hello, darlin'."

"Oh, John, you're home." Mary rushed over to give her husband a hug and kiss. "I've been worried."

"Worried?"

"Yes."

"Why?"

"I didn't want another member of my family shot at today?"

"No shooting involved, dear. However, I'm sure Bernhard White and I have come to an understanding."

"You didn't hurt him, did you?"

"No, just had a talk with him."

"And you kept your temper?"

He looked down at the floor. "Well..."

"Jonathan Ryan—you didn't—did you?"

He smirked. "I best check on Patrick."

Mary smiled. "How convenient to leave our conversation. But your son has been waiting for you."

John gave his wife's upper arm an affectionate squeeze and then went upstairs and knocked at his son's door. "Patrick?"

"Hi, Pa."

John walked into his son's room. "How's the ankle?"

"Sore."

"I bet."

"How did it go at Sylvia's? Did you talk to her pa? Was she there? Did you see her?"

"Whoa, slow down there. I talked to Bernhard, alright. I told him if he ever shoots at you again, he'll answer to me. As for Sylvia, I planned on asking about her, but the sight of him, I... I just let my temper take control."

"Pa, it makes no sense. I've gone over and over it in my head about where she could be. I have checked everywhere I can think of, but nothing. What could have happened to her, Pa?"

"I don't know, Patrick."

"Do you think he... he killed Sylvia?"

"No. Now, don't go thinking crazy. There has to be a logical explanation."

"Like what?"

"Maybe she went to see a family member out of town."

"I'm sure she would have said something. I remember her telling me the only relative she has is an aunt in California."

"Perhaps, her aunt took sick, and Sylvia's gone to help her."

Patrick didn't look convinced. "I sure hope Miss Kimball can find out something."

"I'm sure she will, son. I'll come to get you when supper is ready. I'm sure you'd like to get out of this bed."

"Yes, sir, I would."

~.~.~

Bernhard peeked out a bedroom window when he heard Miss Kimball's buggy. After opening the drapes, he went to answer the front door.

Emma started to knock, but the door opened abruptly, and she found herself standing face to face with Bernhard's scowl. "Oh... oh... my goodness!" Her hand flew to her chest as if to silence a beating drum while gripping Sylvia's homework. "You startled me, Mr. White."

His expression didn't waver. "Can I do fer ya?"

"Well, Sylvia wasn't at school today—"

"Sick."

"May I see her?"

"'Tagious."

"Excuse me?"

"'Tagious—might catch it."

"I brought her homework and would like to explain it to her if you don't mind."

He held out his hand. "I'll take it."

"Oh... why, yes, of course. Thank you." She handed him the reader.

"What pages?"

"She needs to read Chapter 12 and then answer the questions."

He started to shut the door.

"Mr. White?"

"Hmm."

"Might I at least peek in on Sylvia—say hello?"

He pointed his finger. "Winder."

A bit confused, Miss Kimball looked where he pointed.

"Oh, I see, you mean Sylvia's window. Okay, Mr. White. Thank you."

Emma walked the few steps, leaned over, and peered into Sylvia's bedroom window. She saw the girl lying on her side, but with her back to the window, and it appeared as if she might be asleep. Her eyes searched the room but noticed nothing out of place.

Upon standing straight, she became aware of Bernhard's hardened scowl. In fact, he had not taken his eyes off her for a second, which caused her to feel uncomfortable while standing in the strange man's presence. "Well, she's resting comfortably. I hope she is well again soo—"

The front door slammed in her face. "Soon."

Shaking her head in aggravation, a chill ran up and down Emma's spine while she walked to her buggy and then climbed up. "Lord, but he's an antagonistic man." She frowned. *Or is it just me? Nonetheless, I feel something isn't right in this place.*

~

Bernhard glanced at the reader, thinking how predictable this teacher had become. When Sylvia was younger, the teacher wouldn't come to the house unless she was absent for several days. Now, she seemed to stop if Sylvia had a sniffle. He wondered what was going on in her head. With his constant scowl, he walked into his daughter's bedroom and threw the book down on the dresser. "Ya heard?"

~

Sylvia remained unmoving—unresponsive while reliving how he had come in from the fields, opened the cellar door, and ordered her to hurry up the ladder as he stood above her. Then he yanked on her arm to help her climb up and out. Even though her body was throbbing in pain, she knew better than to say a word. He further demanded that she hurry into her room, lie on the bed with her back to the window, and not move. If she did or tried to say anything to Miss Kimball, he threatened to throw her back into the cellar.

"Get to yer chores." He closed the door.

She remained still while assuming her father had grabbed his hat to leave the house when hearing the front door slam shut. She groaned while it took everything inside her to sit upright, where she waited for a moment, trying to gather herself. When standing on wobbly legs, she walked over to the dresser, picked up the vanity mirror, and then turned it around to see her reflection. "HUH!"

Her hair was a tangled and matted mess, but at least the egg-shaped bump on her forehead was not very noticeable. Rubbing fingers over her cheek, she felt the slight green-purplish haze over the eye and cheekbone, which was a remnant of her father's fist.

What she desired most was a long, hot bath to soothe her aching muscles. Not to mention her stench from relieving herself where she lay, because she could hardly move, let alone crawl to a corner and take care of business. She also had many bug bites on her legs, arms, and a couple on her neck, which stung and were red. She stifled a sob, knowing a bath had to wait, as well as tending to the bites with unguent.

So, instead, she trudged out to the barn to start her chores. First up, she hauled the extra manure out of the stalls, as her father did not do chores in her stead while he had her locked in the cellar.

Once the stalls were clean, she put feed out for the animals and cleaned the hen house. After feeding the chickens, she gathered eggs, which he hadn't done either.

All she had left was to pump buckets of water at the outside faucet and then carry them to all the animals. She'd bring the last bucket into the house. After pouring the water into the washbasin, she grabbed a towel and soap to wash her face and arms first. Then she repeated the process since the dirt had come off in layers, causing the water to turn muddy. After tossing it outside, she refilled the basin with clean water and then placed it back in its usual spot on the kitchen's small table. She also put the soap with a fresh towel beside it for her father. Then she hoped and prayed she did nothing to pique his anger.

~.~.~

While Mary Ryan took laundry off the clothesline, she heard a horse and buggy coming up their lane. She looked between the hanging clothes to see Miss Kimball returning. "Well, hello, Emma. Heading back home now?"

"Yes, I am. Would you give Patrick a message, please?"

"Of course, but you're welcome to go in and see him."

"I best get home since I have papers to grade. And it will be dark soon."

"Oh, of course."

"Would you tell him Sylvia is ill but fine?"

"What a relief. Yes, I'll tell Patrick."

"Thank you, Mary."

"You're welcome. I appreciate you coming back to tell us, since Patrick has been so worried about her."

"Yes, it's been difficult for everyone."

"Is it serious?"

"An excellent question. Sylvia's father would only tell me she was contagious, so I couldn't go inside the house to see for myself."

"Oh, we'll be praying for her to recover."

"Thank you, Mary. I certainly do believe she could use it. Well, I must go." She was off with a quick tap of the reins.

"Good day, Emma."

~.~.~

Sylvia started to prepare supper but had difficulty finding items, as the pantry was next to being bare. She knew, however, not to question her father, so she made do.

Bernhard came into the house, hung his hat on the hook, then washed up in the basin of water. When finished, he sat down at the table, where they ate their meal in silence.

Once Bernhard was done, Sylvia could feel his stare fixed on her. Although when he stood, she feared what he'd do—or say.

"You'll stay here t'morrow." He didn't wait for a response—just left the room and then closed his bedroom door.

She sighed and threw her fork onto her plate. Oh, how she missed Miss Kimball and Patrick. It had taken every ounce of strength she had to stay quiet and not communicate with her teacher when she was outside her bedroom window. *They must be worried sick.*

The idea of having to spend a whole day at home with her father from hell, which is how she thought of him now, petrified her. And she had to make sure she did nothing to upset him for fear he'd throw her back into the cellar. Although when down there, she didn't have to fear what he'd do to her next.

Overwhelmed by her undeniable situation, unexpected tears flowed down her cheeks. Sylvia thought she had cried herself dry. So, with elbows on the table and face cradled in her hands, she let built-up sobs slip out as her body shook—quietly so—lest he hears her. *What have I done to deserve him for a father? And, oh, to have a hot bath, then sleep in my own bed again.*

When Sylvia felt like it wasn't possible to cry another tear, she sat up, dried her eyes, and cleared the table. Once the dishes were washed, and the kitchen was put in order, she could finally enjoy a bath.

Sylvia gathered wood from the porch before stoking the fire on the kitchen stove. After filling and toting buckets of water into the house to heat up, she walked to the barn to grab the wooden bathtub, then flipped it upright.

It took several trips back and forth until Sylvia emptied the last bucket into the tub. Then, after trekking into the house to gather soap, towels, a nightgown, and a nightcap, she took them out to the barn. After removing her clothes and stepping into the bathtub, Sylvia leaned her hand on the edge of the tub. She closed her eyes with a sigh.

Her thoughts drifted to Patrick and the time they had spent together, from lunches at school to their talks when he walked her home. And of the times they went fishing too. When the water went tepid, she reached down and grabbed another bucket, but it also was lukewarm. Laying her head back again, she closed her eyes and continued with her thoughts where she left off—with Patrick. She smiled, reliving the day they kissed.

Sylvia had drifted off to sleep but was startled awake with a strange sensation she wasn't alone. Her eyes were drawn to the barn door, but it was still closed. Only darkness stared back at her through the window. Her eyes darted around the barn but still didn't notice anything unusual. *It must be my nerves mixed with my exhaustion or an overactive imagination.*

The animals were all chewing their food and paying her no mind. Holding her breath, she went under the water to rinse her hair and then surfaced to thoroughly scrub her entire body. One final rinse from the bucket, she dried her hair and then wrapped it up in a towel.

After drying off, she pulled on her nightgown, gave her hair a final rub of the towel, and then put on her nightcap. After stepping into her boots, she emptied the bathtub to put it back in the corner.

Sylvia went inside the house and straight to her bedroom, then let out a sigh of relief while leaning against the closed door—there had been no altercation with her father. After lighting the lamp on her nightstand, she sat down and brushed her hair, and with every stroke, her body continued to relax even more from her bath. Not only were her muscles feeling soothed, but the bites on her body were no longer stinging after rubbing unguent on them. And just as happily, she had no stench about herself. She climbed into bed but only glanced at the reader on the nightstand. However, a yawn changed her mind, and she found it hard to keep her eyes open. After extinguishing the lamp, she fell fast asleep almost before her head hit the pillow.

~.~.~

When John Ryan sat down at the dining room table, Mary served up a tasty meal of roast, potatoes, and carrots. John closed his eyes while inhaling the aroma. "Mary, I do believe you have outdone yourself."

She smiled. "Thank you. How was your day, dear? Did you finish up at the widow Barlow's?"

"I did, but she always has another job for me to do."

"It must be hard without a man around the place. It's good you can help her."

"Well, she does pay me well to do so, which helps supply these wonderful meals."

He smiled at his daughters. "Well, how was school today, girls?"

"Fine, Pa," they answered in unison.

He looked concerned. "How's your ankle, son?"

In his own world, Patrick just stared at his plate while pushing a potato from side to side.

"Patrick?"

"Hmm?"

John frowned. "Something stuck in your craw?"

"Oh, sorry, I was just thinking, Pa."

"About the girl?"

"Patrick's in love," the girls chimed in while giggling.

He glared at his sisters. "Be quiet!"

Mary gave a disapproving look. "That will be quite enough, girls."

Patrick's attention went back to his father. "Yes, sir. All I can do is think about Sylvia."

"Oh, no, Patrick. I forgot to tell you... Miss Kimball stopped by before supper. She said Sylvia is ill."

"Did she see her?"

"She said she couldn't go into the house—something about her being contagious."

"Well, what's wrong with her?"

"He didn't say exactly."

"Will she be okay?"

"I'm not sure. I did say that we would pray for Sylvia's recovery."

Later, Patrick couldn't get comfortable in bed, so he gave up, rolled over on his back, and stared up at the ceiling. He sighed as his thoughts became fixated on Sylvia. *Why did I have to hurt my ankle? What's wrong with Sylvia? Will she be okay? Did Miss Kimball even see her? Ugh, I can't take not knowing!*

After a while, Patrick lit the lamp, sat up, and picked up a book. However, he kept reading the same paragraph over and over since he couldn't focus on the words—let alone comprehend them. His agitation caused him to toss the book across the floor. "Ugh."

Patrick heard his mother's footsteps coming down the hall, followed by a quiet knock on his door before opening, then closing it. "Is your ankle hurting you?"

"No, Ma."

"Can't sleep?"

"No."

"You can't stop thinking about Sylvia—can you, dear?"

"No, I can't, Ma. I'm so worried about her."

CHAPTER FIFTEEN
Impatience

Sylvia ended up staying home from school for the rest of the week until the bruises on her face healed. Her father did not want to deal with anyone meddling.

Miss Kimball stopped by on Thursday with more homework. And to check that Sylvia hadn't taken a turn for the worse.

Bernhard had anticipated another visit from the teacher, so he made sure to keep his daughter inside after school hours. Upon her arrival, he informed her that Sylvia was better and would be back at school on Monday.

~

It was difficult for Sylvia to remain in the house after hearing the exchange between her father and Miss Kimball. Yet, she knew the consequences of defying her father. Nonetheless, Sylvia longed to return to school, her only safe place. And it was where she fell in love with Patrick.

After finishing her chores in the barn, Sylvia returned to the house and prepared supper. Once she had finished washing the dishes and putting the kitchen in order, she was, at last, able to retreat to her room. When she sat on the edge of her bed, the realization of her deplorable life had only two escapes open. The best one was reliving her time with Patrick. She couldn't wait to see him on Sunday, even though they wouldn't be able to speak, let alone look at each other.

The only other thing to keep her sane was being thankful to Miss Kimball for dropping off more of her homework. She had become an avid reader. Although it came second to doing her father's bidding. Sylvia even hoped to push past her class.

On Friday and Saturday, Sylvia paid extra attention and made sure she didn't step out of line with her father in any way. So, in-between her morning and evening chores, she kept busy in the kitchen, baking apple pies on Friday, and then served a vegetable stew with freshly baked bread on Saturday.

~.~.~

Patrick's ankle was still sore and somewhat swollen, but he had gone back to school after a few days, where he would wait outside, hoping Sylvia would come walking down the path toward school.

He knew Timmy was happy about Sylvia's absence because he had convinced Patrick to shoot marbles before and after school. It was clear to see how happy Timmy was to see Patrick without his girlfriend. Even told him it was just like old times.

During class, Patrick kept staring at her vacant seat. He couldn't help wonder if she was sick or if her crazy father had done her harm. After all, he had seen the wrath of Bernhard White firsthand, which made him wonder if he would ever see her again. Miss Kimball told him she had only been privy to seeing Sylvia's backside, so she had not seen her face or spoken to her.

"Patrick?"

Hearing his name startled and snapped him out of his contemplation. "Uh... yeah... um... sorry." He shook his head.

"Do you know the answer?"

"Sorry, Miss Kimball. What?"

"To the question, Patrick."

"I'm sorry, which one?"

She sighed. "The second question on the front board."

He read it. "No, ma'am."

Abigail's hand shot up like a blast from a cannon. "I know. I know the answer."

Miss Kimball ignored her. "Sam, do you know the answer?"

"No, ma'am."

The teacher looked around the room. "Does anyone else know the answer to question two?" No other hands were raised, and when she looked back at Abigail, her arm waved in the air like a flag. She frowned. "Yes, Abigail."

After a two-minute explanation, the girl stopped talking.

"You are correct."

"My mother says I'm the smartest in the class."

Miss Kimball sighed. "Thank you, Abigail. Class, it's time for lunch. But, Patrick, I would like to speak with you for a moment."

She walked to the back door, waited until the last child exited, approached Patrick, and then sat across from him. "How's the ankle?"

"It's still sore but getting better every day."

"I'm glad to hear it. Listen, I know you've been through a tough time of late, dear. I also know you are worried about Sylvia, but you need to focus in class."

"I'm sorry, outside of Sylvia, I just can't put my thoughts together. What if she's getting worse?"

"Let's just try and believe the best."

"Okay."

"And in the meantime, hard as it is, try paying attention."

"Yes, ma'am."

A smiling Miss Kimball stood with an understanding hand on her student's shoulder, then continued to the doorway to check on the students.

The rest of the day went well enough. Patrick shot marbles with Timmy after school, then walked home. He did his best to keep busy until Sunday, but it wasn't easy. No matter the attempts to keep his thoughts off the girl, he fell head over heels in love with, his heart ached. And he felt sure he had joined Sylvia's father in the certifiable department as well.

~.~.~

A sudden loud crack filled the air on Sunday morning when the Ryan family was halfway to the church. It caused their wagon to lean right. "Whoooa there... whoa."

"Oh, no, what is it, John?"

"We must have hit a rut in the road and broke an axle. I best see how bad it is." John stepped down and then walked around the wagon to find the problem on Mary's side. He knelt to assess the damage while rubbing his forehead in frustration, then stood with a nod to his wife. "Just what I was afraid of—we have a broken axle all right. You go on ahead and take the kids to church, Mary. If I'm lucky, it'll be an easy fix. Then I'll come back and pick you up."

"Yes, of course, dear. That is a very good idea."

He smiled. "If Reverend Brooks is long-winded as usual, I should be back in time to catch the end of the sermon."

Mary giggled. "John Ryan, you're incorrigible."

He grinned. "I know, but you love me anyway."

Her smile broadened. "Yes, I suppose I do." She turned to the children. "Come on, kids, we're afoot from here."

~.~.~

Sylvia remembered her nervous anticipation while getting ready for church and how she was even dressed and ready to go before her father called to wake her. The temptation to run out of the house was great, but she restrained herself and walked as calmly as possible. After climbing into the wagon, Bernhard had tapped the horses with the reins, and then they were on their way.

The closer they got to the church, the more nervous Sylvia became as her heart raced, and her palms were clammy. When they neared the church, her heart sank, all while stifling a gasp. Her eyebrows furrowed as she sought out the sight of Patrick amongst the horses and wagons. *Oh, no! Where are they? How can they not be here?* If she didn't get to see him today, it would be agonizing. *Maybe, they hadn't arrived yet. Oh, please, Patrick... please be on your way. I've missed you. I need to see you.*

After stopping the horses, Sylvia's father helped her down from the wagon, just as Miss Kimball's horse and buggy pulled up beside them.

Miss Kimball's smile was subdued. "Mr. White."

Bernhard scowled while nodding.

Her smile grew. "Sylvia, it's so good to see you."

"Hi, Miss Kimball. It's good to see you, too."

"How are you feeling, dear?"

Sylvia glanced at her father and then looked down at the ground. "Mmm... much better. Thank you."

"I'm so glad to hear it."

"I appreciate you for dropping off my homework again, Miss Kimball."

"You're welcome. I didn't want to see you get so far behind in your studies. Well, I look forward to seeing you at school tomorrow, so take care."

"Yes, ma'am."

Emma climbed out of the buggy. "Good day, Mr. White."

He grimaced. "Miz Kimbul."

They walked up the steps, greeted the reverend, and were seated. Sylvia glanced back at the door twice, but she had to stay collected so as not to anger the deranged man. A few minutes into the service, she had a premonition someone had eyes locked in her direction. She only hoped it was the one she loved.

~.~.~

As Mary and the children approached the church, Patrick could feel his senses heighten, and it felt like fireflies danced in his stomach. He searched the horses and wagons until he found what he wanted. Mr. White's wagon was parked in its usual spot to the left of the church. *Question is—did he bring Sylvia with him?*

Since Reverend Brooks wasn't outside the door to greet the congregation, it meant service was about to begin.

Mary, Patrick, and the twins climbed the stairs and entered the building. They stopped while Mary looked for open seating.

Meanwhile, Patrick searched for Bernhard White, but just as he spotted him, his mother had chosen the pew where they would sit. Once seated, Patrick held his breath while looking through the crowd for his girl. At least, that's how he had come to think of her as such. When spotting Bernhard again for the second time, his heart skipped a beat. Sitting to the right of him was the most beautiful girl he had ever seen... his Sylvia.

Instinctively, she must have known his eyes were glued to her as she turned in his direction—their gazes met. She smiled, and relief washed over Patrick.

He was desperate to speak with her, as so many questions raced through his mind. *Where was she when he went to her house? Why couldn't he find her anywhere? What illness did she have? Was she even sick, or did her pa do something to her?*

Within seconds, she glanced at him. And even though he motioned toward the back door, she grimaced while shaking her head.

Common sense told Patrick there was no way Bernhard White would allow him to talk to Sylvia after church, but he just had to try. He also knew he couldn't risk going to her house either. Besides, his ankle wasn't back to normal, so the last thing that he wanted was to be a repeat target practice for Bernhard and his rifle. He would have to settle for waiting until tomorrow. Nonetheless, Patrick was slowly going stark raving mad. He decided it was the single-most thing to have ever tested his patience. *What if something happens to her tonight, and she doesn't make it to school tomorrow? One sure thing is, I can't take this waiting much longer because the anxiety is brutal.*

~

Sylvia relived the moment when she had turned, and their eyes met, sending shockwaves throughout her body. And when he motioned to meet outside, it took everything she had in her not to run out the door, fall in his arms, and beg him to take her away... far away from her father.

Sylvia shook her head back to her present dilemma, even though she realized her pain and agony showed in every crease of her face—she just couldn't help it. From the corner of her eye, she saw her father turn and study her. Luckily, she had already shifted back to Reverend Brooks' sermon when declaring, "He gives strength to the weary and increases the power of the weak."

No matter how hard it was for Sylvia to concentrate on the spoken word, she seemed to look through the reverend as if he was a giant piece of glass.

"Even youths grow weary—the young men stumble and fall," the reverend went on to say. However, she found herself tuning him out.

~

Patrick's gaze fixated on the reverend pacing behind the pulpit—although he didn't listen to the words, "But those who hope in the Lord will renew their strength."

He stole a glance at Sylvia, but Bernhard's scowl and dark, beady eyes seemed to look right through him. No matter how he tried to concentrate on the sermon, he couldn't hear the reverend, "And they will soar on wings like eagles; they will run and not grow weary; they will walk and not be faint."

At last, with the sermon finished, the congregation was asked to stand and sing 'Amazing Grace.' As they arose, Patrick looked at his ma and noticed his pa had joined them, but he had been so engrossed in his thoughts about Sylvia, he didn't notice his arrival.

After the song ended and the congregation was dismissed, Reverend Brooks made his way to the exit, shook hands, and made small talk with the townspeople.

Patrick watched Sylvia and Bernhard stand then walk to the exit. He longed to get close to her—perhaps touch her hair or shoulder. However, when Sylvia's father walked close behind her, he could've sworn Bernhard was holding Sylvia's arm like he was guiding her. It made Patrick uneasy. *Why does he have her by the arm? He's holding her like... like she's his wife.* By the time Patrick reached the door, Bernhard had taken her hand while she stepped onto the wagon.

"Good morning, Patrick," the reverend greeted. "And how are you this fine day?"

"I'm fine, sir," Patrick said, shaking his hand, even though his eyes were still fixated on Sylvia, as the wagon pulled away. "I... I mean, Reverend." Then he moved on.

"Good morning, Sadie and Sarah. I believe you two are taller and prettier every time I see you."

They beamed while thanking him for the compliment.

"Mornin' Reverend," John said, shaking hands. "Sorry for my tardiness. A broken axle on the wagon needed fixin'."

"Lucky for you, my sermons are long-winded, John."

Mary chuckled. "It was a fine sermon today, Reverend."

"Thank you, Mary." He leaned down with a lowered voice. "It's good to know some folks listen and aren't nodding off."

Laughter followed from the three adults.

"How about having supper with us, Reverend?" Mary asked.

"That would be lovely, Mary. I do need to stop by the widow Barlow's this afternoon, but I could drop by this evening."

She smiled. "We'll see you then."

~.~.~

As Bernhard and Sylvia left town, she tried to distract her thoughts by looking at the scenery. However, it was unsuccessful when they passed by the same path she walked on every day to school, along with everything familiar, down to the wildflowers. Sylvia had a notion about jumping off the wagon and running back to the church to find Patrick. She imagined what it would be like to kiss and embrace him— never let him go. *How wonderful it would be if I could live with the Ryan's. They seem like such friendly people. They had to be since their son is so wonderful. I wish I lived with them.*

"Sylvia?"

"Hmm."

"Ain't gonna ask 'gain," Bernhard grumbled.

"What, Papa?"

"Weren't makin' eyes at 'im, were ya?"

"No, Papa."

"Were ya?"

"No."

"Told ya t' stay 'way."

"I am."

"Ya know what'll happen?"

"Yes, Papa."

After they returned home from church, Sylvia did her usual chores before fixing lunch. Afterward, she knew her homework would take all afternoon until it was time to make supper.

~.~.~

The Ryan family enjoyed a lunch of bean soup, salad with fresh vegetables from the garden, and warm buttermilk biscuits. Afterward, Patrick played catch with the twins outside. Meanwhile, Mary cleaned up the dishes.

John sat on the porch and smoked his pipe while watching the children play. "All right, kids, it's time for chores before the reverend comes for supper."

"Yes, Pa," Sadie said.

"Oh, okay," answered Sarah.

Patrick walked over and sat down next to his father.

"What's ailing you, son?"

"Well, Sylvia was back at church today."

"Yes, and I thought you would be happy about it."

"I am, but—"

"But what?"

"Well, something just isn't right, Pa."

"What do you mean?"

"He held her arm... like this." Patrick grabbed his father's left elbow with his right hand. "Then he escorted her out as if she were his wife."

"Maybe he was in a hurry to get home."

"I don't know, Pa. Like I said, there's something not right."

"Have you asked Sylvia if he's done anything to hurt her?"

"Yeah, but I think she's scared of him and won't say anything."

"You've always had good instincts, Patrick. If you think something's off, I trust you."

"What can we do about it?"

"Well, son, without evidence, I don't see what we can do."

Patrick sighed. "There has to be something."

"I don't want you going back over to the White house. Her father has made it clear how he feels about you."

"I know. I guess I'll try talking to Sylvia again. Maybe I can get her to open up to me."

"It sounds like a good place to start. Now, you best get your chores done. The reverend will be along soon, and I don't want to be late for your ma's famous fried chicken."

"Yes, sir."

Reverend Brooks arrived while the children did evening chores. When they finished, everyone gathered around the

Ryan table to enjoy the delicious supper that Mary made. From her famous fried chicken, scalloped potatoes, and fresh corn on the cob, along with warm biscuits and honey.

When the meal was finished, Reverend Brooks placed his napkin atop the table. "Mary, this is a wonderful meal. You are truly a fine cook."

She smiled. "Glad you liked it, Reverend."

"Mmm, he's right. I think you've outdone yourself tonight, dear."

Mary smiled. "Thank you, John."

He winked with a cockeyed grin. "You're welcome."

While the adults enjoyed their coffee, everyone ate warm gooseberry pie for dessert. Afterward, John played the violin, Patrick played the harmonica, and Mary strummed a zither. Sadie and Sarah danced and twirled while the reverend clapped along in the festivities until he left sometime later.

However, Patrick couldn't sleep because of his anxiousness about tomorrow—when he could not only see his Sylvia but hold her in his arms.

CHAPTER SIXTEEN
Reunited

Sylvia tossed and turned all night because of her excitement over reuniting with Patrick, so she didn't try going back to sleep when waking up early. Instead, she just got up, dressed, did her chores, and made breakfast.

Her father was seated across the table and had inhaled half of his breakfast before glancing at his daughter. "Up early, weren't ya?"

"Yes, Papa. Before school starts, I need to get the rest of my homework from Miss Kimball."

He glared while pointing his finger. "Stay 'way from 'at boy."

Downcast, she looked up from her plate. "Yes, Papa." Sylvia resumed eating her breakfast. Once the dishes were washed and dried, she put her coat and bonnet on, then grabbed her books and her lunch pail.

"Sylvia?"

With her hand on the doorknob, she froze. "Yes, Papa."

"Anyone asks, ya had 'fluenza."

"Yes, sir," she said with a subdued voice while closing the door behind her. And as much as she wanted to fly like the wind to school, more so to Patrick, she knew better. The premonitions she always had about her father were usually correct. And realizing such a fact, Sylvia was sure she could feel his eyes fixated on her through the window. So, hard as it was, she forced herself to walk the two-path track as if it were any other day. But when starting down the other side of the hill, and out of her father's sight, Sylvia picked up speed. In no time, she was in a dead-on sprint. She only hoped Patrick had the same idea and would come to school early.

Nearing the schoolhouse, she walked slower, hoping to see Patrick. Sadly, all was desolate, even the schoolyard. She walked toward the steps but came to a standstill when she heard her teacher's voice calling to her.

Sylvia turned with a smile while waving. "Hi, Miss Kimball."

The teacher beamed. "It is so wonderful to see you, dear. Are you feeling well now?"

"Better, ma'am," she answered while walking up the steps. "It's good to be back."

"Since you're early, we have time to go over the rest of your missed assignments."

However, something caught Sylvia's eye, causing her face to light up. "I'll be there in just a minute, Miss Kimball."

The teacher turned around to find Patrick approaching them with a grin, like an excited kid in the mercantile candy section. With a smile, she turned back toward Sylvia with a hand on her shoulder. "Why don't we go over your lessons at lunchtime?"

"Okay," Sylvia said happily without altering her gaze.

Emma walked up the steps, but she glanced over her shoulder at the reunited couple before entering the building. She saw them giggling with each other. It made her smile.

Patrick grabbed Sylvia by the hand and then hurried her off to the rear of the building. When they rounded the corner, he pulled her in close to wrap his arms around her. "I've missed you so much."

"I've missed you, too."

He cupped her face with his hands. "Are you okay?"

"Yes, why?"

"I was so worried about you."

She smiled. "I'm fine now."

"Did he hurt you?"

"I was just sick."

"Did he do something to make you sick?"

"No."

"What was wrong with you?"

"I was sick, Patrick."

"What did the doctor say was wrong?"

"I... I didn't see the doctor."

He scowled. "You mean you were so sick for a week, but your father didn't insist that Doc come to see you? Why didn't he?"

"No. Papa thought it was influenza."

"Oh, so he's a doctor now, is he?"

"Patrick, why do you have so many questions? Papa just thought he knew what it was."

"Sylvia, you could have died!"

"But I didn't."

"Well, you could have. Would your father even care?"

She started to cry. "Patrick, why are you so mad at me?"

He embraced her again and kissed her forehead. "Sylvia, I'm not mad at you. I just... well... I love you."

Sylvia pulled back and looked into his soft, brown eyes. "You... you love... me?" She had never heard those words in her lifetime.

He shrugged. "Well, now, you know."

She smiled and blushed. "I love you, too. Patrick."

"I couldn't stand it if anything happened to you." Then he leaned in and kissed her.

They were interrupted by children playing and the bell ringing. "I suppose we should go," she said.

"I guess. Hey, or we could go somewhere."

"Where?"

"Maybe by the fishin' hole."

"No, we can't. Miss Kimball already knows we're here."

"We could tell her we both got sick."

"I don't know. I just missed a whole week."

He grabbed her hand, and then they walked toward the front of the schoolhouse. "I suppose you're right. I'd just rather have you all to myself."

She beamed. "I feel the same way about you, too, Patrick."

They walked hand in hand up the steps. Once inside, they paused while Patrick squeezed her hand before releasing it.

She beamed while taking her seat. It was difficult to wait as minutes seemed to pass in slow motion until lunch. Yet, they stole glances and smiled at each other throughout the morning.

~.~.~

After they were dismissed for lunch, Sylvia stayed in her seat, waiting until the schoolhouse was empty, before approaching her teacher's desk. It didn't take more than a few minutes to go over the homework assignments since Miss Kimball already had a list made up for her.

Sylvia hurried outside and paused halfway down the stairs. However, her pleasant smile turned into a frown when she saw Abigail sitting next to Patrick.

When he looked up to see her, he grinned, then motioned for her to join him.

Patrick reached for her hand as Sylvia walked toward them. "Okay, Abigail, you need to move now."

She scrunched her face. "But you said I could sit by you."

"I told you it was Sylvia's spot."

"You said she was inside with Miss Kimball."

"I said she was inside for a few minutes."

Seeing there was nowhere for her to sit beside Patrick, Sylvia said, "It's okay; I'll find somewhere else."

Patrick stood. "No, I'll go with you." Without a word or backward glance, they walked together while holding hands. The two decided to stay away from the others and ended up sitting behind the teeter-totters.

"Sorry, Sylvia. I told her not to sit here because this seat was for you, but she did anyway."

"It's okay, Patrick."

"Something good came from Abigail."

Her eyebrows furrowed. "What do you mean?"

"She handed out peppermint sticks. Here, I got one for you, too." He gave her the candy.

She smiled. "Oh, thanks."

They talked and laughed while eating their lunch. However, Patrick couldn't help but notice how she kept checking the road, then the mercantile too. "Are you looking for him?"

She was silent and looked at the ground.

"Your pa doesn't like me, does he?"

"It's... well, Papa's just protective."

"What would he do if he saw us together?"

"I don't know."

"While you were gone, I sprained my ankle bad."

"Oh, no. How did it happen?"

"Your—"

The bell sounded.

"My what?"

Patrick sighed. "We can talk about it later."

They stood and walked back into the schoolhouse.

When school let out, Patrick and Timmy talked as Sylvia walked past them and headed for home. She was on the outskirts of town when she heard Patrick calling her. She stopped and turned toward him.

"Hey, wait up. You left without saying goodbye."

"You were busy, and I didn't want to interrupt."

"I was makin' plans to go fishin' with Timmy."

"Today?"

"No, Saturday."

"Oh."

"Can I still walk you home, or at least to the usual spot?"

"I don't know. I have to be careful."

"Well, I didn't see your pa anywhere in town, so he must be at home."

"Okay, but maybe you should turn around before the ridge, just in case."

He nodded. "Deal."

They continued down the road while talking along the way. "So, you were going to tell me something earlier."

"Yes. Well, there's no easy way to tell you."

She looked confused. "How'd you hurt your ankle?"

"Do you remember when we went fishing, and we heard the noise?"

"Yeah."

"You seemed spooked afterward. I was afraid you might have gotten into trouble because of me. So, I came to your house."

She stopped in her tracks. "You did what?"

"I came to your house. I wanted to make sure you were okay."

Her stomach clenched. "When?"

"The same night."

Her concern intensified. "Did my pa see you?"

"Not at first."

Sylvia looked terrified. "So, he did see you?"

"Yes, but only after sneaking up to the house when I could not find you anywhere. I even looked in every window but couldn't see inside what I thought was his bedroom. Then, I climbed onto the woodpile and was just about to look in when the whole thing went down like a line of dominoes. Of course, the noise got your pa's attention. And, even though I hid from him, he kept calling because he knew someone was there. When I snuck off around the side of the house, and he took off along the other side, I made a break for it. After clearing the fence, I took off toward home."

"So, how did you hurt your ankle?"

Patrick looked at her with a distraught expression while weighing if he should tell her. "You see, I stepped in a hole and twisted my ankle. I thought it was broken, but it was just a bad sprain."

"Oh... I'm glad it wasn't broken."

"Thanks. Sylvia...?"

She had started to walk. "Yes."

"Where were you?"

"I... I don't know what you mean. I better go. I'll see you tomorrow."

"Sylvia?"

She didn't turn back, just rushed off and left him standing alone.

He sighed. "See you tomorrow."

CHAPTER SEVENTEEN
A Bold Move

Sylvia sprinted like prey from a pack of wolves straight to the porch, entered the house, and then slammed the door. Leaning against it with her arms outstretched, she panted like an overheated dog, feeling relieved after taking some deep breaths over dodging Patrick's questions. At least, for the time being. She hated not being able to answer him with the truth but knew her father's secret couldn't be divulged. *I can't risk it, my love. There's no telling what he'd do to me... or worse... if he did something to you or your family. I couldn't bear it.*

Bernhard's bedroom door opened, but she didn't hear until he loomed at her from the entryway. "Whater ya doin'?"

She jumped. "Oh, Papa, you scared me. I'm was just catching my breath."

He pointed at the door. "Harvestin'."

"Yes, sir." After hurrying to her room, she changed from her school dress into an everyday one. When she stepped onto the porch where he had been waiting, he pointed to several large piles of wheat in the yard. "Get straw and tie 'em."

"Yes, sir."

When she came back out from the barn, Sylvia carried several bands to tie the bundles of wheat sheaves, which had been cut with the sickle.

Bernhard would then transport the bundles by wagon to the Clintok Mill in town, where they were ground into flour and then sold to Stoope Mercantile. The excess would then be shipped to larger cities within and out of the state.

After the wheat was harvested and delivered, corn would be next. After Sylvia pulled the corn off the stalks, he would follow behind, shocking the stalks before placing them in baskets.

Then, by the wagonload, corn would be taken to the mill, where it would be ground into cornmeal, and the rest processed into feed for the animals.

From now until winter, Sylvia would work from the moment she woke up until the time she went to bed. From helping with the harvest until near dark, followed by other chores, mealtime, clean-up, and then homework.

Oft-times, she fell asleep before completing her homework. Many of the boys and some of the girls who lived on larger farms were taken out of school. They would be required to help their families with the harvesting of crops.

As for school, Sylvia and Patrick continued to sit together for lunch. Unless her father was seen at the mercantile or somewhere else in town. He also escorted her part of the way home every day. Although Sylvia decided it best to keep the walks shorter. Not only was it to feel safer about her father not seeing them, but from further probing by Patrick into her father's treatment of her.

~.~.~

Patrick and his pa were harvesting, too, so after leaving Sylvia, he'd go help in the fields, do his chores, then homework. He was still concerned—frustrated about Sylvia and her father but didn't know what else to do. Every time he brought it up, she acted weird and avoided his questions.

Thankful though he was because it had been a month since the last incident where Sylvia was not at school. Luckier, no red flags were causing Patrick or Miss Kimball to expect anything afoul.

~.~.~

It was the last day before Thanksgiving break, and the kids were filled with anticipation. Each student had been given a writing assignment on the things they were grateful for in their life. They took turns reading their two to three-minute-long presentations after lunchtime, as they had done all week.

"Okay, class, quiet down, please," Miss Kimball said. "Today, we will continue with our presentations of 'Things I'm Thankful For.'" She slid her finger down the classroom ledger for whose turn it was next. "Let's see. Patrick, I believe it's time for your story."

He stood and walked to the front of the classroom for his presentation.

As Sylvia listened to him list everything that he was grateful for, she couldn't help but once again wish she was a part of the Ryan family. Patrick made them sound so wonderful. In the end, he listed good friends and how they were always there for each other. He grinned, and his eyes revealed she was the only one present in the room.

Miss Kimball smiled. "Thank you, Patrick. Let's see the next person... is... Sylvia."

Abigail raised her arm. "What about me, Miss Kimball? Ryan, Stoope, and then White. It's my turn before Sylvia's."

"Oh, well... um... yes, of course, Abigail."

She marched up to the front of the room and then spun on her heel to face the class. "'Things I'm Thankful For,' by Abigail Stoope. I am very thankful for my parents, William and Eliza

Stoope. Not only because they own Stoope's Mercantile, but my father is the banker at Clintok Bank. My parents are the richest people in town—in fact, probably all of Missouri, too."

Miss Kimball rolled her eyes, rested her head in one hand, and placed her pencil in the other one. She held it atop the ledger, giving the illusion of grading the report.

Abigail stood taller. "My parents see to it I have the best of everything. We have the nicest house in town, the finest china and silverware, linens, and fabrics. My mother orders lovely dresses for me, so I don't have to look plain like everyone else. I also get all the free candy I can eat, along with expensive dolls, as well as anything else I want. One day, I will run Stoope's Mercantile. We also have the best and most expensive livestock in Clintok."

Miss Kimball found herself watching the minute hand turn on her watch. If the girl went a second over three minutes, which Emma knew the girl would, she was ready to cut it.

~

As Sylvia listened to the presentations throughout the week, she felt like each one was better than the last. It was clear she was the only person in the entire school who lived without a mother. She wondered if these kids were maybe embellishing fiction or if they truly lived in the families they described.

Why am I so different? Have I done something wrong? Am I a bad girl? Papa says I am. Abigail's report didn't bother Sylvia, as she knew it was unique to every other student in the classroom. However, she wondered what it would be like to have some of the finer things like Abigail described in great detail.

Sylvia hadn't felt quite herself today, although she couldn't pinpoint it to any one thing. She just hoped it wasn't really influenza she had fibbed about to everyone. As Abigail chattered at a rapid pace, Sylvia found it hard to focus on the

189

words. Either her ears were playing tricks on her, or Abigail seemed to be alternating between muffled to concise speech. Even her vision blurred and then cleared. Now, her stomach began to feel queasy. Maybe it was because she had been dreading for weeks when it would be time to give her report. She would have to make up a story—the real one was too ugly.

"Thank God," Emma whispered.

Abigail scrunched her nose. "Excuse me, Miss Kimball?"

"Oh, I said, thank you, Abigail. You may return to your seat now."

"Yes, ma'am." She beamed while doing as the teacher asked her to do.

"Sylvia? I believe you are the last one."

Swallowing hard, Sylvia stood as her stomach tightened, and her palms felt cold and clammy, along with her vision blurring. She took one step, and the room swirled. Another step led to her eyes closing as she fell face first, like a tree chopped by an ax. Everything went black.

Miss Kimball gasped and jumped to her feet. The class was stunned, and a few girls screamed.

A panicked Patrick, who was closest to her, slid on his knees beside her and grabbed a hand. "Sylvia! Wake up... Sylvia. Come on, you have to wake up... please."

Miss Kimball knelt on the opposite side. "Sylvia! Sylvia!" Emma patted her flushed cheeks. "Patrick, go and bring me some water. Hurry."

"Yes, ma'am."

Emma tapped Sylvia's cheek, along with wiping her sweaty forehead, but still no response. She looked up to find a few of the curious students had gathered around to see what had happened. "Children, please, go back to your seats and remain in them. We need to give Sylvia some room."

Patrick returned with a bucket of water.

Miss Kimball grabbed a handkerchief from her pocket, dunked it into the water, then wiped Sylvia's cheeks and forehead. "Please, wake up, dear."

Soon Sylvia stirred, and her eyes began to flutter before opening.

Emma smiled. "Welcome back, Sylvia. You gave us quite a scare, young lady." She stood and said, "Patrick, will you help me take Sylvia back to her seat?"

Once Sylvia was situated, Emma checked her pocket watch. "Class, it's early, but you are dismissed. Have a wonderful Thanksgiving. See you on Monday."

After the room cleared, she turned her attention back to Sylvia. "How do you feel?"

"I'm okay now."

"Do you think you can walk over to the doctor's office?"

"Oh, no. I don't think it's necessary. I've just been tired lately."

"Well, I insist. Come on, we'll walk with you."

~.~.~

After delivering a calf from across town, Doctor Parker had just stepped down from his buggy. He smiled. "Well, hello, Emma, Patrick, and Sylvia. What brings you all here?"

"Hello, Doctor Parker," Miss Kimball said. "Sylvia passed out in class, so I thought she should be seen."

"Of course. It was wise to come, so let's get you into the exam room, my dear."

"Do you mind if we wait?" Miss Kimball asked.

"Not at all. Have a seat," Doc said, then left to tend his patient.

Meanwhile, they sat in silence for a few minutes. "Do you think Sylvia will be okay, ma'am?"

"Oh, I'm sure she will be just fine. Although we must remain patient and wait for the doctor's diagnosis."

After what seemed like forever, the doctor opened the curtain and then reclosed it.

He glanced at the teacher, over to Patrick, and then back to Miss Kimball, prompting them both to stand.

"Patrick, would you mind stepping out for a moment? I need to speak with Miss Kimball."

"What's wrong with her, Doc?"

"It's okay, Doctor. You can include Patrick."

"Are you sure, Miss Kimball?"

"Yes. Patrick is her beau."

He looked surprised. "Oh, you are?"

"Yes." Patrick frowned. "Please, tell us what is wrong. Is Sylvia going to be okay?"

Doctor Parker removed his glasses with a sad and concerned expression, then paused before answering. "She's... well... she's with-child."

~

As the words came out of Doctor Parker's mouth, Patrick heard them, but in slow-motion, and garbled at best. He tried to form the word, 'What?'—ask the doctor to repeat what he had said, yet he couldn't bring himself to speak. The thumping of his heart was beating so loud he couldn't think, and his body went numb. The urge to turn tail and run as far away as possible came to mind. Instead, he was frozen to the spot, as if having a block of ice on each of his feet.

"Patrick, have you and she...?"

The expression on his face changed as if he had swallowed a teaspoon of castor oil. He shook his head. "No... no... I... we... no." A wave of nausea enveloped him—yet, he bolted from the room.

~

"Oh, dear God." Miss Kimball turned pale and felt weak in the knees, so she sat back down in her chair—unbelieving for a moment. She was in complete shock.

"Are you all right, Miss Kimball? You look as if you've seen an apparition."

"I... I'm... afraid... I'm speechless."

"Do you think Patrick is...?"

There was a knock at the door. "Open up!"

Doctor Parker answered it, and Bernhard stepped into the office.

"Where is she? Sylvia? Sylvia?"

Doctor Parker nodded with a frown. "Mr. White, just wait a moment; I was caring for your daughter in the examination room."

Bernhard stepped forward, but Doctor Parker placed a hand on his chest. Bernhard looked down at the blockade and back to the doctor.

"We need to talk."

"Don't need talkin'. Just Sylvia."

"You'll want to hear what I have to say."

He scowled but remained still. "Well?"

"Sylvia is..."

"Is what?"

"Your daughter is with-child."

Bernhard's eyebrows raised, and his eyes popped open. "Sylvia?" He was silent for a moment. "Sylvia!"

"Yes," she answered, timidly before Doc could say anything.

"Let's go."

Pulling the exam room's curtain open and without a word or backward glance, Sylvia walked past Miss Kimball and Doc. She continued on through the doorway and then over to the wagon.

"Mr. White, I know you are not fond of doctors, but I must emphasize, it is imperative I see your daughter throughout this pregnancy."

"Back t' settle."

"Mr. White... I also need to—"

~

Bernhard turned on his heels and hurried to the wagon. He was loading it and taking inventory of his supplies, which is when he overheard Eliza Stoope. She had been gossiping to a customer about seeing Sylvia being helped into Doctor Parker's office.

He checked and made sure the busybody didn't try to cheat him out of anything in his order. Bernhard never trusted the nosey woman, be it in business or otherwise. "Good fer nothin' meddler."

A subdued Sylvia sat staring into nothingness with a blank expression as Bernhard whipped the horses into a gallop and headed out of town.

~

Doctor Parker watched Bernhard White all but manhandle his daughter onto the wagon and then race out of town. He closed the door, shook his head, and turned back to the visibly shaken teacher.

"Miss Kimball, are you okay?"

"I'm not sure."

"Would you like a glass of water?"

"Y... yes, thank you."

Doctor Parker poured water from the pitcher into a glass and handed it to her.

She sipped it while studying the wall as if she were doing a mathematical equation in her head.

"Miss Kimball, you said Patrick is Sylvia's beau?"

"Hmm... yes."

"Do you believe he is the father?"

Miss Kimball looked at him. "No. He is a good boy—comes from a good family. Patrick doesn't lie, either, so I believe him. Plus, did you see the way he reacted?"

"Yes, I did."

She frowned. "Well, I should be going. Thank you, doctor."

"You're welcome."

After the teacher left, he sat at his desk, removed his glasses, and sighed. "Never in all my years as a doctor have I witnessed anything like this."

CHAPTER EIGHTEEN
Bewildered

In the barnyard after a day of harvesting, a concerned John watched his wife rush toward him. "What is it, Mary?"

"Patrick didn't come home after school. And the girls said Sylvia passed out in class."

"Well, I'm sure he'll be along soon."

"He's over an hour late, John. He's never late."

"All right, calm down, dear. I'll go look for him."

"Thank you."

John hurried to the barn, grabbed a bridle to put on a horse in the corral, jumped on bareback, and then raced off. After checking at school and then the doctor's office with no luck, it occurred to him where he could find his son.

As he approached the fishin' hole, he saw Patrick sitting on a big rock, as if in a trance while staring at the water. When he reached the rocks, he could tell from the frown on his face, his first impression was correct—something was very wrong. Taking it slow, John walked over and sat on a rock beside Patrick. Before speaking, he skipped a couple of stones. "You know, son, your ma was worried when you didn't come home after school."

"Sorry."

"Want to talk about it?"

"Nope, but I reckon I'll have to sooner than later."

"When I came looking for you, I heard in town there was an incident at school today, involving Sylvia. Is she okay?"

"I guess... I mean," Patrick said, skipping his own stone, "unless you consider having a baby not okay?"

John was quiet for a few minutes, then looked at Patrick. "Is it yours, son?"

"No, sir. We only went fishin', and hardly spend any time together, with her pa and all."

"Well, I can see you're quite upset."

"How could she do this? I thought she cared about me."

"I'm sure she does care for you. Do you have any idea who the father could be?"

"That's just it. I don't know. I've been over and over things in my head. I mean, we sit together every day at lunch, and I even walk her home after school. Well, I can't walk her all the way, since her pa won't like it, so it only leaves the weekend. If her pa doesn't let me go to the house, I can't imagine he'd let anyone else there either."

"It doesn't seem like it."

"Then, who, Pa?"

"I'm not sure. Did you talk to the doc?"

"No. I was too upset. I just bolted."

"Maybe, you should talk to Sylvia first."

"I don't want to see her right now."

"Then, maybe Doctor Parker is a good place to start. You know, son, it's always best to give people the benefit of any doubt until you hear them out. Sometimes, things aren't as they seem. Could be more going on than you know." He stood and placed his hand on Patrick's shoulder. "I'll tell your ma you'll be back in time for supper."

~.~.~

Back home, while the twins peeled potatoes and carrots for the beef stew, they had been filling their mother in on the drama at the schoolhouse earlier.

"You should've seen it, Ma. She went down like a wall of bricks," Sadie said.

"Yeah... wham! And just like that, she landed smack-dab on her face," Sarah added.

Mary frowned. "Did someone go get the doctor?"

Sarah shook her head. "No. Miss Kimball woke her up, then walked Sylvia over to see the doctor."

"But before that, the teacher told us we could go home for the day," Sadie concluded.

"I'm sure your brother will have some more news when he gets home. "When the door opened, she looked up with a smile. "Well, hello."

John walked inside. "Hi, dear."

Then, he looked at his daughters. "Girls, how was school today?"

They both chimed, "Sylvia fainted."

"Yes, I heard. But right now, I'd like to see you outside for a moment, Mary."

Worried, she dried her hands on a dishcloth. "Girls, please set the table while your pa and I step outside."

"Do we have to?" Sarah asked.

"Girls, mind your ma, now."

"Yes, sir," Sadie replied.

Mary shut the door. "John, did you find Patrick?"

"He's upset and down by the fishin' hole. He'll be home soon."

"Is Sylvia ill?"

"Yes and no."

"I don't follow you."

"Well, it's not an illness per se."

"It must be more than exhaustion from harvesting."

"She's pregnant."

Shocked, Mary's hand flew to her mouth, "Oh, goodness!"

"He says it's not his."

She gave a sigh of relief. "Thank God. But who, then?"

"He's not sure."

She placed her hand over her chest. "Poor, Patrick. It's no wonder he's devastated."

"When is supper?"

"About a half an hour or so. Go on in and get washed up, dear, so I can speak to our son for a moment when he gets home."

~

Her husband nodded and then went into the house. Soon enough, Patrick walked up the path. Mary gathered her thoughts as he came closer.

"Hi, son."

"Hi, Ma."

"Your pa told me what happened. I'm sorry."

"I don't understand it, Ma. How could she do that to me?"

"Have you talked to her about it?"

"No."

"Well, I'm sure there's an explanation."

"I don't want to see her right now."

"I understand you're upset. Maybe you will feel different about it in a couple of days."

"I don't see how."

"Patrick, I'm not sure about what happened. Although I don't get the impression that Sylvia has had an easy life. I can tell you, things will get harder for that girl, so she could use a friend. Right now, supper's near to ready, so wash up."

~.~.~

Sylvia hung onto the side of the wagon as her father urged the horses to go faster. It was as if they were on a late-arriving stagecoach. Once home, he abruptly unhitched the horses.

Meanwhile, Sylvia hurried into the house. Once the horses were put away, she could hear her father grumbling while marching into his bedroom, then loud noises erupted. After changing her school clothes, she heard a door slam shut.

"Sylvia, get out here."

Her stomach clenched, and she considered hiding under the bed or making a break for it out the window.

"Sylvia!"

She opened her bedroom door but hesitated before joining him in the dining room, although with her head downcast. Glancing up from the floor, she felt her face turn beet red to panic-stricken in an instant.

"Told ya t' stay 'way from 'im. Told ya was trouble."

"I did."

His whole body started to shake. "You didn't!"

"Just like yer mother. Men 'tracted to 'er like bears t' honey. Don't care if 'ey get stung."

He pointed his finger at her. "You was flirtin'. Askin' for it."

She shook her head. "No—no, I didn't."

He charged toward her with a backhand across the face and then grabbed her arms and squeezed. "Ya did. Now, you'll reap wha' ya sew."

Tears streamed down her cheeks. "Why do you hate me?"

He grabbed her by the throat with a tight grip. "Ya killed 'er. Died cuz o' you."

Years of feeling responsible for her ma's death brought tears as he confirmed in his own words what she had always feared.

With a tighter grip on her neck and feeling lightheaded, her eyes rolled back in her head as things began to go black. Then he released his grip, leaving her bent over while coughing and gasping for air.

"Yer just like 'er. Drawin' in menfolk."

She shook her head while moving away from him.

Bernhard lunged at her. "Now, you'll pay." Once again, he backhanded his daughter.

Sylvia placed her hand on her cheek to stifle the stinging while stepping back toward the door.

His eye twitched, and a vein popped out on his forehead. "Yer a whore!"

As soon as the words left his mouth, her jaw dropped open, and he might as well have driven a knife through her heart. Something snapped inside her like a twig, and no longer did she see her father, but someone else... a sinister monster standing over her.

Turning away from the savage, she sprinted to the door and flung it open. Even though Bernhard clutched her by the shoulder from behind, Sylvia could break away and bolt through the door. She ran for her life as fear mounted while attempting to escape his wrath. Although with no idea where to go, she just knew to turn back now was not a good idea.

Bernhard chased after her, but he was tipsy from the liquor he had guzzled in his room.

It didn't take Sylvia long to veer off the path and into the open fields. As soon as she determined he wasn't following her anymore, she slowed down—only to have a rude awakening in the cold. Sylvia realized she didn't have her coat or bonnet. *Where should I go? Oh, Patrick. I want to be near you, but you must hate me. Maybe, I could go to Miss Kimball's. No, Papa will look there. I can't put either one of them in danger. There has to be somewhere else.* She thought for a minute. *Oh, I know just the place.*

Along the way, she went past Susie Evan's house, where she noticed laundry hanging on the line. After looking around to make sure no one was about, she sneaked up to the north side of the house. Lucky for her, it further appeared as if no one was home. Even though she saw no coats hanging on the line, she did find a blanket. Luck was with her—it was dry. "Sorry, Mrs. Evans." She snagged it from the line and then continued on her way towards town.

She saw an abandoned barn located about a mile from the schoolhouse. It was the old Heides' place, where a tragic fire occurred many years before when Mrs. Heides went out of town to visit a sick relative. It was decided the three children would remain home with their father, so they wouldn't miss school.

However, because Mr. Heides was well-known as the town drunk, the final determination for the cause of the fire was two-fold. He had consumed too much whiskey, which acted as an accelerant after falling asleep while smoking his pipe. The fire ignited, spread to the curtains, then furniture, until it engulfed the whole house, burning to the ground.

Folks said Mr. Heides probably never woke up, and with the two boys and one girl being found in their beds, they were likely taken by smoke inhalation.

When Mrs. Heides received the wire, she returned home to make burial arrangements. After the funeral, she couldn't bear the thought of living in Clintok anymore—a constant reminder of the family she lost. So, she sold the livestock and put the property up for sale. Sylvia wondered what had become of Mrs. Heides and if she still owned the property. Over the years, the story changed many times. Some folks even believed the property was haunted by the ghosts of Mr. Heides and his three children.

Sylvia knew about the vacant barn that still remained on the property as she passed it on her daily walk to and from school. Knowingly, she knew it was somewhat dilapidated on the outside but hoped the inside conditions would be in better shape. Unfortunately for her, since it was not summertime, a fire was out of the question since it would give away her whereabouts. She hoped the blanket and her thoughts of Patrick would be enough to keep her warm throughout the windy night.

When she got there, the sides of the barn reminded her of a house of cards, which looked ready to collapse inward. *Well, I've got nowhere else to go.* She pushed the door open and looked over the area. There were gaps between many of the boards, with a few large holes in some, but it seemed to be intact when she noted the roof.

Making her way to the back, she found what appeared to be an old stall of some kind. It was the least drafty spot in the entire place and furthest away from the door. After draping the blanket over the stall wall, she took the time to pick up some fallen boards to lean against some of the more significant gaps. She hoped they would stay put and help to block out some of the wind. After a while, her stomach gurgled. *I'm hungry. Where can I get some food? Should I risk searching?*

~.~.~

The Ryan family gathered at the supper table but didn't eat until after John prayed. Then, the biscuits were passed around the table while Mary spooned beef stew onto each plate, placed the pot back on the stove, and then seated herself.

While enjoying their stew, a loud knock interrupted them, with Mary and John exchanging curious glances.

He placed his napkin on the table, scooted his chair back, got up, and walked to the door. Although before reaching it, he heard a familiar voice.

"Open up, Ryan!"

John opened the door to an angry Bernhard White standing in the kitchen doorway with a shotgun pointed at him. "What's going on, Bernhard?"

Mary all but jumped out of her chair while the twins gasped in surprise.

Patrick placed his hands on the table, bracing himself to back up his father if needed.

"Where is she, Ryan?"

John raised his hand to stop the belligerent man from entering the house.

"Mr. White, I'll ask you to lower your weapon. I assume by 'she,' you mean your daughter?"

"Sylvia."

"Well, you can see she's not here."

Bernhard's eyes glared. "Got t' be here."

"Mr. White, please lower your gun. She is not here."

Bernhard lunged at John like a wild grizzly. "Liar! Where is she?"

John charged, knocking him onto his back, then swiped the rifle out of Bernhard's hands. They rolled in the dirt like two pigs in the mud.

Bernhard continued to fight like a crazed animal.

It took John a couple of right hooks across the cheek to stop the attack. Then he pushed himself up on his knees while pointing. "Enough! Enough, Bernhard!"

The winded man rolled onto his side. "Can't find 'er."

John stood and held out his hand.

The enraged man grabbed John's offered hand and allowed him to pull him to his feet, avoiding eye contact.

"I'll help you look."

Bernhard jerked his head toward John with an arched brow.

"Just let me get a few things, and I'll be right back." John went inside and found Patrick standing by the window while holding his father's shotgun in his hands. A sense of pride warmed John's heart as he patted his son on the shoulder. "Thanks, Patrick." Then, he went to the bedroom, returned with more shells, and then put on his hat and jacket.

Mary frowned. "John, what is it?"

"Sylvia's missing. I'm going to help him look for her."

Patrick's heart sank. "Pa, I wanna go."

John glanced at Mary, and then Patrick. "I don't think it's a good idea, son. Not in Bernhard's state of mind. I'm sure it won't take long to find her, so I'll be home soon."

Mary handed John a wrapped cloth. "Warm biscuits."

He grinned. "Thanks. Maybe, you can keep that stew warm for me."

"I will." She kissed him. "Please be careful, John."

"I will, darlin'."

While John saddled up his horse, Bernhard stood beside his, then the men rode off together. It dawned on him, Sylvia's father seemed more like an angry man than worried about his daughter's safety or whereabouts.

Meanwhile, Mary and the children finished supper, and then it was time to complete chores and homework.

After finishing his chores, since Patrick didn't have homework, he walked to the house and peeked through the window. When seeing his ma and the twins engrossed in a project at the kitchen table, he decided on returning to the barn, grabbed a lantern, then disappeared through the fields. While his pa and Bernhard looked for Sylvia, he would search the one place they wouldn't think to look... the house.

CHAPTER NINETEEN
Laudanum & Whiskey

Patrick surveyed the barn first and saw one horse missing. It accounted for Mr. White being at his home earlier. However, he didn't find anything else out of the ordinary. He grew more afraid by the minute of what Sylvia's father had done to her. Visions of him doing her harm, then covering it up by accusing his family of hiding her ran through his mind.

As he walked to the house, his eyes surveyed the area for any signs of Bernhard's return but saw none. Once at the front door, he knocked while calling for Sylvia, but there was no answer. After another knock and call out was met with no response, Patrick turned the handle but paused and took a deep breath to muster his resolve to enter the house. First, he started his search in the kitchen, the living room, and then what he thought might be Sylvia's. Meanwhile, he continued to call out her name as his worry intensified.

Patrick paused outside the other bedroom that he thought could be Bernhard's. Sighing, he took a deep breath and pushed the door open. "What in the...?" Patrick could not believe the room in such disarray, so unlike the rest of the house. There were bottles scattered all over the room, mostly on the floor. Some were dark and round—others square and clear—and in varying sizes. He picked up one of the exact square bottles. He shook his head in puzzlement.

The label read, 'Pure Rye Whiskey,' *Whiskey? It's true... he's a drunk.* Placing the bottle back on the floor, he looked at the nightstand to the right of the bed.

On the left side of the desk was the matching chair, but it was almost unnoticeable, as several dresses were draped across it. Patrick had never seen Sylvia wear any of them.

On the opposite side of the bed, a dresser located in the right corner held an ivory-colored, porcelain washbasin with a pitcher on top, but nothing else.

He noticed a desk with two large vertical drawers on the left side of the desk. After opening one, he found it filled with liquor bottles. When he opened the smaller, horizontal drawer underneath the table, there were many smaller, clear bottles. He picked one up to read the label with red lettering—

LAUDANUM—Poison, Each Fluid Ounce Contains 45% GRAINS OPIUM and 40% ALCOHOL.

Laudanum? He slid the bottle into his jacket pocket, but when he started to close the drawer, something shiny caught his eye. In the empty spot where the bottle had been was a gold chain. After pulling it out, he saw a locket. Upon opening the clasp, it revealed a picture of a beautiful woman. *Sylvia? No, no, it just looks like her.* He sighed. *This has to be her mother. That son of a...* He sighed, shook his head, and slipped the locket into the same pocket as the bottle.

Patrick searched the dresser drawers—only finding Bernhard's clothes. He went to the nightstand, where there was a single drawer. Inside ... more laudanum. *Why does he have so much of this?* He left the room, closed the door, and then stood by the front door for a moment. He gave the kitchen and dining room a look-see. *Where are you, Sylvia? What has he done to you?* He groaned while leaving the house to head for home.

He returned home and started to shut the kitchen door—

"Patrick Jonathan Ryan, where have you been?"

He closed the door, then spun around to find his ma standing in front of him with a scowl and hands on her hips, which was never a good sign.

"I went to Sylvia's."

"You went to... you did what? Are you nuts? Or have a fever? You know how crazy the man is and what he tried to do to you the last time you wandered over there. What on earth is the matter with you? It's like all common sense has left your mind. You had me worried half to death."

"Sorry, Ma. I would have told you, but I—"

"You thought you could go over to the White home, then sneak back here without me knowing about it—thinking the whole time you were out doing your chores. Does that just about sum it up?"

"Well..."

"Well, what?"

"I guess."

"You can forget about me not knowing what's going on around here because I've got eyes in the back of my head, young man. I swear, if you weren't twice my size, I'd take you over my knee and knock some sense into you."

Patrick smirked.

She shook her finger at him. "And you can just wipe that smirk off your face. As long as you're in this house, you will show me some respect."

He became subdued. "Yes, ma'am."

Mary took a deep breath. "Well, are you hungry?"

"Yes, I am."

She softened her demeanor and tipped her head at the table. "Well, have a seat. You can tell me what you found while I heat up some stew."

He pulled out a chair. "Thanks, Ma."

"You're welcome." Mary began stirring the stew to prevent it from scorching. "So, what did you find at the White place?"

"I didn't find any sign of Sylvia. It's like... she just vanished."

"Well, you're lucky her pa wasn't there to shoot at you like the last time. Besides, with your pa, and Mr. White out looking for her, it wasn't likely you would find her at the house."

"I knew he wouldn't be back for a while since he was with Pa, so I wanted to make sure Sylvia wasn't there. For all we know, he has her hidden somewhere. Besides, I went into her pa's room this time."

A flabbergasted Mary looked up from the stew. "Patrick! Oh, good grief!" She sighed. "Well... what did you find?"

"It was a complete mess. There were bottles everywhere."

"Bottles? What kind of bottles?"

"Whiskey."

"So, it's true?"

"Yep. The man is a drunkard, alright." Patrick got up and walked over to his coat hanging by the door, reached into the pocket to pull out the small bottle, then a locket, although he put it back for now. He rejoined his mother, who had poured hot stew into a bowl, then held out his hand. "I found this too."

Mary took the bottle and read the label. "Laudanum."

"What's it for, Ma?"

"It's for pain—the same medicine prescribed for your ankle."

"Well, her pa must have a lot of pain because there's bottle after bottle in his room. Maybe this stuff is why he's crazy, too."

She raised her eyebrows while handing it back to her son. "Did you find anything else?"

"Yes. I found a locket on a chain. I have a feeling it might be Sylvia's—the one she thinks is lost."

"So, you think her pa took it?"

He nodded. "I think so."

With crossed arms over her middle, she rubbed her upper arms as if to ward off a chill. "It doesn't make sense that her father would take it. Why would he do such a thing? I mean, just to begrudge his daughter a remembrance of her mother." She shook her head in confusion.

"I don't know. Sylvia told me it was the only picture she had of her ma. Come to think of it, I saw pictures on his dresser, but just of him and Sylvia's mother. Nowhere else in the house were there any other pictures. Not even one of Sylvia anywhere. Isn't that strange to you?"

"Well... um... yes, I guess it is." Mary gazed at the pictures on the fireplace mantle. It had their wedding picture, one of Patrick soon after he was born, as were there a picture of the twins.

~.~.~

Sylvia couldn't take her hunger pains any longer. Although she did make herself wait till dusk to leave the barn. When she walked over to where the house was before the tragedy, she paused a moment. The thought of it sent shivers up and down her spine.

Not far away, she spotted an abandoned apple orchard. *I don't recall the Heides having an orchard. Please let there be some apples on the trees.* She ran over to the trees like a ravenous cat. Many red apples were scattered beneath the tree, with smaller than normal ones hanging above, and all looked edible. After picking one up off the ground and biting into it, she decided it was fine. Sylvia picked up a few and cradled them in one arm while continuing to eat the one in her other hand. En route to the barn, she heard voices, which halted her dead in her tracks, so she stopped chewing to listen.

"Bernhard, I'll head into town and check there."

"Be lookin' here."

Sylvia heard the sound of hoofbeats racing away on the dirt road. Panic-stricken to hear her father's voice, she tossed the apples on the ground and ran back into the orchard. She found a tree with a wide trunk, so she crouched behind it and stared back at the barn, waiting and praying for her father not to go inside. Better yet, he would leave soon.

It seemed like an eternity before the horse and rider returned. "No sign of her in town. Did you find anything?"

Bernhard held the blanket in his hands. "This."

"Do you think it could be your daughters? Of course, someone else might have been here and left it too."

"Not sure."

Sylvia heard them leave and made her way back to the barn. *Oh no! The blanket! They know. Where can I go now?*

~.~.~

After the men called it a night when darkness began to overtake them, John returned home since he didn't live far from the abandoned barn. Famished, he quickly unsaddled his horse, then put it back in the stall. He smiled at smelling his wife's stew when his foot hit the porch steps, which heightened his appetite. Although when opening the door, John found and anxious-looking Mary.

She smiled at the sight of her husband.

"Hi, darlin'."

"Hello, dear. I'm so glad you're home. Any sign of Sylvia?"

"No. Bernhard found a blanket inside the old Heides' barn, but nothing else."

"Where do you think she could be?"

"I have no idea. Bernhard appears to be worried about Sylvia."

"Maybe she left town."

"I wouldn't think so. Where would the girl go? What would she do? I doubt she has any money to speak of either. Bernhard said she left with nothing."

Mary shook her head in bewilderment. "Are you hungry?"

"Ravenous."

"Good. I kept your supper warm. I figured you'd be back soon."

He grinned. "I knew there was a reason I married you."

With a heartwarming smile, she handed him a bowlful of stew. "And for any other reason?"

"Just one of many."

She smiled while kissing him. "You are a smart man with an excellent answer."

"Everything okay here?"

"For the most part—other than your son deciding to go back over to the White place tonight."

"He did what?" John's brow furrowed, along with a growing frown. "I told him to stay here."

"He thinks Sylvia's pa did something to her."

"Bernhard says she ran away."

"Whatever happened, I have to think it was serious enough for Sylvia to feel as if she must leave. I'm more concerned, too, after what Patrick found at the house tonight."

"What did he find?"

"Her pa's room is so full of whiskey and laudanum bottles, and they're scattered all over the place."

"So, it's true. I have heard a few folks say they saw the man coming out of a tavern in Saranac. That'd explain the whiskey, but laudanum?"

"It's clear he's been using it for a while from the number of bottles Patrick found."

~.~.~

Although Bernhard kept looking for Sylvia, it went without success. On Saturday, he stopped at Doctor Parker's on his way out of town to settle-up on his bill.

The doctor smiled. "Oh, Mr. White. Please come in."

Bernhard stepped into the office. "Come t' pay."

"Thank you. I appreciate it. But I also need to speak with you."

"'Bout what?"

"Well... it's about Sylvia."

Bernhard's temper showed as he slid two small burlap bags on the table, one with flour—one cornmeal. "That 'nough?"

The doctor looked at the bags. "Why, yes. Thank you."

Bernhard turned to leave.

Doctor Parker slid between him and the door, holding his hand up to stop the disgruntled man.

Bernhard glared as if he could squash Doc like a bug. "What?"

"This was the first time I examined your daughter. I must admit that... I ... I've never seen anything like it."

"Outta my way."

"Mr. White, I noted there are several bruises and various scars... uh... well... burn marks too."

Bernhard grabbed the doorknob. "Clumsy girl. Outta my way."

Doctor Parker noticed a vein pop out on his forehead, so he stepped sideways.

Bernhard flung the door and stomped over to his horse.

Doctor Parker chased after him. "Please, Mr. White. I will need to see Sylvia to care for her and the baby."

Bernhard ignored the doctor, climbed onto his horse, and rode away without a backward glance.

When Eliza Stoope stood near the doctor's front door, she saw Bernhard leaving the office. But after Doctor Parker called to him, she stopped suddenly weak-kneed and gasping as her hand flew to her chest. "Oh, gracious, Doctor Parker! Did you really just say... baby?"

Doctor Parker sighed. "Now, what do you need from me, Mrs. Stoope?"

"Well... I... um—"

"Mrs. Stoope, what is it you need?"

"I believe my gout has flared up again, Doctor Parker."

"I just gave you medication for your gout the other day, Mrs. Stoope."

"Well, I don't feel it's working anymore."

"Then, you will need to schedule an appointment with me next week. I have a house call to make."

"But—"

"I will see you next week, Mrs. Stoope." He grabbed his hat and jacket, then left the building.

She stood enraged. "Oh, how rude!"

~.~.~

Patrick searched everywhere for Sylvia during the holiday weekend. Even the dilapidated barn at the old Heides' place.

When he arrived at school on Monday, he knew Sylvia would not show. Had she left Clintok? Or was she somewhere he hadn't looked? He had been all over town and outskirts but to no avail.

Was it his imagination, or were kids whispering while eyeing him behind his back? Patrick had the strangest feeling they knew something he didn't. When he walked into the building again, all eyes watched him in what appeared to be with great interest. Once seated, the whispers and snickering grew, as did his anxiety. Although he still didn't know why.

To Patrick, it seemed like forever until Miss Kimball dismissed the class for lunch. However, she caught Patrick before he could leave the classroom.

"Patrick, please stay. I'd like to speak with you for a moment."

He remained in his seat while his teacher approached.

"How are you?"

"All right."

"How is Sylvia?"

"I haven't seen her."

"Oh, so you're not sure if she's returning to school?"

"Haven't you heard?"

"Heard what?"

"She ran away."

"Oh, my goodness." Emma's expression showed her distress at the news. "Do you think she's still in Clintok? Of course, she must be because Sylvia wouldn't leave town without telling someone."

"I don't know, ma'am."

She sighed. "Well, there is nothing to be done without more information, so you better go eat your lunch before the class takes up again, Patrick."

"Yes, ma'am," Patrick said. Wearing a noticeable frown, he picked up his lunch pail, walked outside, and noticed a group of children gathered in a circle. The closer he got to them, it became clear what the commotion was all about.

Johnny Prescott stood in the middle of the circle on bended knee with a kickball underneath his shirt. He had a hand on his back while mocking in a high-pitched voice. "Oh, Patrick, our baby's coming!"

Then Timmy ran over and grabbed Johnny's arm. "Our baby's comin'! Our baby's coming!"

Patrick threw his lunch pail down and then shoved his way through the crowd. When he reached Timmy, he wasted no time in punching him on the right cheek. "You take that back, Johnny! Now!"

The kids chanted, "Fight—fight—fight!"

Johnny pushed the ball out from under his shirt, only to have Patrick tackle him to the ground. They rolled around in a ball with limbs flailing, and then Patrick suddenly landed an on-target punch on Johnny's nose.

Miss Kimball pushed her way through the crowd. "What's going on here? Stop it! Stop it, you two!" She tugged on Patrick's shirt.

"Get back!" She noticed he had fared better than Johnny, who had his hands over his nose. "Get on your feet this very instant, boys!"

Johnny stood frozen while holding his hand to his face. "I think he broke my nose."

"Children, go back inside and stay in your seats. I'm going to take Johnny over to Doctor Parker's." She pointed her finger at them. "When I come back, I don't want to find one person out of their seat. Do I make myself perfectly clear?"

"Yes, Miss Kimball," they answered in a random reply while starting back to their classroom.

A while later, when Miss Kimball returned, she directed her attention to one person. "Patrick, I need to speak with you." Then she looked at the other children with a scolding expression. "I do not want to remind the rest of you to stay seated."

Patrick headed out the door, where Miss Kimball waited with her arms folded over her chest. "Well, Johnny has a broken nose. What do you have to say about that?"

"He made fun of Sylvia."

"Patrick, you must be under a great deal of strain. And I do understand, still—"

"Johnny made fun of Sylvia being pregnant," he answered with frustration evident in his voice and on his face. "I couldn't let him get away with his teasing."

She sighed with a frown. "I know Johnny can be difficult. And understandably, what he did wasn't right either, but you shouldn't have hit him, Patrick."

"But he deserved it, Miss Kimball."

"Well, whether he needed it or not, you must realize that I have to ask you to stay after school?"

"I know. It's fine."

"All right... well... head back to your seat."

"Yes, ma'am."

CHAPTER TWENTY
Sylvia Discovered

After class, the room cleared, except for Patrick, Miss Kimball, and Susie, who walked over to the board and picked up an eraser.

"It's okay, Susie. You can go home. Since Patrick has to stay, he can erase the boards today."

Susie put the eraser back. "Yes, Miss Kimball." She grabbed her books and lunch pail from her desk.

"See you tomorrow, dear."

"Bye, Miss Kimball... Patrick."

Emma watched Patrick walk to the board and pick up the eraser, where he absentmindedly began to clean them all. She watched him for a moment as a companionable sadness came over her, for the boy and poor Sylvia. Sighing, she placed her elbows atop the desk and cradled her head.

Once he finished erasing the other board, he approached her desk. "Do you want me to erase the other one, too?"

She lifted her head. "No. Sit down for a moment."

He took a seat in front of her.

"When I ask someone to stay after school for fighting, they have to erase the boards and write on them, 'I will not fight.' I won't ask you to do it today. Although I should." She shook her finger at him. "And don't think this gets you off the hook if it happens again—which I hope it does not."

"Yes, ma'am, I know." He looked at the floor for a moment, then his teacher. "It's just... well, I'm worried about Sylvia."

"I know you're worried like I am. How can I help you?"

"I don't think so. I've looked everywhere. Sylvia's pa and my pa searched. No one can find her."

"All right. Well, I sure hope the poor girl is okay. You go on home, Patrick. I'll see you tomorrow."

He stood. "Thanks, Miss Kimball."

"You'll keep me posted?"

"Of course."

"And Patrick?"

"Yes?"

"No more fighting."

"Yes, ma'am." With weary smiles from both, he went home.

The rest of the week went without incident for Patrick, both at school and home. He and Johnny made a point to steer clear of each other after their fight.

In turn, Johnny was careful not to get into any more fights all week while he nursed his broken nose.

The other children were afraid of Patrick, so they made sure not to tease him.

Timmy ended up with a shiner over his right eye, along with a broken nose, but on Friday, he couldn't take how Patrick ignored him. So, he set out to approach his best friend at recess. "I'm sorry, Patrick. It wasn't right to make fun of Sylvia like we did. Especially me."

"Why'd you do it?"

"I dunno."

"Where'd you hear about the baby?"

"Abigail."

"I should've guessed. You know, I expect such a thing from Johnny, but not you. I thought we were supposed to be friends."

"We are."

"You got a funny way of showing it."

"I said, sorry. It won't happen again."

"You better see to it doesn't if you want to remain friends." Patrick walked away.

~.~.~

Later, as the Ryan family ate supper, there was a knock at the door. John wiped his mouth, placed his napkin on the table, and went to the door. "Hello, Doc. Would you like to join us?"

"Oh, no, thank you. I'm sorry to come at suppertime, but, John, may I have a word with you?"

"Sure. Have a seat."

"Um… could we talk out here?"

With an expression of confusion mixed with worry, John and his wife glanced at each other. "Of course, Doc." He closed the door behind him and went outside. "Okay, what is it?"

"It's about Sylvia."

"What about her?"

"Well, I've been trying to decide what to do since last week, after I examined her."

"I'm not sure I follow."

"I'm not in the habit of sharing a patient's findings with anyone. However, I find there are exceptions in some cases, and this one certainly is that."

"I'm sorry, Doc. You're going to have to help me out here. What do you mean?"

"I've never examined Sylvia before last week."

"Never?"

The doctor grimaced. "No. Bernhard has never brought her in for a physical. I've never even seen her for a cold."

"If you've come to tell me about the baby, I already know."

"Well, thanks to Mrs. Stoope, I'm afraid the whole town knows, which is all my fault. I was discussing things with Bernhard in the office, but he pushed his way out the door. I had no idea Eliza was on her way to my office. Unfortunately, she overheard me mention the baby, so you can guess the rest."

"So, is this what you've come to tell me?"

"Not exactly. There's no easy way to say this—"

"Please, Doctor Parker, just say it."

"Well, when I examined Sylvia, I've never seen anything like it in all my years of practice. The girl had bruises, scars, and worse, what appeared to be burn marks on her body."

John winced. "Did you really say burn marks? What do you think caused them?"

"I think Bernhard has been... well... harming the girl. And I... I think he's been doing it for years."

"I don't know what to say, Doc. But he did shoot at my son. A man who could do such a thing is..." John couldn't finish—just shook his head.

"What if I organized a town meeting regarding Bernhard?"

"You know, I think you just might have a good idea."

"All right, then, I'll talk to some others and see if we can get something scheduled. Thank you for talking with me. It has helped. I'll let you get back to your supper."

"Okay, thanks."

"I'll be in touch. Goodnight, John."

"Goodnight, Doc."

~.~.~

Patrick opened the door to the root cellar and froze in his tracks, his mouth gaping. He moved the lantern out in front of him to make sure his eyes weren't playing tricks on him. He squinted, and his mind raced while searching for what to say. "Wha ... how?"

"I had no place to go," she said in a weary and timid voice.

Anxiety, anger, fear, and relief swirled in him at the same time, like a tornado. Before he could make sense of things, he set the lantern down and then grabbed hold of Sylvia in an all-encompassing embrace. With eyes closed, he savored their shared moment—it felt like home to have her in his arms. After a while, Patrick pulled back, cupped the side of her face, and kissed her forehead. "I've missed you so much. Where have you been? I looked everywhere."

"I've missed you, too, but I didn't know where to go. I... I thought you might hate me. So, I—"

"Sylvia, I could never hate you."

Her tears flowed. "I had to get out of there. I can't live with Papa anymore. He hates me."

"What happened? What did he do to you? And what's this mark on your face?"

"He called me names—such awful ones."

"Did he do this to your face?"

"I don't want to talk about it." She hung onto him. "I just want you to hold me. Can you just—"

He shoved her. "No more secrets. Did he do this to your face?"

"Please, please. I can't—"

"Sylvia, tell me now! Did he do this?"

Sensing his anger growing, she broke away from his grip to make a break for the door.

He caught hold of her arm to pull her toward him.

She fought like a caged animal to break free by flailing her arms on his chest.

"Don't fight me, Sylvia. I would never hurt you." He hugged her to his chest.

With her energy waning, she relaxed in his arms as the pain in her body took its toll as well.

"It's okay. You're safe with me." He held her tight with one arm and stroked the back of her long dark hair with his free hand. "Shhh... shhh. You'll always be safe with me. It's going to be all right."

When she was finally quiet, he eased her back. "Do you want to go into the house?"

"Oh, no! Please... please don't tell your folks that I'm here. They might tell him and send me back. I just can't be near him. Not now, Patrick. Besides, I'm a filthy mess. I can't even stand myself."

"Okay... okay. You can stay here, but I've got to get back. As far as you being a mess. I don't care. I'm just glad you're safe. We'll sort this all out, Sylvia. I came out here to get some apples for Ma. They'll begin to wonder what's taking me so long. Later, I'll bring you a blanket and some water. Are you hungry?"

"No, I ate some of your food. Sorry."

He smiled. "Yeah, I forgot you're in a room full of food." He grabbed the small wooden bucket by the door and filled it with apples. "I'll be back later—just as soon as I can get away without my folks suspecting."

When Patrick walked into the house, set the bucket down on the table, and found his folks talking. His mother sat in the rocking chair mending clothes, while his father sat at the table filling his pipe. John looked up. "Well, we were beginning to wonder what happened to you, son."

"I started chores and then forgot I promised to bring the apples in for Ma since she talked about making a pie, so I did it before I forgot."

"True, but I completely forgot about mending the girls' dresses, so I need to get that done. The pie will have to wait 'til tomorrow."

"Do you have any homework to do before Monday?"

"No, Pa, but I still have some of my chores to finish."

His pa nodded. "All right."

Patrick cleaned the horses' and cows' stalls and the chicken coop. Afterward, he went back to the house and peered in the window to see if his folks were still seated in their usual places at the kitchen table. Patrick didn't see them when stepping inside but heard his parents helping his sisters with schoolwork in the sitting room. Feeling confident that he'd go undetected, he sprang into action.

He opened the old wooden chest at the foot of his bed and found a quilt, snatched it up, and tiptoed down the hallway. He lifted the bucket to pump some fresh water from the kitchen faucet and then grabbed a cup from the cupboard. When he reached the root cellar door, he paused, knocked twice, opened it to find Sylvia seated against the wall, and faced him as he walked in to greet her.

Her face lit up when she saw him. "Hi."

Patrick's smile glowed in return. "Hey. I brought you water and even a warm blanket, too, since the nights are getting a lot colder. I figured you would appreciate it. Especially after what you've been through lately."

"Thank you." While she drank her fill, he walked amongst the bushels of red and yellow apples, potatoes, and various vegetables for canning to the back of the cellar. "Hey, what's this straw doing back here?"

"I... I took it from the barn. It's warmer in here."

"How long have you been here, exactly?"

"Since Friday."

"A whole week?" He smirked while shaking his head. "I searched the entire town, and all this time, you were right under my nose."

"Well, at first. I was at the old Heides' barn, but I barely escaped."

"So, you *were* there? Your pa found a blanket in the barn."

"I couldn't go to Miss Kimball's or anyone else. I just couldn't put anyone at risk. You can't tell anyone I'm here either."

"Well, you can't live in a root cellar. It's not good for you... or the baby."

"I switch to the loft in the barn during the day. I never know when your ma will come in to get something."

He went silent—in deep thought.

"Patrick, what is it?"

"If I ask you something, will you tell me the truth?"

"I've never been dishonest with you."

"Is there someone else?"

She looked confused. "What do you mean?"

"You know... have you been... well, seeing someone?"

"No. Why would you even ask me such a question after all the time we have spent together?"

"Well, because you're going to have a baby, and—"

"PATRICK."

He snuck over to the window. "It's Ma. She's halfway to the barn. I have to go, but I'll come back in the morning with more food." He gave Sylvia a hug, then reached the barn just as his mother did.

"Well, there you are. Wherever have you been, Patrick?"

"The outhouse, Ma."

"Are you okay, son?"

"Just thinking."

"About Sylvia?"

"Yeah."

"I'm sure she will turn up again, but I hope she's safe."

"Yeah, me too."

"Are you finished with your chores?"

"Yes, ma'am."

"Come on, your pa is ready to read a new story tonight."

With hands in his pockets, they walked back to the house, even though his unsettled thoughts were scattered.

Later, when Patrick went to bed, he tossed and turned with thoughts of Sylvia running through his mind. While thankful she was safe for now, he knew staying in the root cellar couldn't be good in her condition. The nights hadn't become too cold yet, but winter was on the way.

He must convince her to come into the house and then ask Ma and Pa if she could stay. He didn't think they would object. But talking Sylvia into it might be difficult. It was a certainty she would be safer from Bernhard in the house. So many thoughts ran through his mind.

Finally, Patrick fell asleep, but the next morning, his senses were awakened to the smell of scrambled eggs and bacon. After dressing and then combing his tangled hair, he joined his family for breakfast.

The twins wore the dresses Ma had mended last night and were chattering up a storm about how they would fix their hair after the meal.

"Well, good morning, sleepyhead," Mary said while spooning some eggs onto his plate. "We were beginning to wonder if you were going to sleep all day."

"Thanks, Ma."

"You don't look as if you slept too well," John added.

"No."

"Son, we all know you have a lot on your mind these days."

"Girls, pass the bacon, biscuits, and jam to your brother," their mother said. "Then, we'll get your hair fixed."

Patrick took three pieces of bacon, along with four biscuits, and spread jam on them. He ate two, then, when his ma left the table to comb the girls' hair, his pa went to the fields. He wrapped the other two biscuits in his napkin. After stowing them on his lap, Patrick finished with breakfast, then snuck out to the root cellar. He knocked twice before entering.

Sylvia stood near the door this time when he entered and looking sleepy.

"Hi, I brought you a little something to eat. I figured you might be getting tired of apples and vegetables. I wish I could have brought more. Were you warm enough last night?"

"Yes. Thank you for the blanket."

"You're welcome. Can I get you anything else?"

"Well, there is something..."

"Name it."

"I'd love to take a bath."

"I can arrange it, but only if you promise me something. There's no debating the subject either."

"What?"

"Let me tell my folks you're here."

"No, they might tell my pa."

"They won't tell since they're worried about you, too. Besides, my folks wouldn't want you staying out here. Neither do I."

"I'm fine."

"Sylvia, you'll be safer in the house."

She puckered her bottom lip. "I'm fine here, Patrick."

He sighed. "Do you trust me?"

"Yes."

"Then, let me take care of you. Just let me talk to my folks."

"I don't know."

"Sylvia, this is no place for you and not in your condition. It's going to be winter soon, and you can't stay out here in the cold."

"Promise me that they won't tell him."

"I can promise you, they won't."

"All right."

"I better get my chores done. I'll talk to my folks and stop back later."

"Okay."

He started to leave but spun around to face her while reaching into his pocket. "Oh, I found something that may belong to you."

"What is it?"

He extended his arm and opened his hand.

"Oh! My locket! Where did you find it?"

"It was on the desk in your pa's room when we all searched for you."

She opened the locket, swiped her thumb over the picture, and closed it. "Could you help me with the clasp?"

"Sure." He took the necklace from her while she gathered her hair out of the way.

She smiled. "Thank you, Patrick."

He nodded. "You're welcome. I better go now, but I'll be back soon." He slipped out the door.

CHAPTER TWENTY-ONE
Ryan Hospitality

Patrick completed all his chores, then visited the outhouse before returning to the house. Since it was Saturday, his ma asked him to make a trip to the mercantile for some staples she had forgotten the day before. As well, she had a couple of errands for him. By the time he returned, his mother was preparing lunch.

He washed up at the basin. "Smells good, Ma. What's for lunch?"

She stirred the black iron pot. "Hope you're hungry. We have vegetable soup and cornbread."

"I'm starved."

"Girls, time for lunch," she called to them.

Sadie and Sarah sprinted out of their room and to their seats.

Mary frowned. "Slow down, you two."

Patrick slid his chair back. "When will Pa be here?"

Mary spooned the soup into the bowls. "It should be soon."

"Good. I need to talk to you both about something—"

"Talk to us about what?" John asked, entering the kitchen.

"It's about Sylvia."

"Let me wash up, then we'll talk." After John sat down, he said, "We'll pray, first." Everyone closed their eyes and bowed their heads. "Lord, we thank you for this food, and we ask you to bless it to our bodies. We thank you for all the blessings you have given us. We ask for you to keep Sylvia safe. We ask for all of this in Your name. Amen." He looked at his son. "So, what's this about Sylvia?"

"Before I tell you, I need you to promise me two things."

John looked at his son with a puzzled expression. "Such as?"

"One... promise me you won't get mad."

John and Mary exchanged glances. "Okay," they said at the same time.

"Two... please promise me you won't tell Sylvia's pa."

Mary looked surprised. "Patrick, do you know where she is?"

"Yes, but you have to promise, please, you won't tell her, pa."

"Okay, son." John looked concerned. "I can understand your worry in such regard, so, where is she?"

"She's here."

Mary looked startled. "Here?"

"Yes. Hiding in the root cellar."

His ma's mouth gaped. "In the root cellar? For how long?"

"Since last Friday... but I only found her yesterday."

"But I've been in the root cellar."

"I know, Ma. She switched from the barn to the root cellar."

"Well, it explains how I've missed her."

"Pa, do you remember the blanket her pa found at the old Heides' barn?"

"Yes."

"She was there too and searching for some food. But when hearing you and her pa, Sylvia ran away and came here. She didn't know where else to go—afraid you might tell her pa if you knew. So, I had to convince her to let me talk to you. She's afraid you might even make her go back to him."

"Well, for heaven's sake, the poor girl can't stay in the root cellar," Mary said. "It's no place for a girl, and not in her condition."

"Please don't make her go back to him. He called her awful names, and there's a mark on her face. She won't admit it, but I think her pa did it."

John glanced at his wife's pleading eyes. "We won't make her go back after what she's endured. But her pa could come looking for her again, son."

Mary went to the cupboard for a bowl and a spoon. "Why don't you bring her into the house, so she can have a proper meal? Afterward, we'll move the girls into the same room, and then Sylvia can have her own room."

Patrick grinned. "Thank you, Ma... Pa."

She smiled. "You're welcome, son. I'm proud of you for taking such good care of her. Now, hurry up and bring her in here before the soup gets cold."

Patrick hurried to the root cellar and knocked twice before entering. He found Sylvia pacing while wringing her hands. She mumbled something to herself, and her face was flushed.

"Are you okay?"

She turned toward him and rubbed her arms like she needed to generate heat. "I'm just nervous. I don't know about going into the house. I don't want to cause any trouble for you and your family or be a burden."

"Sylvia, it's okay. My folks insist I bring you into the house. Ma sent me to bring you in for a proper meal. Then she'd like to get you settled into your own room."

"I don't want them to go to a lot of trouble for me. And what if my pa comes looking for me? What will they do then? I can't go back there. I just can't."

"Well, he's not going to find out you are here. They promised."

"They did?"

"Yes. I told you to trust me. I won't let anything happen to you. There's vegetable soup and cornbread if you're hungry."

"That sounds wonderful. I am hungry."

Patrick grabbed the blanket, closed the root cellar door, then led Sylvia to the house.

The closer they got, though, the more apprehensive she felt. She scratched her left forearm with a nervous hand.

Patrick opened the door, where his family was seated around the table. His pa stood while nodding. "Well, hello, Sylvia. I'm John, and this is Mary."

His ma smiled. "Hello, Sylvia."

"Hi, ma'am... sir."

John pulled a chair out for Sylvia. "Please have a seat. I think you know Patrick's sisters."

Sadie and Sarah stared at Sylvia with wide-eyed wonderment.

"Well, girls, mind your manners and say hello."

"Hello," they repeated.

"Hi." Sylvia gave a nervous smile.

Mary spooned the soup into a bowl and then placed it and the remaining cornbread in front of Sylvia. "Help yourself, dear."

Sylvia picked up a piece of cornbread.

"Would you like water, tea, or milk to drink, dear?"

Sylvia smiled. "May I have some milk, ma'am?"

"You may, on one condition."

The smile turned to a frown on Sylvia's face. "Yes, ma'am?"

"You stop calling me ma'am and call me Mary."

She grinned nervously. "Of course, ma'am... I mean, Mary."

"Good. After eating, the twins will wash the dishes while John and Patrick go back to the field. Then I'll get your room ready while you freshen up, my dear."

"I don't want to be a burden. I was fine with the root cellar."

"Nonsense. The root cellar is no place for anyone, and in your cond... Well, you'll be more comfortable here." She chuckled. "Besides, the girls jabber back and forth between rooms at night anyway, so they will love the arrangement. At least, now, with them in the same room, they won't have to shout to hear each other. Isn't that right, girls?"

The twins giggled. "Yeah! We'll like you staying here, Sylvia," said Sadie while Sarah bobbed her head in agreement.

After lunch, Patrick gave Sylvia an affectionate smile before leaving with his father for the fields. And the twins cleared the table and started in on the dishes as was told, and without argument.

Meanwhile, Mary looked at Sylvia, who still sat at the table. "Are you all right, dear? You look flushed."

"I'm fine. Just tired, I guess. May I help you?"

"No. It's quite all right. Once you freshen up, I want you to come and sit in the rocking chair by the fireplace. Maybe, you can doze off for a while."

"I guess I am sleepy. Your vegetable soup and cornbread were the best I've ever had."

"Why, thank you, dear."

After Mary drew water in a pail, got a bar of soap, and a towel, Sylvia put it to good use. Meanwhile, Mary stripped the bed and put fresh linens on it. Then she put the soiled ones in the hamper to wash later.

With the twins chuckling and clowning around while doing the dishes, Mary found Sylvia in the rocker beside the fireplace and had fallen fast asleep. Mary got a heartfelt twinge and shook her head while watching their guest. Her motherly instinct kicked in as she brushed a straggly hair off of her forehead with a sigh; *Land sakes, you poor girl. I'll just bet you haven't known any kindness in a very long time—such a life you must have had without a mother.*

When the men returned, she would ask them to kill and clean a chicken for supper. Tonight, she decided, would be a special occasion. Sylvia deserved some pampering since she doubted the poor girl had ever been treated well.

After peeling the potatoes and putting them in a pan of water on the stove, so they were ready to cook closer to supper, she had made a crust for the pie. After peeling and slicing the apples, she sprinkled them with spices, then put the top crust on it.

Sylvia awoke, and the pie was out of the oven, with the table set for supper.

John and Patrick returned from the field, and as was their usual task, they defeathered a chicken. Then, while Mary coated and fried it, Sylvia added bacon and onions to the green beans to simmer before mashing the potatoes. The ease she felt in the Ryan home was evident with her broad smile.

After everyone washed up and were seated at the table, John said a prayer.

Sylvia's mind wandered to mealtime with her pa, but not one recollection of him ever praying before a meal.

"You are in for a real treat tonight, Sylvia. My wife makes the best-ever fried chicken in the state of Missouri."

"Oh, John. I'm not sure about that." Mary blushed.

Sylvia took a bite of the chicken and fast discovered she had a lot to learn about cooking.

"Oh, Mrs. Ryan... I mean, Mary, this is the best-ever fried chicken I have ever tasted."

Mary smiled. "Well, my goodness, with all these compliments, I'm liable to get a big head."

The moment was interrupted by a knock at the door. Sylvia stopped chewing, with her eyes darting back and forth between the door and then Patrick. With her heart racing, she turned flush as her palms began to sweat.

Everyone gave each other a nervous look.

Mary thought fast. "Sylvia, dear, go into the bedroom for safety's sake."

Sylvia bobbed her head and hurried out of the kitchen.

John swallowed his food, wiped his mouth with a napkin, then answered the door. "Well, hello, Doc."

"Hello, John." Doctor Parker nodded to everyone.

"What can I do for you?"

"I'm sorry for interrupting your supper again, but might I speak with you alone, John?"

"Sure." He turned to Mary. "Be right back."

John closed the door behind him, then listened to what the doctor had to say.

"I've taken the liberty of speaking to most everyone about having a town meeting regarding Bernhard White. I've been able to reserve the church for Thursday evening since several families plan to attend. Can I count on you and Mary to attend at 7 p.m.?"

"We'll be there, Doc."

"That's good. I'll see you then," Doc said, turning to leave.

Patrick opened the door. "Doc Parker."

"Yes?"

"May I speak with you?"

"Why, of course, Patrick."

He closed the door behind him to join his pa and Doc.

John put his hand on his son's shoulder. "I'll leave you two."

Patrick nodded. "Thanks, Pa." After John left, he walked down the steps. "Doctor Parker, I'm sorry I ran out of your office the other day. It's just ... well, the news was ... shocking."

"I understand, Patrick."

"Can I ask you a medical-related question?"

"Of course."

"What exactly would someone do with lots of laudanum?"

"Well, it's used for a broad range of ailments such as cough, diarrhea, rheumatism, cardiac disease, and delirium tremens. It can also be used as a painkiller for gout and other maladies."

Patrick studied his face. "Could it be used for anything else?"

Doc arched a brow. "It's sometimes used as a sleeping aid."

"Could it put someone into a sound sleep—very sound sleep?"

He raised an eyebrow. "Put someone to sleep? Do you mean, without their knowledge?"

"Yes, I do."

"It could be. Is there something you want to tell me?"

"I found a lot of bottles of laudanum in Mr. White's room."

"It can be purchased at any mercantile," Doc answered.

"I also found lots of whiskey bottles."

"I've heard about Bernhard's drinking for years, but he's never been in for an examination." He sighed. "Well, it's for certain we'll have plenty to discuss this Thursday night."

"What's Thursday night?"

"A town meeting."

"Excuse me?"

"Yes. I've called on folks to attend a meeting about Bernhard."

"Hmmm... my folks didn't mention it."

"Oh... well, perhaps it slipped their minds. I just confirmed the meeting tonight. If that's all, I'll let you get back to your supper."

"I think that should do it. Thank you, Doctor Parker."

"You're welcome, Patrick. Goodnight."

"Night."

CHAPTER TWENTY-TWO
No-Show Bernhard

Patrick rejoined the family, as did Sylvia return to the table, where they all finished their meal together. Then the family joined in with the preparations for the weekly Saturday night bath in the big wooden tub in the barn. They always wanted to present their best at church by wearing their Sunday finest clothes.

Sadie and Sarah pumped water from the kitchen spigot into wooden buckets, then carried them outside to their ma.

Mary would then dump the water into a big iron pot over an open fire pit. Once heated, she would pour the water back into the wooden buckets with a large, long-handled pail so she wouldn't get burnt.

Patrick would then carry the buckets out to the barn, where he'd dump the water into the tub. When there was enough water in it, bath time started with the youngest, ending with the oldest. But tonight, Sylvia would go before anyone else since she was a guest in the Ryan's home.

As Patrick emptied the last bucket into the tub, he became aware Sylvia had moved to the barn and was unlacing her boots. He froze while surveying every inch of her body as she continued.

He'd seen females dressed in pantalets, petticoats, and crinolines when he was younger. Although it was by thumbing through magazines at the mercantile. However, he had always been curious as to what was underneath those garments. Once, he looked up to find his ma standing over him with her arms crossed over her chest, looking like she'd like to skin him alive. He knew when she stood in such a position, and with a particular look on her face, it meant trouble. Without a word, he had closed the magazine and then stepped away as if he had done nothing wrong.

Now, with Sylvia standing in front of him, his thoughts strayed to her bathing. It stirred unfamiliar sensations within every fiber of his body. As she looked up at him, he felt a strong urge to scoop her up and kiss her.

"I can't wait to take a bath. I must have a month's worth of grime on me."

"Um... uh... do you need anything else?"

She smiled. "No. I don't think so, but thank you for being so thoughtful."

"You're welcome. Okay, I'll leave you to your bath." After he closed the door and leaned against it, he closed his eyes while taking a deep breath. It failed to calm his runaway thoughts and desire because they still surged throughout his body as if lightning were streaking through the sky in full force.

Sylvia opened the barn door, and before he knew what hit him, Patrick landed on the ground and ended flat on his back with a thump.

She giggled. "Oh, I'm so sorry. Are you all right?"

He jumped up. "Of course, I... I'm good. I just had to catch my breath from carrying all those buckets."

"Well, you did haul a lot of them. I hate to trouble you, but I don't have a towel."

Oh, dear God. This girl drives me all kinds of crazy! "I'll go and get one from Ma."

"Okay, thanks."

After he hurried to the house and returned with a washcloth and towel, Sylvia carried on with her bath so Sadie and Sarah could take theirs next.

John preferred to bathe in the creek and did so often. He dressed and heard the crackling of leaves and spun around to find Patrick approaching. "Oh, you startled me, son. Is everything all right?"

"Yeah, I thought I might try the creek."

"I'll warn you, it's cold."

"Sounds perfect to me. I'm hot... uh... from carrying all the buckets of water."

"You might want to make it quick. It'll be dark soon."

"Yes, sir."

"See you back at the house."

Patrick started for the water but turned back. "Pa?"

"Yes."

"You didn't tell me about the town meeting on Thursday."

"Oh, yes. Sorry, I didn't want to mention anything until Doctor Parker knew for sure. He had to check with folks in town and stopped by to let us know the meeting has been scheduled."

"It's a good idea. What do you think will happen?"

"I don't know, son. The purpose of the meeting is to discuss Bernhard."

"Pa, do you think he's the father. You know, of the baby, I mean?"

"I don't know, son, but I'm guessing it may be discussed. Has Sylvia said anything to you?"

"No. I couldn't even get Sylvia to admit that her father put the bruise on her face. I just don't know what to think, Pa. There are so many unknowns about Sylvia's father. It's just downright scary."

"Well, I'll tell you one thing. The truth has a way of coming out eventually, one way or another."

Patrick nodded.

"You best get in that creek while you can still stand it."

"Yes, sir."

Patrick removed his clothes and stepped into the ice-cold water. He sure hoped this would cool his thoughts about Sylvia soaking in the bathtub.

~.~.~

Sylvia had the desire to soak in the bath all night but realized she couldn't dawdle as the rest of the household waited for their turn. Upon hearing a knock on the barn door, she sunk down into the tub, so only her eyes peered over the top.

When the door swung open, Mary poked her head inside. "I hope I didn't alarm you, dear, but I brought a nightgown. I thought you might want something fresh to wear tonight."

Sylvia had pushed herself up higher. "Oh, thank you, Mary. It's kind of you."

"Well, it may be too big, but it's clean. After my bath, I'll wash your dress, so it will be clean for you tomorrow."

"It's all right. I don't want to be a burden."

"Nonsense. You need a clean dress until I can get some fabric to make another one."

"Oh, no, you don't have to."

"You'll need some clothes, my dear. Well, I'll leave you to it."

"Thank you."

"You're welcome."

Later, after Mary finished her bath, she washed Sylvia's dress, then put it by the fireplace to dry.

Meanwhile, Patrick had returned, so everyone gathered by the fire, where John made popcorn for the family. However, they had waited for Mary to join them in the nightly reading of Louisa May Alcott's short story, 'The Mysterious Key.'

John wasn't far into the story when Sylvia yawned in the same rocking chair she sat in earlier and fell fast asleep within minutes. When John finished the chapter, he closed the book with a nod. "All right, girls, time for bed."

Sadie made a face. "Oh, do we have to, Pa?"

Sarah frowned as well. "Yeah, Pa, can't you read us another chapter?"

"Girls, you know we have church tomorrow. Now off to bed."

Disheartened, the girls answered. "Yes, sir."

"We'll come soon to tuck you in, girls," Mary said, then walked over to place her hand on Sylvia's arm. "Dear, it's time for bed." She turned toward John. "Poor girl is plumb tuckered."

Patrick got up and stood by her side. "Is she okay, Ma?"

Mary watched Sylvia's heavy breathing. "The poor dear, I suspect she's just exhausted. How about carrying her into her bedroom, son."

"Okay." Patrick scooped her up in his arms, then off he went.

Mary hurried behind Patrick until reaching the room, where she made haste in turning down the covers, so he could lay her on the bed. Once she was tucked in, he kissed her on the forehead. "Goodnight, Sylvia."

Mary smiled as she took notice of Patrick's affection for the girl. She knew he liked her since his deeper feelings were becoming evident. *This may just be my future daughter-in-law.*

As they both took their leave, Patrick's expression was one of gratitude for his family. "Thanks for taking her in, Ma."

Mary gave her son a warm smile. "Well, we certainly couldn't have her living in our root cellar, could we?"

He grinned. "No, ma'am."

"Patrick, I think you and I and your pa need to talk about what should happen tomorrow."

"Okay." As they entered the dining area, John had gathered the bowls and was picking up popcorn kernels off the floor.

"Dear, I just told Patrick we must make a plan for Sylvia tomorrow while we're at church."

"I had the same thought, Mary. Let's talk about it at the table." Once seated, John sat back in his chair with an unlit pipe in his mouth while cogitating. "Well, it's obvious that Sylvia can't go to church with us, or her pa will know where she is."

Mary looked worried. "I agree. Maybe I should stay with her."

"You're always with us at church, so if you aren't tomorrow, he may think it suspicious under the circumstances."

"You could say I'm not feeling well if anyone asks."

"I won't lie, Mary."

"Jonathan Ryan. You know I don't condone lying, but we've got to help this girl. She can't go back to that man after what he's done!"

John held up his palm. "Calm down, Mary. I'm not suggesting we send her back to Bernhard. But there's got to be a way to do it without being dishonest."

"What if I stay at home with Sylvia?" Patrick asked from where he sat at the opposite end of his pa.

Both parents shook their heads. "No, no," John said. "If you're not there, it would be the first thing to alert her pa. I think she will be safe here in the house. Bernhard should be at church, anyway, so, if the whole family shows up, it'll look normal, so no suspicion can fall our way."

"What if he does show up here, Pa?"

"I don't think he will, Patrick. He's looked all over the place for Sylvia. Maybe he's given up the notion she's in town by now."

Mary yawned. "Let's get some shut-eye then."

"Goodnight, Ma... Pa." Patrick stood.

"Sleep well, son," they both said.

The next morning, the family enjoyed fried ham, scrambled eggs, and fried potatoes. Near the end of the meal, Mary looked at their guest with a smile. "How did you sleep, Sylvia?"

"I don't recall falling asleep or going to bed, but I sure do feel better."

"Glad to hear it, dear. I believe your dress is dry, but after thinking about it, we just can't risk taking you to church for fear your pa guesses you're here. That will never do."

Sylvia frowned. "It' okay. I didn't plan on going."

"Are you okay, dear?"

"I'm fine."

"We're afraid if one of us stays with you, it may alert your pa to your whereabouts, as well. Will you be okay here by yourself?"

"Yes, I'll be fine, Mary."

"Girls, finish up, then I can brush your hair because it's nearly time to go."

John looked at their guest. "Sylvia, please stay in the house, and don't answer the door or go anywhere."

"Yes, sir."

"Mary, it's time to go."

"We'll be right there, John."

With a nervous smile, Patrick clasped Sylvia's hand and gave it a gentle squeeze. "Just remember what Pa says and stay in the house. And don't answer the door if someone knocks."

Sylvia forced a smile. "Okay."

~

It had become commonplace for Patrick to drive the wagon to Sunday service. But, John observed the visible anguish on his son's face and the haphazard actions he showed for morning chores, so he drove—assuring a timely arrival.

In the meantime, Mary said it was a good time for her to plan out their meals for the day so she couldn't dwell on Sylvia's dilemma either.

As they arrived at church, Patrick noted Bernhard's wagon was not present. *Where is he? Maybe, he's running late.* After the Ryan family greeted the reverend, they took their seats.

Sadie and Sarah got permission to sit with their friends while John and Mary greeted other church members.

Patrick kept an eye on the door, but there was no sign of Bernhard. Unable to shake the gnawing feeling in his stomach, he leaned over, "Pa, Mr. White isn't here. I think I should go back."

"You stay, son, I'll go."

"I'm going with you."

John hesitated. "Oh, alright, let's go." He tugged on his wife's arm. "You and the girls stay here. We'll come back and get you."

Mary didn't hide her worry. "Okay, but just be careful, John."

He nodded, "I will, darlin'."

CHAPTER TWENTY-THREE
Picking Blackberries

Sylvia sat in the rocker, and not only did she rub her stomach but her arms too, as if by doing so, her aches and pains would suddenly disappear. And even though her whole body ached, she was restless. Maybe in part, it was ignorance about having a baby. That reality scared her mightily. She also assumed, along with her present circumstances, accounted for why she was so jittery. Whatever, she stood and began to pace like a caged lion at the circus. *Although the Ryans's told me not to leave, I have to do something, but what? I need to get out of here, or I'll go crazy. Since Papa will be at church, I'm perfectly safe from him finding me.*

Feeling chilled, she grabbed Mary's shawl from the rocking chair and wrapped it around her shoulders. While doing so, a small, metal bucket to the left of the door caught her eye. *I could pick some fresh flowers or maybe, some ripe berries for a treat, or maybe a pie. Yes, I'll make the family a pie.* She grasped the handle of the bucket and then headed for the creek bed.

Sylvia walked along the length of the creek until she came to the opening in the forest. She stepped in amongst the trees and glanced at their towering height. The sun peeked between the majestic treetops, and a gentle breeze touched her face.

An uneasy feeling washed over Sylvia, who spun on her heel to look around. Even though the only thing she saw were trees everywhere, she could not shake the feeling someone watched her every move. Deciding to shrug it off, she assumed it was just her imagination.

When approaching the center of the forest, she saw a thicket of bushes growing. However, the closer she got, there was a flock of birds that flew up. Her splayed hand flew to her chest in surprise. "OH! Oh, my goodness!" To settle her nerves, she took some deep breaths.

Once calmer, she walked into the thicket and then noticed some berries growing all over the bushes. "Wild blackberries—enough for the pie." She busied herself by picking them while quickly getting lost in her task.

When Sylvia heard the snap of a twig, she whirled around to see his tall, dark presence. It terrified her as she dropped the bucket at his menacing stance. "Huh."

He continued to tower over her—a frightening, dark menace. "Hidin' from me?"

She swallowed hard while frozen with fear. Even though she tried to speak, she couldn't, let alone bolt, but no matter how hard she tried to move her feet, they just wouldn't cooperate.

"Think I wouldn't find ya? Hidin' with 'at boy."

Sylvia shook her head, her heart pounded, and her chest felt heavy. She was short of breath, and all the color drained from her face while feeling dizzy and nauseated. Even her legs went weak. It became too much when the trees spun around her, and then, unable to control it, she bent over and vomited. While stepping backward, everything suddenly went black.

~

Bernhard lifted Sylvia's upper body and dragged her to the wagon parked just off the two-track road. After dumping his daughter into the buckboard, he secured her wrists and ankles with a rope, then jammed a cloth into her mouth. Once he climbed into the wagon, he looked back to make sure she was still out, then charged homeward.

Even though she awoke once on the way, she tried to squirm her way out of the bindings while trying to scream for help, but it did her no good. She kept gagging.

Bernhard stopped the horses, grabbed a small bottle out of his pants pocket, then removed the cloth from her mouth. He took the cap off the bottle and put it to her lips. "Drink it."

Sylvia's eyes darted back and forth from his face to the bottle, but she made no attempt to move or drink from it.

"Drink." He pinched her mouth, forcing it open so he could pour the liquid down her throat. Sylvia choked and spit, but Bernhard was persistent. Although she tried to fight it, she couldn't. After replacing the cloth in her mouth, he put the bottle in his pocket, then climbed back into his seat.

Tears streamed down her cheeks, and no matter how hard she fought the cloth in her mouth, all she could manage to do was more choking and gagging.

Minutes later, Bernhard turned to see Sylvia had passed out again.

Once home, he carried her from the buckboard into the house, then lowered her into the cellar. After removing the gag and bindings from her wrists and ankles, Bernhard climbed up the ladder and closed the cellar door. It gave him a sense of great satisfaction to have his daughter home... his possession.

~.~.~

When Patrick and John returned home, they hurried off the wagon. "Son, you check the house. I'll check the barn and cellar."

Patrick rushed into the house. "Sylvia?" He became much more frightened when she didn't answer. "Sylvia!" He found no sign of her in the house, so he raced outside and met his father halfway between the house and barn.

"She's not in the house, Pa."

"No trace of her in the cellar or barn, either."

Patrick was panic-stricken. "Where could she be, Pa? Where?"

"You must stay calm, son. You check by the creek—I'll search the forest."

Patrick took off on a dead run for the creek.

~

John surveyed the forest not far away for any clue to lead him to Sylvia's whereabouts. In the middle, amongst the trees, he saw a thicket of wild blackberry bushes, where he discovered the small, metal bucket from the house. It was tipped on its side, in front of the bushes. While reaching for it, John noticed some scattered blackberries on the ground and inside the bucket.

As he turned to go back, he saw two parallel drag marks in the dirt, not far from where the tracks started, then stopped. Back at the opening of the trees, he spotted some boot prints in the thicker mud. He measured his boot next to one of the prints and pressed down in the mud. However, it turned out to be an exact replica of his boot.

He met Patrick outside the tree line. "Anything?"

John held up the bucket. "I found this, and there are also some drag marks in front of the blackberry bushes."

"He's got her!"

"We don't know for sure, Patrick."

"Why would she come out here, Pa?"

"I'm sure she thought her pa was at church, and she was safe."

"Where else would she be? No one knew she was here. How did he find her?"

"He may have been watching us... biding his time."

"We've got to go get her!"

"Patrick, you need to calm down, son. We have to think rationally. First, we need to bring your ma and sisters back home. Then, we can think about our next move. The town meeting is in four days."

"Four days! Who knows what he will do to her by then. We have to get her now... today!"

John grasped Patrick's right shoulder. "Son, I know you care about this girl. But trust me. You must keep a level head here, or you will be no good to her. Understand?"

Patrick sighed. "Okay, I... I guess."

"Good. Let's go."

~.~.~

Mary and the twins started walking home and just outside of town when John and Patrick met them on the road. She knew by their straight faces, all was not right—she feared the worst.

John stopped the wagon and helped his wife up. Meanwhile, Patrick moved to the back of the buckboard to help his sisters onto the wagon.

"What is it, John? What happened?"

"I'm afraid she's gone, Mary. There's no sign of her at the house or the barn."

"Oh, no! Do you think he has her?"

"I'm not sure, but it appears, since I found our bucket in the forest, she decided to pick some blackberries, as there were marks in the mud like she'd been dragged."

"Why would she leave when we told her to stay in the house?"

"I'm sure she thought Bernhard was at church and must have felt safe."

Her eyes revealed such anxiety. "We have to get her back, John."

"How, Mary? We can't just rush over there and tell him we're taking his daughter."

"I'm sure if we put our heads together, we can come up with something."

CHAPTER TWENTY-FOUR
Gone

The situation weighed heavily on the family, so they were somber en route home. When the wagon stopped, Sadie and Sarah bolted to their rooms and discovered Sylvia was, in fact, gone.

Mary changed out of her Sunday dress and put on a plaid one, then began preparing lunch. As much as she hated it, she realized they might have to wait to make any plan concerning Sylvia until the town meeting and then see what happens.

John unhitched the team and put the horses in the corral. He knew they couldn't barge into Bernhard's house and demand he let his daughter go home with them, so he debated whether he should ask Doctor Parker to move the meeting up from Thursday night.

Meanwhile, Patrick wandered off to the creek to formulate his own plan. He saw no other way around it. Tonight, after the family ate supper, he would go by himself to the White house. One way or another, he was determined to get Sylvia back.

The Ryan family ate their lunch of homemade squash soup and Mary's famous buttermilk biscuits and honey. Gloom had fallen over them all, as the scraping of spoons in their bowls were the only sounds heard through the shroud of silence.

While John tried to come up with some answers in mind's eyes, Mary's focused gaze could have burned a hole through the table. It was clear to see that Patrick was lost as if his heart were drowning at the bottom of his soup bowl.

Mary became resolute as she sat straight up in her chair. "Well, how do we get Sylvia back?"

John frowned. "Much as I dislike the idea, I think we just have to wait until the town meeting."

Patrick shifted in his chair. "Pa, we can't wait. Who knows what he will do to her by then."

"I told you, son, we can't barge over there and demand her back."

Mary tried to smile, although it came out more like a frown. "Sad to say, but I have to agree with your pa, Patrick. I'm not so sure there is much we can do until the meeting on Thursday."

Patrick grimaced. "I can't wait 'til then."

"Son, I know this kills you. Please don't do anything stupid."

"You remember what happened the last time you went over there half-cocked. Bernhard nearly killed you."

Sadie interrupted. "Ma, me and Sarah finished. Can we be excused?"

"Yes, girls. Clear your plates."

"Yes, ma'am."

Mary patted her son's arm. "We have to trust the good Lord will protect her, Patrick."

"I don't know if I can do it, Ma."

"You—"

"Ma, can we go outside and play?" asked Sadie.

Mary sighed. "Yes, girls, you may."

The twins raced each other to the door, flung it open, and then disappeared.

"Girls... the door!"

Sarah reappeared in the doorway. "Sorry, Ma." She closed it, then joined her sister, where they squealed while chasing each other in circles out in the yard.

A heartwarming smile came across Mary's face while thinking about her daughters at play. She shook her head to refocus attention back on her son. "I can see you love Sylvia very much, don't you?"

Patrick hesitated. "Yes... I do."

John leaned closer. "What are your intentions toward this girl? The way things stand, you don't think her pa will allow you to be with her, do you?"

"I don't care what her pa thinks, we're going to be together, and there's nothing he can do about it."

"What about the baby?"

He grimaced. "Thanks to Mrs. Stoope, everyone in town thinks I'm the father, anyway, so—"

"But, Patrick, you're not," Mary said in an empathetic voice. "Are you prepared to help raise the child, along with all the gossip it will entail?"

"It's a part of Sylvia. So, yes... yes, I do."

"And you mean to get married?"

"Yes, ma'am."

John sat forward after moving his plate aside and then leaned his forearms on the table. "Your intentions are all well and good, son, but there is a lot more to consider than just your feelings. How will you support them?"

"I'm going to graduate soon. I'll get work."

"And where will you live?"

"I was hoping we could live here... I mean, just until we can afford our own place."

John nodded. "Well, I can see you have given this a lot of thought."

"Yes, sir. I guess I have."

"Well, for now, you best get to your chores."

"I will, Pa."

After Patrick was outside, John turned to his wife. "Mary, do you think this baby is Patrick's?"

"He said it isn't, and I believe him. Don't you?"

"I do, which means the father of the baby has to be... *him*."

Mary grimaced. "Maybe, there's someone else."

"Like who?"

"I don't know."

"Patrick said she couldn't have been involved with anyone else. She goes to school, and when he walks her home, he can only go halfway because her father is strict and won't allow her to have friends, be they a girl or boy. He says her father doesn't permit her to do any dallying after school, let-alone letting her go anywhere socially."

Mary let her tears fall. "Land sakes, that poor girl. I can't imagine what she's gone through at the hands of such an... an awful tyrant."

"I'm inclined to think along the lines with Doctor Parker. He believes Bernhard has abused her for quite some time."

With eyes closed, she shook her head. However, they suddenly popped open. "John, he's crazy—evil, and needs to be removed from this town."

"I agree, my dear. We should suggest it at the town meeting."

"Good. Then, we'll see to it Sylvia has a proper home."

He smiled. "Mary, you never cease to amaze me."

She smirked. "Well, we can't have her living in our root cellar or worse, on the street."

~

After supper, while the family cleared the dirty dishes, Patrick slipped out the door. He headed through the fields and came to the spot where he had fallen after twisting his ankle.

He swallowed hard, recalling the bang of Bernhard's rifle shots, which gave him pause for thought. However, with determination, he continued on until reaching the back of the house. He sneaked over to the barn, where he entered and conducted a thorough search of the stalls, haymow, and anywhere else he could think to look. One of the horses was gone, just like the last time. Patrick reasoned then, it must be a regular Sunday night occurrence for the old man to leave for a while—but where?

He took a less guarded approach to the house, turned the door handle, and entered. He checked Sylvia's room first, but it looked in perfect condition. A look-see in Bernhard's room revealed the same barrage of bottles as the last time.

He went to the kitchen and dining room with hopes of finding some kind of a clue as to where the cruel man might have Sylvia. This time, in the back corner of the kitchen, Patrick discovered a door. It seemed newer than the last time he was here. He found the wall's shape around it had a strange configuration because it didn't match the rest of the house. *How did I miss this?* When he turned the handle, it didn't surprise him that it was locked. *Why is this so odd? And why is it locked? Does he have her locked away upstairs?* Patrick shuddered at the thought as he ran his hand over the top of the door ledge but found no key. *If I was a crazy ole coot, where would I hide it? His bedroom—it has to be there.*

The nightstand drawers beside the bed turned up empty, as did the desk drawers. *It has to be in the dresser... unless the man keeps it with him.* The first drawer contained socks and his unmentionables. The more he continued to rummage through the drawers, Patrick's grimace intensified.

The second drawer was filled with shirts and the third drawer with trousers. Underneath the last pair, then Patrick's fingertips felt a small, irregular shaped piece of metal. *A key?*

He dodged around the trail of bottles, then back out to the kitchen door. As luck would have it, the key fit into the lock. He turned the doorknob. *Got it!* He opened the door to find stairs leading to the second floor. Without second thoughts, he hurried up the staircase, where he found two doors on each side of the landing. Patrick stopped at the first one on the left and opened it to find a dusty nursery. He found it complete with a bassinette and rocking chair. *This must have been Sylvia's room as a baby.*

He closed the door and moved to the second room, where he found a dark, cherry dresser covered in powdery dust on each side of the window and a large bed to the right of the door. The bedroom appeared untouched for quite some time.

Patrick moved to the other side of the stairwell and then opened both of the doors. The first room revealed a cabinet of books against the wall, a rocking chair near the window overlooking the backyard, and a small table and chair with fabric garments draped over it—like the ones in his room.

The last room was empty. Patrick took a deep breath, exhaled, and then shook his head. *Where can she be? It's like she disappeared into thin air, just like the last time.* He sprinted back down the stairs, closed and locked the door, then returned the key back to its place in Bernhard's dresser drawer. After moving the drape back from a window, he surveyed the yard to find the closed barn door. There was no sign of Bernhard or anyone else approaching on horseback.

Patrick walked to the front door but paused for a moment, closed his eyes, and then turned his head upward. *Where are you, Sylvia?* He opened his eyes and slipped out the front door. Not giving up, he continued to inspect the area around him while making his way back to the field. He ran until he was sure to be out of gun range and then slowed down to a walk. En route home, he kept replaying it in his mind, rechecking the barn and house. *What has he done with her?*

~

Patrick didn't discover the rug under the dining room table, which covered the trap door. Otherwise, he would have found Sylvia—in the cellar, where she lay beside a bucket of the laudanum-laced water Bernhard left for his daughter. However, it was losing its effect as she began to stir.

~

If not for hanging onto the saddle horn, Bernhard would have fallen off his horse after his usual Sunday night outing at the Saranac Tavern. He was fortunate the horse knew the path home because he barely held onto the reins. As his head swayed, he had brief moments of dozing off, interrupted by a case of hiccups or belching. When his mount walked to the barn door, where it stopped in the usual place, Bernhard swung his right leg over the horse, but too fast, and his foot slipped from the stirrup. He slid to the ground and landed on his backside.

The horse side-stepped to the right, then turned its head and snorted. It was as if he were looking at the spectacle of the man on the ground.

"What 'er ya lookin' at?"

The horse answered by way of a sneeze, with blowing droplets of clear discharge mixed with dirt onto Bernhard's face and shirt. Bernhard scowled, wiped his face on his sleeve, and then wobbled to his feet. After leading the horse into the stall, he removed the saddle and bridle and then set them down in the straw.

Bernhard staggered up to the house, but he stopped to pause while listening for stirring from the cellar once he walked inside the front door. He considered paying Sylvia a visit but decided he was far too drunk and passed out on his bed instead.

~

A motionless Sylvia roused down in the cellar but soon became fully awake as hunger pains hit her. When hearing the kitchen door close upstairs, she locked her eyes on the trap door. After snacking on two apples, she hoped her father would lower a fresh bucket of water down to her. Even though lightheaded and feeling very queasy, she was still hungry. Sylvia ate one more apple, then sucked as much juice from the cores as possible. She was more scared than she could ever remember.

Meanwhile, thoughts turned to Patrick and his family—how she was sure they probably enjoying a wonderful hot meal together. Later, with no concept of day or night, Sylvia envisioned the Ryan's. They were most likely eating popcorn while in front of the fireplace and listening to John read 'The Mysterious Key.'

Her tears fell while thinking about Patrick's kindness—his gentleness toward her—yet, furious why she wouldn't admit what her father had done. Nonetheless, he held her close and whispered to her softly in a tender way—convincing her to come into the house.

John and Mary had been so accepting of her being in their home. They never questioned her situation—just welcomed her with open arms. *Mary even gave me a lovely nightgown to wear. And it was so soft and fresh smelling. No one has ever been that nice to me before.*

One of the twins had given up their own room just to have a warm bed and her own space. *Oh, how I miss them all.*

~.~.~

Patrick peeked into the front window to find his mother sitting alone in her rocking chair in the living room. He could see and almost feel the tension on her face and knew what it meant. He drew in a long breath, then exhaled before opening the door.

Her face changed instantly from worry to relief, then dread as Mary leaped from her rocking chair to stand with arms folded over her chest. "Patrick Jonathan Ryan! Please tell me you didn't go over to the White home?"

He closed the door. "Okay, I won't."

She looked at him with a quizzical eye. "Oh, don't get cute with me, young man."

"Yes, ma'am."

"Well, I don't see any bullet holes. How'd you get so lucky this time?"

"He wasn't home."

"So, you *did* go there? What's it going to take for you to realize how dangerous Bernhard is?"

"Don't you see, I do realize it, which is why I have to find Sylvia and get her away from him."

Her tone softened. "You didn't find her?"

He frowned. "No. It's just like last time. I searched everywhere, and it's as if Sylvia packed up and left town."

"You could have at least asked your pa to go with you because he's out right now looking for you. Honestly, Patrick, what do we need to say and get through to you?"

"I know—it's clear you and Pa wanted to wait until Thursday. But, Ma, I can't. If there is the slightest chance I can find her, I'll take the risk."

Mary sighed. "Patrick, it's not that we don't want to do anything. We just don't know what we can do until the town meeting. Action without all the facts is not wise."

"Well, what will they do?"

"We're going to do our best to get him thrown out of town."

"And then what?"

"Then, Sylvia can live with us."

He smiled. "You mean it?"

"Yes." She waved a finger at him. "But you will keep things respectable. Understood?"

He grinned. "Yes, ma'am."

"We'll be watching to make sure you do."

"Yes, ma'am." His grin widened.

~

When John came in, he hung his hat on a hook in the kitchen, then walked into the living room. He found Patrick seated across from his mother, next to a drum table. His ire showed through his eyes and stance while pointing. "Patrick! I have been looking all over for you. The whole time, I thought you might be shot and left for dead in a field somewhere. What possessed you to pull such a foolhardy stunt again? Well? Can you tell me that? Has the slightest bit of what I've just said sunk into that mind of yours? Not to men—"

"John, would you like a cup of coffee?"

Without taking his eyes off his son, John's impatience showed in the stern set of his jaw and in his rigid stance. "Not right now."

Worry became instantly evident on her face.

"I mean, what goes through your head, Patrick? Do you want to get yourself killed?"

"Dear, I've already gone over this with him."

John held up his hand. "Mary, it's about time I speak up because our son needs to hear a few things."

She nodded with understanding.

"Are you trying to get yourself killed? It's a simple question."

"No, sir."

"Well, there's a starting point. Do you mind telling me why it is you keep going back to a crazy man's house? Son, you have to get it through your head to stop acting on your emotions, and instead, use good old common sense?"

"Pa, I know he's crazy, which is why I can't leave Sylvia there any longer. Don't you see, he may have hurt her in a bad way—even do her more harm if I don't find her."

Frustrated, John took a deep breath. "Yes, Patrick, I do. And I know you love this girl—want to protect her. But you have to be smart about it. Going there alone is not safe. For goodness sake, son, if you're dead, you certainly can't help Sylvia. Then what will become of her?"

"I know, and I'm careful, Pa."

"Will you promise me that you will not go back over there until Thursday?"

He hesitated.

"Patrick?"

"Oh, all right."

"No, I want you to say it."

His shoulders slumped. "I promise you. I won't go back over there until Thursday."

"Good." He glanced at Mary. "Where are the girls? I'd like to say good night to them."

"I've tucked them in already."

"I'm going to go say goodnight to them, and then I'd love to have your offered cup of coffee."

"I'll heat it up, dear," she answered as John left the room.

"Thank you, Ma."

She placed her hand on her son's arm with a smile and a gentle squeeze. "I know it's difficult right now, Patrick, but it'll be okay."

"I hope so."

"I just know she's alive."

"How do you know?"

"I've been praying about the poor girl, and now I have some peace about it. I believe the good Lord watches over Sylvia."

"I wish I had your faith, Ma."

Meanwhile, Patrick remained in his chair in the living room, hanging onto Sylvia's thoughts and his mother's words.

CHAPTER TWENTY-FIVE
Town Meeting

The next three days were difficult for the Ryan family. Not only were they concerned for Sylvia's safety, but for the well-being of her unborn child as well. Still, they all went about their daily routine, but with heavy hearts.

The tension mounted, and Patrick felt Thursday would never arrive. Each night, he was tempted to wander back over to the White house and resume his search for Sylvia. And many times, he came close but remembered the promise to his father and stayed home.

Thursday evening, the family's supper was vegetable stew and cornbread. John said grace but also prayed for a positive outcome of the town meeting. The room became thick with nervous anticipation. No one could bring themselves to speak.

It broke Mary's heart to see her loved ones unhappy. She decided to break the silence. "So, how was school today, girls?"

"Okay," Sarah answered in a dull voice.

"Fine," Sadie added, just as downcast.

"Patrick, you haven't touched your stew. Don't you like it?"

"It's fine, Ma. I'm just not hungry," Patrick said while staring into the bowl, his unease over Sylvia evident on his face.

"Please try to eat something, so it doesn't go to waste."

"Yes, ma'am."

John sat back with his pipe in hand. "Let's hope the town can decide on a plan for Sylvia's father."

Patrick pounded the table with his fist. "He deserves to die!"

"Now, you just hold on a minute, son. Granted, he's done awful things, but it's not up to us to decide his fate. That's up to God."

"Well, I don't see how God can allow a man to do such awful things to his own daughter."

"A man has choices. Don't blame God for Bernhard's actions."

"I suppose."

"It's not fair, what happened to Sylvia, but I can tell you, God will make it right in the end."

"I hope so, Pa."

John backed away from the table and grabbed his hat. "Mary, we best get a move on if we want to be on time."

Mary untied her apron and removed it from around her waist. "We'll be back as soon as we can. Girls, will you please clear the table and clean up the dishes for me?"

"Yes, Ma."

"Don't forget your homework."

"Yes, ma'am."

John nodded at Patrick. "Girls, listen to your brother. He is in charge until we get home."

"Yes, sir," they both answered.

Mary rested her hand on Patrick's shoulder and smiled for a moment before leaving.

He watched his folks climb into the wagon and head down the two-track road. As soon as they were out of sight, he grabbed his coat but paused at the door. "You girls stay in the house. I'll be back in a while."

Sarah's mouth gaped. "Where are you going?"

"For a walk."

After closing the door, Patrick put his coat on while recalling the promise he made to his pa about not going over to the White house. *I promised I'd stay away until Thursday, and now it's Thursday.*

~.~.~

As John and Mary neared the church, they noted a buggy and two other wagons parked outside. John took his wife's hand and helped her to the ground.

Just then, the reverend pulled up next to them in his buggy. "Good evening, John and Mary."

"Hello, Reverend Brooks."

Meanwhile, Susie's parents, along with Joshua and Lilly Evans, arrived. After greetings were exchanged, they walked inside the church to find the Stoope's already seated in the front row, on the left side.

Also, present and sitting in the pews was Doctor Parker beside Miss Kimball. Timmy's parents, Benjamin and Rachel Logan sat nearby. While waiting to see if anyone else would attend the meeting, some polite conversation could be heard.

Joshua, Lilly, John, and Mary took a seat on the right side to exchange pleasantries with the others.

Reverend Brooks made his way to the podium, hoping all who planned to attend were present. He wanted to call the meeting to order.

The last to arrive for the appointed 7:00 p.m. meeting was Johnny Prescott's folks, who came in without saying a word. They quietly took a seat behind the Stoope's.

Reverend Brooks checked his pocket watch. "Excuse me, but may I have your attention, please?" It didn't take long before the chatting ceased. "I want to thank everyone for coming tonight. I believe more families were invited, but I imagine some couldn't break away since it is harvest season. We're here to discuss some recent events, which have taken place in the community. I'm afraid it involves Bernhard White and his daughter, Sylvia. Having said so, I would like to give each one here the opportunity to speak. Then, once all the facts are laid out to you this evening, it is my hope that together, we will be able to reach a decision."

~.~.~

While the town meeting was due to begin, Patrick entered the barn at the White residence. There was one horse in each stall, and he knew at once, Bernhard was home. Realizing that he should return home, something told him not to leave, even though nothing was amiss in the barn. So, he closed the door and left.

Once inside, he checked each window around the perimeter but saw no evidence of Sylvia or her pa. *Where could they be? Upstairs? The outhouse? They both wouldn't be in there?*

Patrick held his breath, turned the doorknob, and pushed open the door. Since it was dusk and there were no lights on in the house, it took on a cold and eerie feeling. Even though he understood Bernhard was home, he didn't hear anyone stirring in the house, so his need to find Sylvia overrode common sense. As he made his way down the hall, his heartbeat raced with each step, yet, the bolder he became.

Something came over Patrick, and before he realized it, he stood at Bernhard's bedroom door. After fisting his nervous hands, he reached for the doorknob, opened the creaky door, and then walked into the room. In an instant, he had the feeling as if he had just walked into the center of an oncoming storm. Nonetheless, not sure what he hoped to find, once again, he began skimming through the desk and end table drawers.

After moving to the dresser, he ransacked those drawers as well. When he located the key in the fourth one, he closed it. Then Patrick sensed a cool blast of air course through the room. When he stood up, it was to come face to face with Bernhard's intimidating and twisted face, lurking in the doorway.

~.~.~

Reverend Brooks continued, "Doctor Parker, would you go first?"

The doctor nodded, came forward, and replaced Reverend Brooks at the podium. "Thank you, Bartholomew. And thanks to all of you folks for taking time away from your families this evening. I'll get right to why we're here. A few days ago, I had to examine Sylvia White for the first time. I can tell you, I have never witnessed anything like it in all my years of medicine. It is my belief the girl has been abused by her father for quite some time."

Gasps came from the women, while the men sat stone-faced.

"Having said that—"

Eliza Stoope smirked. "Now see here, Doctor Parker, how can you be sure? After all, Mr. White is a member of this church and our community. You cannot spread such innuendo with no certainty of fact he is guilty of any wrongdoing. And for the sake of mercy, above all, one must remain civilized."

"Mrs. Stoope, I assure you that the evidence speaks for itself. I don't make a habit of divulging patient information, but in this case, I feel I must. On examination, findings revealed multiple bruises and scars on her arms, legs, and torso. Also, there appeared to be burn marks on her arms."

The women gasped at the words filling the air, and once again, sniffles flooded the room.

Amos Prescott, the town drunk, added his two-cents worth. "Maybe, she's just clumsy, like my boy. That's just kids—they have accidents."

His wife gasped. "He's not—"

Amos nudged his wife. "Quiet, woman!"

Doctor Parker looked miffed. "Mr. Prescott, I assure you, this is no accident."

Once again, Eliza jumped to her feet. "Doctor Parker, it seems to me, it's your intention to smear the name of a good man, and under an unfortunate circumstance! He lost his wife, for heaven's sake. And he's had to raise the girl on his own, as well."

"Mrs. Stoope, I assure you, I mean him no harm. I am only concerned about Sylvia's safety and well-being, so it imperative that something must be done."

"Well, perhaps it is a simple matter of her father taking a more effective way of disciplinary action. I mean, after all, she's gallivanting around town with the Ryan boy. It's no wonder he's got her into trouble."

Mary Ryan closed her eyes, swallowed hard, and took a deep breath, doing her best to remain level-headed—although her endurance was waning.

John catapulted from his seat. "Now, see here, Eliza! My boy only walked her home from school. He's been nothing but a gentleman."

"Well, so-called gentleman, do not make a young girl with-child, John Ryan!"

"Oh, my good gracious!" Lilly Evans cupped her hand to her mouth as tears filled her eyes.

"Mrs. Stoope," Miss Kimball said while standing, "I can attest to the fact Patrick has been nothing but a good friend to Sylvia. He doesn't even walk her all the way home. He isn't gone very long until I see him walk back past the school. There has never been anything inappropriate between them."

Eliza stuck her snooty nose in the air. "Well, what about the weekends? And since she is with-child, who's to say she has not taken it upon herself to do personal harm—just for the sake of sympathy in her present condition?"

John's ire had him seeing red. "First of all, I can assure you, Bernhard doesn't let Sylvia out of the house for any reason over the weekend. But most importantly, she's a good girl and would never do what you're insinuating, Eliza."

"Well! Maybe your son sneaks over to her house."

~.~.~

Bernhard's face contorted, and the harsh glare in his eyes became accentuated by the shadows from the lantern in his hand. "You!" He stepped into the room, set the lantern on the desk, and then lurched toward Patrick in one swift but awkward motion.

Patrick's adrenaline surged when he took two steps forward but had to duck as the crazed lunatic took a swing at him, even though Bernhard staggered.

He returned a right hook of his own, which connected with the side of Bernhard's jaw, but only stunning him a second. Shaking like a wet dog, in slow motion, he turned toward Patrick with a sinister smirk before lunging at him. Bernhard took another swing at Patrick's face, but this time it was blocked. Instead, they locked arms like antlers on two bucks butting each other. However, Bernhard shoved Patrick backward, where he hit the dresser behind him.

When Patrick charged forward, the two began to tussle. Although he managed to break an arm free, then fisted his hand and slammed it into Bernhard's ribs, causing the big man to recoil, which allowed Patrick to force him backward.

Bernhard rebounded with a direct jab to Patrick's side.

At the same time, a blow hit Bernhard's left cheek, with its momentum sending the old man reeling and stumbling over empty whiskey bottles scattered on the floor.

Patrick wasted no time in targeting a blow to Bernhard's face, knocking him into the desk. The force tipped the lantern over, whereby shattering it into pieces.

~.~.~

Mary Ryan had reached her limit over the accusations toward Patrick. "I disapprove of your spiteful attack on our son, Eliza Stoope. Furthermore, we are always aware of where he is on the weekends, as well. And he does not spend them at the White residence."

Eliza sighed while rolling her eyes. "Mary, you see through a mother's eyes, of course. Do you doubt Doctor Parker when he says the White girl is with-child?"

"I don't deny she is with-child, but our son is not the father."

"Well, how do you know for sure? It is quite obvious she is not a young innocent in her condition. Huh—and need I remind you, it will become more obvious very soon?"

"Mrs. Stoope, I know my son well. When he says that he is not the father. John and I believe him. Perhaps you should think of what Sylvia has endured. Notwithstanding what she is now facing, without any motherly guidance—yet, you condemn her."

"Um… perhaps we should hear what Miss Kimball has to offer," Reverend Brooks suggested.

The teacher stood while clearing her throat, but with a smile as she stood at the podium. "Thank you, Reverend Brooks. I've gone back through my school ledger, and there are several unexplained absences for Sylvia. More this year than any other student. I wouldn't have made too much of it, but then I looked back over other years, and the same pattern of Sylvia's absences are more than anyone else. I would also like to add, Patrick Ryan is an exemplary student who has gone out of his way to be kind and a good friend to Sylvia White." She nodded and returned to her seat.

"Well, it's obvious he certainly *has* gone out of his way," Mrs. Stoope mumbled.

Mr. Stoope glared at his wife.

Reverend Brooks smiled. "Thank you, Miss Kimball. Does anyone else have anything to add?"

Eliza Stoope was back on her feet. "I have something to say. I think John and Mary Ryan want to cover up the predicament their son has gotten this poor girl into!" She smirked. "Well, it's what you all are thinking. I just stated the obvious."

William Stoope gritted his teeth. "Sit down, Eliza, right now. You have said quite enough."

The reverend shot Mrs. Stoope a dirty look.

Benjamin Logan raised his hand. "Reverend, may I speak?"

"Of course, Benjamin, the floor is yours."

"Well, the Mrs. and I have known Patrick since his family moved here. They're good, solid folks. And, they got a mighty fine boy. He just wouldn't get anyone in trouble."

Rachel Logan nodded in agreement while standing. "I must second what my husband has said about Patrick Ryan. There should be more boys in this world just like him. And Mary is right. We should show compassion for poor Sylvia. She simply must be found."

~.~.~

As the lantern shattered on the floor, bright orange flames rose, knocking him onto the bed. Before he could move, Bernhard's hands were coiled around his neck, feeling as if they were a snake constricting the air from his lungs. All the while, Patrick could smell the drunk man's sick, foul breath as he fought for life.

The fire spread quickly across the desk, surrounding the floor as smoke billowed throughout the room. Patrick saw silver stars dancing before his eyes, and the fear of death loomed. He hadn't been able to get the dead weight of the drunkard off his body. In a desperate effort attempt, he reached his right hand behind his head and searched for something... anything. His fingers connected with something cold, hard, and smooth near the head of the bed. It was round... maybe a bottle. He didn't care what it was as he grabbed it, then smashed it over the evil man's head.

Bernhard slumped over Patrick's right shoulder before landing on the bed.

Patrick choked and gasped for air while moving the lower half of his attacker's limp body off his legs. Then he bolted into the dining room. "SYLVIA! SYLVIA!"

~.~.~

Reverend Brooks said, "Thank you, Benjamin. Does anyone else have anything to say?" No one offered to or even moved. "Well, then... shall we move on to deciding what to do?"

Joshua Evans stood. "I motion we evict Bernhard White."

Eliza's mouth gaped. "Evict him from our town? For mercy's sake, but I do not believe there is enough evidence to do such a thing!"

John glared at the woman. "I second the motion."

Eliza scowled. "Well, of course, you would."

This time, William Stoope grabbed his wife's forearm and forced her back on her seat. "Sit down, Eliza! You just never give up, woman. Always causing trouble."

Even though it was not the Christian thing to do, Reverend Brooks found himself grimacing at the irritating woman. He sighed. "Well, folks, let's begin the voting for *Nay*."

With puckered lips, Eliza Stoope raised her hand. "Nay!"

Meanwhile, her husband shook his head with a scowl aimed at her and with his hands at his sides.

Amos Prescott raised his hand, then elbowed his wife, who raised her arm to half-mast.

"And the ayes? Let me see a show of hands." Reverend Brooks finished his count. "The ayes have it. Bernhard White will be evicted from town—effective immediately."

A timid Rachel Logan spoke up, "What's to become of the girl?"

Mary stood. "We'll give her a home. Sylvia has stayed with us recently after running away from her father."

Reverend Brooks smiled. "Very well, then. I want to thank you all again for coming out tonight to deal with such a delicate matter. With everything settled—this meeting is adjourned."

After Prescott's exited the church, the others followed.

Lilly Evans pointed to the billowing smoke in the sky. "Look! Over there!"

Rachel Logan, who had just taken a step forward, looked up to follow in the direction of the smoke. "Where could it be coming from?"

The color drained from Miss Kimball's face as she turned to John. "Oh! It's the White residence."

"I'll head over there," John said.

Mary grabbed his arm. "I'm coming with you."

Doctor Parker said, "Bartholomew, and I'll follow in my buggy."

The Logan's and the Evans's followed to the White home to lend a hand in fighting the fire.

~.~.~

The more Patrick called out to her, the more he panicked. "SYLVIA! SYLVIA! SYLVIA!"

At last, he heard a faint reply... "Help."

"SYLVIA!" He thought he heard a banging somewhere, but he wasn't sure where it was coming from.

Again, there was a muffled response. "Help me."

"SYLVIA... where are you?"

"Down here!"

"Down where?"

"Under the table!"

Under the table? When looking under the table and chairs, he saw the rug bouncing. Hurrying to the table, he slid the chairs and table away, flipped the rug back, and there it was—a trap door. Patrick pulled it open to find Sylvia standing on a ladder. He reached down, gripped her by the arms, and then pulled her up onto the floor.

Sylvia wrapped her arms around him, and he could feel the heat on his back from the approaching flames and all but burning his skin.

Patrick turned to realize there was no way to get out through the front door. He scooped Sylvia up in his arms and searched for an alternate exit. He was able to get around the flames easy enough, then into her bedroom, where he stood her next to the window and out of harm's way. "Stay right here and be ready for me to get you, Sylvia!"

She nodded through her tears.

Patrick grabbed a towel from the nearby washbasin, wrapped it around his hand and arm, and then smashed the window.

Next, he yanked the bedspread off her bed and launched it through the shattered window, so he could dive out and over the shattered and jagged glass. After jumping to his feet, he picked up the bedspread and then stood. "Sylvia, come on!"

She stood weak-kneed at the window, but this time Patrick got a firm grip on Sylvia through the window, pulled her through it, and then ran with her a safe distance away from the house. He set her down and held her face in his hands. "Are you okay?"

She nodded through her endless tears.

"Stay here," he ordered in a stern voice and then went back to the window, but saw no safe reentry into the bedroom, so he ran around the right side of the house. He hoped to find another way inside, where the fire hadn't spread to yet. Nonetheless, there was no way to rescue Sylvia's father in reality since he was in front of the house where it was engulfed in flames.

"Patrick!" John yelled as he halted the wagon, then jumped off and rushed to his son. "Patrick, where's Bernhard?"

"He's still inside, Pa. I can't get to him."

John took off to check the house's perimeter, looking for a safe point to enter, but Patrick was right; there was none.

As women pumped buckets of water, the men would relay them, attempting to put out the fire, but it was too late. They had no choice but to watch the house burn.

Meanwhile, Mary hurried out of the wagon, unable to run fast enough. When she reached her son, she gave him a hug, then turned to embrace Sylvia. "Thank God, you're all right, my dear. I'm so grateful both of you are safe."

Patrick wrapped Sylvia in his arms, kissed her forehead, and kept holding her in his arms.

~

Sylvia leaned into Patrick's chest while watching as the only home she had ever known burned to the ground. Yet—she felt nothing.

Patrick held her close to him. "No matter where I looked, I couldn't figure out what he had done with you. And all the time, you were there all along, Sylvia... in the cellar."

-The End-

AVAILABLE NOW
Melissa's other book
Amazon: http://amzn.to/295I9QA-

'Broken Heart: *The Blessed Road to Healing'*

ENJOY PREVIEW OF
Book 2—Sylvia: *A New Life*

-ALSO-

...STATISTICS & AUTHOR NOTES...

PROLOGUE

BOOK 2
Sylvia: A New Life

A few days after the incident, Doctor Parker, John Ryan, and Reverend Brooks returned to the White house. They surveyed the ashes and found the charred remains of Bernhard White. A standard pine box was built at the lumberyard and transported by John to the scene. Doctor Parker and the others put on gloves and then began the arduous burden of sifting through the ashes where they loaded them into the box. Then they returned to town with the remains of Sylvia's abusive father.

Patrick had been cleared of any wrongdoing since he rescued Sylvia and attempted to find a way back inside the engulfed home to retrieve his attacker.

It was also confirmed by the other eyewitnesses since John Ryan also searched for a possible entry point but to no avail.

The next day, Sylvia, the Ryan's, Logan's, Prescott's, Evans's, Stoope's, Miss Kimball, and Doctor Parker attended Bernhard Henry White's funeral. Reverend Brooks pulled from within his spiritual guidance to give the best service he could. Even though the deceased was had a tormented soul. Afterward, Joshua Evans and John Ryan covered the pine box with dirt.

Other than morning sickness, Sylvia remained unspoken since the night of the fire, as if in a trance. Some nights, she'd wake up screaming, fighting an unknown force in her nightmares. Even though Mary and Patrick took turns tending her, nothing brought her out of her present state of mind. So, she continued to stare off into the distance—unable to communicate or just refused to speak.

Doctor Parker examined Sylvia, then spoke to the Ryan's, and of course, Patrick. "I'm afraid the poor girl is in shock. It's a normal response to the terrible years of abuse she's endured. Even though her father is gone, he was the only caregiver she's ever known."

The doctor sighed. "I have no idea how long Sylvia's state of silence will last, although I am certain it won't be forever. The pregnancy appears normal, but there's no telling what kind of impact the abuse and smoke she inhaled will have on the baby."

Miss Kimball stopped by once a week to check on Sylvia and offer Mary and Patrick's help and encouragement. Each visit, she hoped to see Sylvia return to a version of her former self. Nonetheless, the longer she remained silent, the more Miss Kimball wondered if Sylvia could recover from all she had suffered.

After Patrick graduated from school, he helped his pa with the crops, and worked at the lumber yard on the weekends, and asked for more hours when they were available. He planned to ask Sylvia to marry him and to take the baby in as his own. However, moving too fast while she was mentally unstable was not a good idea. He couldn't help but wonder if she would ever again be the person he knew and loved.

When he thought about what Bernhard had done to his own daughter, he regretted looking for a way back into that house. He also wished he could've gotten a few more punches in or somehow made him suffer more. The fact he was unconscious through the fire seemed much too humane a way for him to go. At least, in Patrick's summation.

A month after her father's funeral, the horrible nightmares continued for Sylvia and her lack of any communication, too.

On a day that Patrick worked at the lumber yard, his sister, Sadie, came running toward him as fast as her legs would carry her. The panic-stricken expression on her face left no room for debate—her visit was anything but good. "PATRICK! QUICK! YOU HAVE TO COME HOME! QUICK!"

Patrick looked toward his sister in distress. "What is it, Sadie?"

"It's Sylvia!"

~

While Sadie ran for her brother, Sarah and John had raced into town for the doctor after Sylvia woke up screaming.

Meanwhile, Mary went to help Sylvia but found the poor girl lying in dark, crimson-stained sheets.

STATISTICS

If you know someone who's been sexually abused or have experienced sexual abuse yourself by a family member or someone else, you are not alone. Nor is it your fault either. Child sexual abuse is rampant in our society.

According to RAINN (*Rape, Abuse and Incest National Network*), one in nine girls, and one in 53 boys under the age of 18, experienced sexual abuse or assault by an adult. The majority of those abused know the perpetrator, and approximately 34 percent of perpetrators in cases of child sexual abuse are family members.

If you have been or are currently being sexually abused or assaulted, please -call the **National Sexual Assault Hotline at 1-800-656-4673 or visit www.rainn.org**, any time, 24/7, and ask to speak to a RAINN support specialist.

It can be difficult to talk about abuse, especially if it was committed by a family member. If you don't tell, it won't stop. If it doesn't stop, you can't heal.

Why is it so hard to report abuse?

You may care about your abuser and be afraid of what will happen to the abuser if you report it.

You may be afraid of other family members' reactions, fearing they won't believe you or that you will be accused of doing something wrong.

You may have been told the abuse is normal, that it happens in every family, or the abuser may be threatening to harm a family member or pet. They may also threaten that no one will believe you.

You may not know whom to tell or have someone you trust.

You may be afraid of getting in trouble with a parent or other family member.

What are the signs of child sexual abuse?
Behavioral/Verbal:

1. Sleep disturbances (nightmares, bedwetting, trouble falling asleep, suddenly needing a night light.)
2. Loss of control of bladder or bowels.
3. Loss of/sudden increase in appetite.
4. Lots of new fears, needing reassurance, clinging, not wanting to be left alone.
5. Returning to younger, more babyish behavior.
6. Unusual behavior shift (from outgoing to withdrawn.)
7. Giving up or throwing away a favorite toy, piece of clothing, or other possession.
8. Sudden turning against one parent, relative, or friend.
9. Increase in school difficulties or a sudden immersion in school.
10. Explicit sexual acting out, obsession with sexual parts or words, inappropriate kissing, or sexual knowledge beyond their age.
11. Vague references to an incident, for example ("I don't like Uncle Joe anymore.")
12. Reluctance to go to a particular place or to be with a particular person.
13. Irritability, crankiness.
14. Use of drugs, alcohol.
15. Running away.
16. Prostitution.
17. Suicidal thoughts, attempts, or self-mutilation.

Physical:

1. Bruising or swelling near the genital area.
2. Blood on sheets or undergarments.
3. Broken bones.

According to the World Health Organization, victims of sexual assault are:

1. 3 times more likely to suffer from depression;
2. 6 times more likely to suffer from PTSD;
3. 13 times more likely to abuse alcohol;
4. 26 times more likely to abuse drugs;
5. 4 times more likely to contemplate suicide.

Silence Protects the Perpetrator—SPEAK OUT!

How to Help Someone Who Has Been Sexually Abused:

First and foremost, believe them! It's extremely rare for a child to lie about abuse.

Thank them for trusting you enough to tell because it took a great deal of courage to break the silence.

Let them know you are sorry this happened to them, and that it's not their fault.

Remind them you are here for them, and you will help.
Let them know this hasn't changed how you see them or feel about them.

How to Report Child Sexual Abuse:
If you know or suspect a child has been sexually abused or assaulted, report it to local authorities or Child Protective Services.

Call the Childhelp National Abuse Hotline to be connected to a trained volunteer. 1-800-422-4453 Childhelp Hotline crisis counselors will walk you through the process of how to report it and what to expect. Make sure to follow up with doctor's appointments, counseling and/or support groups.

AUTHOR'S NOTE

Sexual abuse is rampant and the best-kept secret in our society. If you've been sexually abused once or multiple times, please know you are not alone. You did not ask for it. No matter what age you were when you were abused, it was not your fault! It was not the clothing you wore, what you said or didn't say, or something you invited. There is nothing you could have done or said to change what your abuser or abusers did. Nothing is wrong with you! The person or persons who abused you is/are the one with the problem(s).-

Sexual abuse affects your mind, damages your body, and kills your soul. But with professional help, healing is possible. How do I know? Because I am a survivor. As a young girl, I was molested, although not by my father, as portrayed in the book. Staying silent only protects your abuser and continues to harm you.

I suffered from anxiety, depression, fear, low self-esteem, self-hatred, nightmares, and suicidal thoughts. I also went through a brief bout with an eating disorder. I tried many different coping mechanisms. Like alcohol, marijuana, perfectionism, workaholism, and nothing worked. Things only got worse. I went through many failed and abusive relationships until I came to the end of myself. It took seventeen years to break the silence, but I told someone I trusted.

I walked down a long road of healing and restoration. It was only when I turned to God and gave all my pain and sorrow to Him that I was healed! I became a counselor to help others who have suffered through abuse heal too. I'm here to tell you if I can be renewed, so can you! It is a difficult process, and there will be days you will want to quit. But if you stick with it, you will find it is the best gift you can give yourself. You are worth it!

If this book has helped you make the decision to break your silence and seek help, or if you have a wonderful story of healing, I'd love to hear from you!

Contact me at*: Melissa@BridleofHope.org.*

God Bless Your Journey,
Melissa

www.ingramcontent.com/pod-product-compliance
Lightning Source LLC
Chambersburg PA
CBHW051244260626
47162CB00002B/600